STATE OF BETRAYAL

VIRGIL JONES MYSTERY THRILLER SERIES
BOOK 2

THOMAS SCOTT

This book is a work of fiction. No artificial intelligence (commonly referred to as:
AI) was used in the conceptualization, creation, or production of this book. Names,
characters, places, governmental institutions, venues, and all incidents or events are
either the product of the author's imagination or are used fictitiously. Any
resemblance to actual persons, living or dead, businesses, companies, events,
locales, venues, or government organizations is entirely coincidental.

For information contact: ThomasScottBooks.com

HIGH ROAD PRESS

— **Also by Thomas Scott** —

The Virgil Jones Series In Order

State of Anger - Book 1
State of Betrayal - Book 2
State of Control - Book 3
State of Deception - Book 4
State of Exile - Book 5
State of Freedom - Book 6
State of Genesis - Book 7
State of Humanity - Book 8
State of Impact - Book 9
State of Justice - Book 10
State of Killers - Book 11
State of Life - Book 12
State of Mind - Book 13
State of Need - Book 14
State of One - Book 15
State of Play - Book 16
State of Qualms - Book 17
State of Remains - Book 18
State of Suspense - Book 19

The Jack Bellows Series In Order

Wayward Strangers - Book 1
Brave Strangers - Book 2

**Visit ThomasScottBooks.com for further
information regarding future release dates, and more.**

For my father, Richard, who taught me how to be a man, and my dear late mother, Judy, who never let me lose sight of the boy I'll always be. What a wonderful combination of gifts. Who could possibly ask for more? Thank you both. This one's for you. God bless.

be·tray·al
bəˈtrāəl, bēˈtrāəl/
noun

—THE ACT OF BETRAYING SOMEONE OR SOMETHING

—VIOLATION OF A PERSON'S TRUST OR CONFIDENCE

—REVELATION OF SOMETHING HIDDEN OR SECRET

CHAPTER ONE

IT WAS THE SEASON OF BAKED ASPHALT, DRY HARDPAN backyards, and boiled over tempers that flared red long after the sun would journey below the horizon. So much change for so many—that summer of heat and Boots—though Virgil Jones knew full well the one name they would never call him again, *Boot*, was a part of his past now. It was also one where the heat barreled on, an oppressive undertow that became the undoing of so many, the death of an unfortunate few.

Virgil was on patrol driving south on US 31 about halfway between Kokomo and Indianapolis. He had the air conditioner set to maximum and that kept the temperature in his cruiser at eighty degrees, give or take. A heatwave had stalled out over the middle of the country a few days ago and if you were outside for more than five minutes, even in the shade, the humidity landed on you like a water balloon tossed from a second-story balcony. It was so bad you could see the air. The blacktop a half-mile out shimmered in the heat and Virgil thought it looked as though at any moment he might drive headlong into a pool of mercury.

His shift was scheduled to end in less than half an hour and he was only a mile away from the convenience store when he got the radio call of two males engaged in a verbal argument that threatened to turn into something much worse. He hit the switch for the light bar, then punched the gas pedal and when he did, the Police Interceptor engine in his Crown Victoria responded with ease. Traffic in the immediate area was light and he ran his speed up to over one hundred miles per hour, the tires gliding across the greasy, heat-soaked asphalt. He would be on scene in less than forty-seconds. If he would have glanced at himself in the rear-view mirror he'd have seen the smile on his face.

The convenience store sat along an access road right off the highway. The entrance was at the far end of the lot and Virgil was forced to drive past the store along the perimeter road before he could turn back into the parking area. The cause of the altercation was clear. Two vehicles —one a clean, dark blue, mid-sized sedan, the other a dull red and rusted pickup—sat nose to tail, the rear bumper of the pickup firmly embedded into the headlight of the sedan. Two white males stood to the side of the damaged vehicles. Virgil tried not to draw any conclusions as to which vehicle belonged to each driver, but it seemed obvious. One of the men wore a pair of cutoff jeans and a sleeveless shirt, the other a business suit. Two small children were in the cab of the pickup, their hands and faces pressed against the rear window, their expressions a mixture of both fear and familiarity. A small crowd had gathered around the front door of the convenience store but no one was making any sort of attempt to curtail a situation that was rapidly escalating out of control. The men, both red-faced and angry pointed their fingers at each other but their words were lost to the road noise and air-conditioning of Virgil's squad car.

Then, in an instant, everything spun out of control when business suit shoved sleeveless in the chest and knocked him to the ground before walking away. Virgil burped his siren to get their attention, but at the same time sleeveless jumped up, reached into the bed of his pickup and pulled out a piece of steel rebar. He hesitated for a moment but the look on his face left little doubt about his intentions or his state of mind. Business suit faced Virgil as he approached, his back to his adversary, unaware of what was about to take place against his person, and even though Virgil pointed at him and hit the siren again as a warning it had no effect.

Virgil braked to a stop right when sleeveless swung the rebar and hit business suit across the backs of his thighs. The suit dropped to his knees and his jaw unhinged with shock and pain. Virgil jumped out of the car, drew his weapon, and pointed it at sleeveless. "Drop the bar. Do it now. No, no, don't even think about it. Drop it right now."

Sleeveless looked at him, but he was too far gone by then, the flat of his eyes a sign of what was to come. He raised the piece of rebar high above his head, his yellow teeth bared, the tendons of his tattooed arms as tight as leaf springs and when he stood up on his toes and started to swing the bar again he left Virgil no choice at all. He fired two shots and they both hit their target. Sleeveless was dead before he hit the ground.

Virgil wasn't smiling anymore.

That was twenty years ago and it was the only time he'd ever fired his weapon as a police officer. It was also his first day out of training—no longer a Boot—riding solo as an Indiana State Trooper.

———

THE MAN VIRGIL SHOT AND KILLED WAS NAMED JAMES Pope. The two children in the truck with him were his five-year-old twins, a boy, Nicholas, and his sister, Nichole. James Pope had abducted his children from his ex-wife's house only minutes before the altercation in the parking lot that led to his death. Virgil never knew what happened to the twins after that day, but he did get a thank-you card in the mail from their mother a few weeks after the shooting. Virgil had hopes that the children would somehow grow up trouble-free, even though they had witnessed the death of their father at the hands of a police officer. When the thank-you card arrived in the mail from their mother, Virgil's hope died as quick as James Pope had. It's one thing to be glad you're rid of someone. But it's something else entirely when you carry such hatred in your heart that you send a note of thanks to the man who killed your ex-husband. Virgil thought the Pope twins were in for a rough ride.

He threw the note in the trash and got on with his life.

CHAPTER TWO

NICHOLAS POPE SAT IN THE DARKNESS OF HIS OFFICE, HIS face illuminated by the dim glow of his computer monitor. Pope was a programmer for the state's lottery, though the job description was something of a sore spot for him. He was not a programmer. Programmers were about one step up from the I.T. guy who kept Excel from crashing every time someone tried to recover a missing file. No, Pope was a coder and a damned good one at that. The distinction was important to him. Programmers and coders did share some similarities—Nicky would grant you that—but it was a bit like comparing a couple of house painters with artists like Renoir, or Monet. They all used paints and brushes, but that was about as far as anyone could extend the comparison. Guys with names like Billie Bob and Monty D. painted houses, but they could hardly be called artists. They were simple laborers. Coders, on the other hand, were true artists, like Renoir, or Monet. One little splash of color here, one little bit of binary there and... well, it made all the difference, whether anyone else noticed or not.

So. Nicholas Pope was a coder who was, at the moment, working on a scheduled update for the algorithm that was the basis for the random number generator, or RNG, for the state's lottery system. Gone were the days of numbered Ping-Pong balls floating about on puffs of air until they popped into a tube on live TV. Everything was digital now, including how the winning numbers were picked. The lottery's RNG algorithm served two primary functions. The first was to pick a total of six numbers at random between 1 and 48 whenever someone bought a lottery ticket and used the 'quick pick' method instead of playing numbers they'd decided upon themselves. The second purpose of the RNG algorithm was to pick the six winning numbers every time a drawing took place, and in the case of the state of Indiana, that was every Wednesday and Saturday.

The RNG algorithm was one of the most complex algorithms that Nicky had ever seen, layer after layer of intricate code that every now and again made someone wealthy beyond their wildest dreams. Nicky was fascinated with RNGs, especially the one he now had access to. The lottery used a true RNG, one that worked by capturing background ambient noise from a variety of ever-changing sources—street traffic, wind, aircraft flying overhead, footsteps and voices in the hallways—then converted those noises into a pattern. Once the pattern was established, it was output and converted into a string code that the system used as the key—or seed—that ran the algorithm. If the key kept changing, as it would with random ambient background noise, then the numbers would always be truly random. Even if they did happen to repeat—though that had never happened and as far as Nicky could tell, never would—they were still random by definition and that's what mattered.

Near the end of his shift, Nicky made note of his place in the program and began to back his way out of the layers of code that converted the noise into its sequential string. He was almost out when he found what he was looking for. Found it by dumb luck. It was right there and had been all along. He'd simply missed it going in. It was hidden, but not all that well. It was, he thought, a little like hiding a tree in the forest.

He double-checked to make sure what he'd found was the right section and when he was sure, he pulled the thumb drive from his pocket and uploaded his own little bit of binary code into the sequential string generator section of the program. He wasn't worried about being traced by the security measures the lottery had in place. He'd been logged in the entire time under his boss's username and password, two little items he'd copied from her phone over eight weeks ago after a particularly feisty night of drinking and well…feistiness. He logged out of the terminal and once clear of the building he took out his cell and called his twin sister, Nichole. "We're in," he said.

"You're sure?" she asked him.

"Oh yeah, no doubt about it."

"Will it work?"

"Of course it will work. I designed it. Hey, Sis?"

"Yeah?"

"We're doing it, aren't we? After all this time, we're going to make them pay."

"You bet your ass they're going to pay, baby brother. They're going to pay big time."

"Hey, a minute and a half hardly makes me your baby brother."

"Be careful, Nicky. Sometimes I think you don't realize what we're up against here."

"No worries, Sis. I'll see you in an hour."

They still had some work to do, but they were almost ready. Almost there.

———

NICHOLE WENT TO HER FRIDGE, PULLED OUT TWO BUDS— the liquid kind—and handed one to her brother. "What about Pearson? Maybe we should let that go."

"Little late for that. Besides, the plan is already in place. Pearson is going to pay for what he did to our family."

Their plan had evolved over the years. It started out as nothing more than a childhood fantasy—a way to get even with Pearson for the altercation he started that eventually led to their father's death by an Indiana State Trooper. Shortly after the Pope twins turned seventeen their mother died and that was when they began to understand a few things, the biggest of which was that they were on their own. They had no other family so they made a promise to themselves; they would take care of each other no matter what came their way.

And that's what they did. Nichole had proven herself to be quite a little thief, a talent she discovered in short order after their mother died. They had to eat, after all. She became a master shoplifter, which, Nichole discovered, required a good deal of acting. You couldn't look suspicious if you were about to steal something, no matter how big or small said something might be. You had to *act* normal. You had to *act* like you belonged where you were, doing whatever it was you were doing. Nichole discovered she was good at it…the acting. She could act like a punk or a princess…a young socialite, or a homeless teen. Her biggest score had been their most elaborate one to date, not counting what they were doing now. She went to the mall, stole the most expensive dress she could find—with matching shoes, of course—then went to one of the more exclusive college graduation parties in nearby Carmel, Indiana. Nicky had hacked into the guest list, added her name and once she was inside she used the list of probable passwords Nicky had given her and cracked the safe hidden in the parent's bedroom closet. That score alone netted them almost fifty grand, mostly in cash and Canadian Maple Leaf coins. The coins didn't have serial numbers, God bless you, Canada.

Of course, that wouldn't have been possible if Nicky hadn't become such an expert coder and hacker over the years, a skill he picked up on the Internet as he began to track Pearson's every move. It wasn't long before he'd found and built backdoors into virtually every area of Pearson's digital life, from bank records to utility bills, personal and professional email accounts, cell phone records and texts, employment records, the works. When Pearson became the governor's chief of staff, Nicky followed him—electronically speaking—right into the second most powerful position in the state.

And that's when things got interesting.

The Pope twins began to completely understand how corrupt and manipulative Pearson really was. They had accumulated massive amounts of data on him. They had proof of bribery, falsification of official state records, evidence that demonstrated election fraud and extortion. The problem though wasn't in the acquisition of the data. The problem was what to do with it. They couldn't simply hand it over to the cops and say, "See…here's a bad man. Arrest him please and, oh, by the way, it's really all about payback for our father. You see…"

No, that wouldn't work. They'd be the ones locked up

for theft, spying, and whatever else the prosecution could think of. They understood that whatever they were going to do, they would have to do it themselves like they always had. Which wasn't to say they didn't have a little help along the way.

Nicky hacked his way into the credit agencies, created a dozen false identities—all with excellent credit—then bought passports and driver's licenses that would stand up to not only human inspection, but machine inspection as well. Those had cost them dearly, but they were worth every penny, or in this case, every Canadian Maple Leaf.

"What is it?" Nichole asked.

"I guess I suddenly realized that if our plan doesn't work, it won't be long before I'm broke and alone in a foreign country."

"Don't worry, Nicky. Everything is going to work out. The code is in place, we've got Pearson by the short hairs and we are all about to be richer than God…if your little bit of code works."

"That little bit of code as you call it took me over two years to perfect."

"But what if your boss gets one of the other coders to dig around and root out your program?"

"They'd never find it."

"But how do you know? For sure, I mean."

Nicky sat down on the sofa. "It's sort of complicated, but the bottom line is this: They won't be able to find it because it's not in the main system. It's buried deep in a tiny subroutine that overrides the security measures at the point of sale. Remember, we don't want or even need control of the main system…only the printer that generates the ticket."

"And that instruction comes from the configured play slip you gave me?"

"Yep. Go get it and I'll show you."

Nichole went to her bedroom, got the slip, and handed it to her brother. "See here," he said as he pointed to the slip. "Every play slip has five boards you can play. Most people don't play that many, but some do. Anyway, see how every board has forty-eight spaces?"

"Yeah. So what?"

"You're supposed to pick six numbers for each board that you want to play. Take a look at the slip. I've played six numbers on each board except the last one. On that one, I've played eight. Not just any eight either. I've got the system set up to bypass the security measures at the point of sale, no matter where that might be. When the bypass occurs, the program will compile, the code within the algorithm will run and the nifty little printer they've got behind every gas station and grocery store counter in the state will print out a post-dated ticket with any numbers we want, which in our case happens to be the six numbers on the last board."

"Boy, Nicky, that's a lot of money we're talking about. I hope you're right."

At just a shade over three hundred million dollars, it

was a lot of money a lot of money. It was the single largest jackpot in the state's history. Week after week not one single person had hit all six numbers, then the momentum started to build. When the amount hit fifty-million people started to notice. When the amount rose to one-hundred-fifty-million, people started lining up at gas stations, grocery stores, mini-marts, and anywhere else a lottery ticket could be purchased. When it hit a quarter billion, people started showing up from out of state, buying tickets instead of paying their bills. Then, when it went to three-hundred-million dollars, the almost unimaginable happened. One person hit all six numbers and won the single largest jackpot in the history of the Indiana lottery.

Except that person never came forward to claim the prize.

At first, the media coverage was almost nonstop. Who was the winner? Why hadn't they come forward? When would they claim the prize? But after a few days of speculation, the media got bored, the losers got pissed and the story began to fade away. Some thought that the winner— the real winner—had lost the ticket. Or maybe they'd passed away, lost it to a house fire, or flood, or some other disaster. Theories of what happened to the ticket were almost as numerous as the jackpot amount, but no amount of supposition produced the winning ticket or its holder. Now, with less than two weeks left before the six-month deadline to claim the prize, the money, if left unclaimed, would quietly go back to the state, like all other unclaimed payouts.

"Oh, I'm right. In a matter of days, you and I are going to be filthy rich, retired, and trying to figure out how to spend the interest on hundreds of millions of dollars."

"It doesn't seem real."

Nicky laughed. "I know what you mean. But believe me, it will seem real enough when you check your account balances. Listen, I have to ask, mostly to make myself feel better...but you know what to do with that play slip right?"

"I do."

"Tell me."

She rolled her eyes a little, then told him.

CHAPTER THREE

IF VIRGIL THOUGHT ABOUT IT—AND HE OFTEN DID—HE'D have to admit the shooting of James Pope still haunted him. After it happened he was still young and foolish enough to believe that the past was the past, and once free from its grasp, he'd not worry over it or attempt to be the arbiter of events outside his own control. Except those types of certainties are a preserve best left to youth, a lesson Virgil thought he might never have to learn. Then before he knew it twenty years had sailed away and now this; a summer like no other, the pain a constant companion as it cut a swath through the jungle of his life, a trail laid bare as if it were his only choice, at once clear and true. It would be a harbinger of things to come, a combination of that moment from long ago and his life now, one he might be able to point to someday and say,

Ah, yes, that's when it turned. That's when it all changed. If only…

A late-afternoon haze drifted across the sun but the air temperature held steady so adjustments to his line depth weren't necessary. The bobber was simple, made from the cork of an old wine bottle and it vibrated in the water if he held too much tension on the line. It reminded him of those old electric football games Virgil and his boyhood friend and brother, Murton Wheeler, used to play when they were kids. They'd line up the little plastic players, hit the switch, then watch the tiny figurines vibrate their way across the surface of the game board. Virgil could still hear the buzzing sound the board made when they toggled the power button and turned it on.

He had a two-pound monofilament line tied directly to an eye-hook at the end of the cane pole. The pole was twelve feet in length and stained dark with age and the regular applications of Tung oil used to maintain its beauty and structural integrity. The pole was one of Virgil's most prized possessions. His grandfather had taught him to fish with it and then had given it to him as a gift a few years before he died. Virgil had a shed full of fishing poles, ones made of boron, graphite, fiberglass, or some other space-age composite, and they were all fine poles. Some were so flexible and tough you could literally tie them into a knot without damaging the rod, while others were so sensitive you could detect a deer fly if it landed on the tip. Virgil didn't know why he continued to buy them. His grandfather's cane pole was the only one he ever used.

When he held the pole in his hands the way he'd been taught so long ago, he felt a connection to his grandfather, as if the linear reality of time held no sway in his existence and he was back in control of himself and his own destiny, his path clear, his choices many.

Virgil knew, at least on some level, that he was a sight this Saturday afternoon. He wore a pair of green cotton gym shorts that hung to his knees, a Jamaican Red Stripe Beer utility cap angled low across his brow, and a pair of brown leather half-top boots with no socks. He sat at the edge of his pond, cane pole in hand, and tried to relax, mostly without any measure of success. The fish were not biting but he didn't really care. He set the pole in the grass next to his chair, reached into the cooler, and took out his supplies. Among them, a plastic syringe with a screw tip on the end, a glass vial of a drug called Heparin, and an odd-looking, round container made of a stiff rubbery material about the size of a baseball. The baseball-like container held a drug called Vancomycin, a powerful antibiotic medication that the doctor had referred to as their drug of last resort.

The glass vial of Heparin was fitted with a threaded female connector that matched the male connector of the syringe on the table. He scrubbed his hands clean with a disposable alcohol wipe, then used another to cleanse the top of the Heparin vial and yet another to wipe the connector that was sutured and taped under his arm. The tube that penetrated his body was a Peripherally Inserted Central Catheter, or PICC Line for short. Once he had everything sterilized he filled the syringe from the Heparin bottle with the required amount of the drug and injected it into the tube.

Heparin, the doctor had told Virgil, was an anti-coagulant drug that prevented the formation of blood clots and helped aid in the healing process of human tissue. In non-technical language, it greased the skids for the real medicine, the Vancomycin.

After injecting the Heparin, he hooked up the Vancomycin container. The delivery process of the Vancomycin would take about thirty minutes as the medicine flowed from the ball and into a vein through Virgil's heart before being distributed throughout his body.

Five months ago, while working a case as the lead investigator for the state's Major Crimes Unit, Virgil had been kidnapped, tortured, and almost beaten to death. In the course of the beating, his leg was broken and required surgery to repair the damage. The surgery went well, or so he'd been told and he was up and around in no time at all. Except one day about eight weeks into the recovery process, he woke in the morning with a low-grade fever that did not seem to want to leave him alone no matter how many aspirin he took. He began to feel worse with each passing day until finally on the fifth morning Virgil's girlfriend, Sandy Small, found him unconscious on their bedroom floor. During the surgical procedure to fix his leg, Virgil had picked up a staph infection. The infection grew in his body where it eventually worked its way into his bloodstream, a condition known as staphylococcal sepsis. He'd been taking the Vancomycin twice a day for the last six weeks to kill the infection. This would be his last dose.

It had been a rough couple of months. During his previous investigation—right after his release from the hospital—the wife of one of the main suspects in his case killed Virgil's father, Mason. She was trying to shoot Virgil, but his father took the bullet instead.

The buzzing in Virgil's head was with him constantly. It had nothing to do with childhood memories and simpler times, nor did it have anything to do with the Heparin or the Vancomycin. It was because of the other drugs he was still taking. Oxycontin was one. He took two of the blue-colored thirty-milligram tablets three times a day. Between doses, he'd toss back two or three Vicodin…both for the pain in his leg.

At least that's what he kept telling himself.

When he thought about the men who kidnapped and tried to kill him, Virgil thought they might yet succeed.

———————————

HE BROKE TWO OF THE VICODIN IN HALF AND SWALLOWED them with a couple of sips of Dew. A few minutes later he felt the chemical rush hit his system the same way a shot of whiskey will burn the throat and warm the blood. He closed his eyes and let the feeling flow through his body and for a few minutes he felt confident and strong and happy and free. But he also knew the feeling wouldn't last, that soon the reality of his situation would once again wrap itself around him like a second skin, one in which he could not seem to find an edge. He thought if he could, he'd peel it away until nothing remained at all.

After twenty-five minutes or so, the Vancomycin container was empty, so Virgil unscrewed the connector and capped it off tight. He had an appointment later in the day to have the tube removed and a blood test to ensure the infection was gone.

When he pulled his fishing line from the pond he noticed that not only was the worm missing from the hook at the end of the line, but so too was his desire to fish. The late morning air was warm and still and when Virgil let his gaze settle on the bowed limbs of the willow tree planted next to the edge of the pond water he saw his father standing there, leaning against the trunk of the tree, his face partially hidden by the leafy, feather-veined fronds. He was shirtless under his bib-style bar apron tied off at his waist and he had a towel thrown over his left shoulder. Virgil could see the scar from the bullet wound at the bottom of his father's chest, the skin around the edges gnarled and puckered, yet somehow pink and fresh like that of a newborn baby.

They stared at each other for a long time, then Mason moved sideways a bit. "I'm worried about you, Son," he said. When he spoke, the buzzing inside Virgil's head went quiet and the absence of the incessant sound was more of a surprise than the vision of his dead father. "You're hitting the meds pretty hard, don't you think?"

"Better living through chemistry," Virgil said, but regretted the words as soon as they left his mouth. The sarcasm didn't seem to bother Mason though; the look of both love and concern on his face remaining steady. "I'm sorry, Dad."

"It's alright, Bud. I remember you told me that day in the truck how the pills were making you cranky."

"That's not what I meant. Why do I think you know that?"

"It wasn't your fault."

"Wasn't it?"

"Of course not." Mason looked away for a moment and wrapped his hands around the trunk of the willow tree. "This is a beautiful thing you did here, Virg. It's more significant than you might imagine."

After Mason's death, the people who meant more to Virgil than anyone else in the world brought his father's bloodied shirt to his house along with the willow tree. Together they buried the shirt and planted the tree on top of it. "Thanks, Dad, but I'm not exactly sure what that means."

"It's okay, Son. You wouldn't. You learn things over

here. It's sort of a timeless knowledge. I can't really explain it. The actual words don't exist."

"Can I ask you something?"

"Sure."

"I don't want you to take offense."

Mason smiled. "What is it, Son?"

"Why haven't I heard from my grandfather?"

"He's been here with you all morning, Virg. In fact, he spends most of his time with you."

"I've never seen him."

"It doesn't always work that way."

Virgil closed his eyes and shook his head. "I don't—"

"I have to go now, Virgil. You have people in your life who are going to need you."

"What do you mean?"

"I mean you've got to be shut of those pills. You're not thinking straight."

"I'm trying," Virgil said.

The smile left Mason's face and Virgil felt as much as he heard the words that came next. To Virgil, it felt as if they passed through him, like a pressure wave from a bomb blast. "*Try harder.*"

"Will you tell him I said hello?" Virgil asked.

"You can tell him yourself, Virg. He hears you. We all do." Then Mason looked toward the house and pointed with his chin. "Say, looks like you've got company." The look on his face was almost mischievous. "Don't worry, Virgil. Everything is exactly how it should be."

"I don't understand, Dad."

"Maybe not yet, but you will. Good-bye for now, Bud."

"Wait, Dad, there's something else I need to know."

"Dad loves you, Virgil. We all do. Stay tuned."

From the time Virgil was old enough to remember, he and his father had acknowledged their love for each other in something of an unusual way. Mason spoke of himself in the third person. He would say, "Dad loves you," and because Virgil was still young enough that he'd not yet grasped the many nuances of the English language, he'd say, "Dad loves you too." Virgil had always considered it one of the best things about his own life—the fact that they both continued to express their love for each other in that particular way: 'Dad loves you...Dad loves you too.'

The footsteps came from behind and when Virgil turned in his chair he saw his boss, Cora LaRue, and the governor's chief of staff, Bradley Pearson, as they approached across the backyard. Virgil put the pill bottles in the pocket of his shorts and stood to greet them, his legs not quite as steady as he would have liked. The air was thick and heavy without any wind and the surface water of the pond as smooth and flat as a tabletop mirror, but when Virgil looked over at the willow tree where he'd spoken with his dead father, he saw a few of the branches sway as if someone had brushed them aside.

The buzzing in his head was back and at that very

moment Virgil knew in his heart he'd do anything to make it all go away.

Anything at all.

———

WHEN THE PEOPLE OF INDIANA ELECTED HEWITT (MAC) McConnell as governor, he answered their concerns over rising crime rates by forming the Major Crimes Unit. He appointed Cora LaRue as the administrator of the division and together she and the governor chose Virgil as the lead detective for all investigative operations. Because of the nature of politics though, Cora spent most of her time dealing with Pearson instead of the governor. As a result, Pearson— the state's biggest political operator—often used this to his advantage in ways that were not only unnecessary but also counterproductive. In short, it was typical politics, which Virgil despised more than almost anything. Cora never let her dislike of Pearson get in the way of her job, though she never tried to hide her feelings either. Pearson, on the other hand, operator that he was, rarely let his emotions show. You could be a friend one minute if it suited any particular agenda, or conversely, if the need arose, you could be an enemy of the state. The problem with people like Pearson, Virgil knew, was that those two things were not often mutually exclusive.

"Jonesy, how are you feeling?" Cora asked.

"I'm squeaking by," Virgil said. His words were

slurred and his tongue felt thick and unresponsive and he had to look away from Cora when he spoke.

"We need to talk to you, Jonesy. I'm sorry about this, I really am."

"Sorry about what?"

"Oh for Christ's sake, Cora, look at him," Pearson said. "It's the right call. He's in no condition. No condition at all. He has tubes coming out of him and he sounds like he's three sheets to the wind. How about we get this over with and get back to work?"

"Hi, Bradley, always a pleasure," Virgil said. "I'm standing right here, you know. How about telling me what's going on?"

Pearson ran his hands across his forehead then up through his thinning hair. He pulled back so hard on his scalp that for a moment the outer corners of his eyes angled upward in a manner that gave him an effeminate look. He started to speak, but Cora cut him off.

"Jonesy, about an hour ago, on direct orders from the governor, you've been replaced as lead detective of the Major Crimes Unit." She paused to let her words sink in and Virgil saw her eyes slide away from his own. "Ron Miles has been appointed by the governor as your replacement."

Virgil sat back down in his lawn chair and looked out at the pond water. When he didn't respond, Pearson filled the silence. "Look at yourself, Jones. What did you expect? You're a goddamned mess. How many pills are you popping these days, anyway?"

"Why are you here, Bradley?"

"To make sure that there is no misunderstanding regarding your situation."

The drugs were still working on him and when Virgil spoke he took no care with his words or their intent. "How much of that is your doing? Never mind, you don't have to answer. We already know the answer to that question, don't we? So here's the deal Pearson…I think I want you to leave. In fact, I'm sure of it. Would you like me to show you to your car?"

"In your condition? I'd like to see you try," Pearson said. He stepped forward and when he did his foot came down on top of the cane pole and snapped it in half. Pearson jumped a little at the sound the cane made when it broke and when he did, Virgil knew he had not stepped on it with purpose. Pearson bent over to pick up the ruined pole, as if the act of lifting it in his hands could repair the damage. "Don't touch that," Virgil said, his voice no more than a whisper. "I really would like you to leave now."

Cora looked at Pearson, then back at Virgil. "Would you two please give it a rest?"

"This is my home, Cora," Virgil said. "I make the rules here. Not him, and not you either." When she didn't respond, Virgil said, "What?"

"There's something else."

"There always is, Cora. Except I can't for the life of me imagine what it might be."

"Your replacement isn't temporary. They're not going to let you come back."

Virgil stood and faced her. "Say that again."

Cora took an involuntary step back, as if in fear. "The state. They're forcing you out."

"*What?* On what grounds?"

"The medical reports for one. You'll qualify for three-quarters disability. With your time on the job, your pension will kick in right away. I've done the math and the truth is you'll be making more by walking away than if you stayed."

Virgil kept glancing over at the willow tree as if something his father had said would somehow help him. He bent down to retrieve the broken cane pole and when he stood, the look on Cora's face seemed as sad and mixed as his own emotions.

"How bad is it?" she said.

"I don't know, Cora. Some things can't be fixed."

She stepped close and placed her hand on the flat of Virgil's bare chest, her eyes inspecting the PICC line. "I'm not talking about the fishing pole, Jonesy."

"I know you're not. Neither am I."

Cora shook her head, then raised her chin, her voice taking on an official tone. "I'm sorry, Detective, but I'm going to have to ask you for your badge."

Virgil dropped the cane pole back in the grass at Pearson's feet, then reached into his pocket, pulled out his badge, and skipped it across the surface of the pond. The badge made it about halfway across before it settled and then sank in the murky depths.

"You want my badge? Go and get it." He turned to walk up to his house, but Cora didn't let it play.

"You break my heart sometimes, Jonesy. Do you know that?"

CHAPTER FOUR

RON MILES DUCKED UNDER THE CRIME-SCENE TAPE AND stepped up to the apartment door, then stopped in his tracks. He peered inside, saw the crime scene techs—seven of them in all, the most he'd seen at one location in quite a while—caught Rosie's eye, then backed out. He didn't want to contaminate the area. *Shit load of blood,* he thought.

Ron had been around. Had spent most of his career as an Indianapolis Metro Homicide cop, so he was no stranger to crime scenes or blood, but still, a hell of a way to start a new job, with that much blood.

———

A FEW MINUTES LATER DETECTIVE TOM ROSENCRANTZ stepped out of the apartment wearing Tyvek coveralls, shoe protectors, and latex gloves. He had bloodstains on his knees, the tops of his shoe protectors by his toes, and the palms of his hands. He unzipped the suit, pulled the hood back, and stripped out of the gear. One of the techs handed him a biohazard bag and he dropped everything inside and handed it back. "Christ, I've never seen that much blood without a body," he said to Miles. "You just get here?"

"Yeah. What do you mean without a body?"

"I mean, there's enough blood in there to do a remake of Stephen King's Carrie, but there's no body."

"Huh. How much blood are they saying?"

Rosencrantz looked over Ron's shoulder. "You get a new car?"

"Yep. Picked it up two days ago. The guys over at the motor pool set me up with the radios, lights and siren, the works."

Rosencrantz smiled at him. "Nice." The car was nice too. A brand new black over black Ford Fusion. "Get the Police Interceptor motor?"

"You mean engine. Motor is electric. Engine is internal combustion. And yeah, did I ever. The goddamn thing runs like a raped ape. All-wheel drive too." Miles glanced at the apartment. "So anyway, how much blood?"

"Here comes Mimi. I'll let her explain it. I guess it's sort of technical. Plus, that voice of hers…"

Miles puffed out his cheeks. "Tell me about it. She could be one of those phone sex broads. Half the time when she's talking to me I feel like I'm about to get busted for sexual harassment because I listened."

Rosencrantz made a rude noise with his lips. "Half? You're doing better than me."

"They still have that, don't they? Those phone sex lines?"

"I'm sure I wouldn't know," Rosencrantz said, his face as flat and blank as a piece of slate.

———————

MIMI PHILLIPS, THE LEAD CRIME SCENE TECHNICIAN, TOLD them in no uncertain terms—all with a voice that sounded like a 30-second satellite radio spot for a porn flick—that whomever the blood belonged to, they were, without question, as dead as the Pope's dick. "Double entendre intended," she added.

"You're sure?" Miles asked.

Mimi reached into her pocket, then folded a stick of gum across her tongue. "No doubt about it," she said. "The human body—and these are averages, mind you, depending on size and so on and so forth—holds about six quarts of blood. The loss of about forty percent or more of that volume will generally require immediate resuscitation. But what you have to remember is the amount of blood loss any one person can withstand is going to depend on their physical condition and cardiovascular shape. Athletes, people who live in high altitudes, and the elderly are examples of disparate groups that will have differing susceptibilities to blood loss. The amount of blood we're talking about for that to happen…it's about a two-liter sized bottle of soda pop. What you've got in there is at least twice that. If it all belongs to the same person, then, yeah, they're dead all right. Deader than—"

"How soon before you can tell us if it all belongs to the same person?" Miles asked.

Mimi bit the inside corner of her lower lip. "Hmm, belonged, I think is the word you want there. Not very long at all to type it out. Three days if you want to match the DNA from the personal effects and we rush the shit out of it. You do want the DNA, don't you?"

"Yes, we do," Miles said. "Rush the shit out of it."

Mimi turned to go back to work, then over her shoulder, "Hell of a way to start a new job, huh? Nice wheels though. Bet that baby scoots."

———

"You talk to him yet?" Rosencrantz asked.

"Who?"

"Who, my ass." He gave Miles a 'Don't try to bullshit me' look. "Have you called him? Anything?"

"Cora asked me not to say anything until she and Pearson had a chance to go over to his place and tell him in person." Miles looked at his watch. "They're probably still there."

"Three things," Rosencrantz said. He ticked them off his fingers. "One, if you haven't figured this out yet, Pearson is a snake and now he's *your* snake. I'd get used to it, I was you *and* I'd watch my back. Two, Jonesy is not only a good guy, but he's our friend. At the very least you owe him a phone call and when I say at the very least, I mean exactly that. Three, it is my belief that there might be something else going on, politically speaking, that put him out and you in. You may want to spend some time with that, you being the crack investigator and all."

Miles reached up and flattened his grey hair with the palm of his hand. "I know about Pearson. This won't be my first interaction with the man. And, I am going to speak with Jonesy, but I thought it might be best to let things settle for a bit. Also, I'm not a political guy. I'm an investigator guy. They tell me to investigate, that's what I do."

Rosencrantz held his hands up, palms out. "Hey, I'm not giving you grief, Ron, But this little squad we've got here, our MCU, it's always been run a little…sideways, if you know what I mean."

"If you mean you make your own rules, keep the intel to yourselves, and don't have too much oversight, then yeah, I've sort of noticed that. That might change too."

Rosie shook his head. "That's not what I meant. What you said is true, but it's more than that. You're suddenly one of the most powerful cops in the state with only two layers between you and the governor himself."

"And?"

"Have you asked yourself why they wanted *you* for the job?"

Miles was starting to get a little pissed. "You work for me, do I have that right?"

"Yep."

"Then how about you do that?"

"Leave the big thinking to you?"

Miles pointed a finger at Rosencrantz. "Now look…"

"Relax, Ron. I'm on your side. No disrespect intended, okay? You're one of the best investigators I've ever known. I want you to think about the situation. Investigate the 'why me?' part of the equation, for your own sake if nothing else."

"And maybe for Jonesy too?"

"Why not?"

"Because based on what I've heard, I don't think it will do him any good at this point."

"Maybe it won't. But I've been a part of this group almost since its inception and if I've learned anything, it's this: We get the hard stuff, the political stuff, the good stuff, as Cora likes to call it. But nothing is ever quite what it looks like. Not when you're this close to the top. Never has been anyway. Not one single time."

Miles thought about that for a minute. "Maybe this one will be different."

Rosencrantz laughed without humor. "Did you happen

to get a look at Jonesy's files yet? In particular, the one I told you about?"

"Yeah, I did. What about it?"

"Anything jump out at you?"

"It looked like a good shoot. The department, the union, the lawyers, hell even IA said it was a good shoot. Plus, it was over twenty years ago. I had to blow the dust off the paper so I could see the ink."

"Did you know it was the one and only time Jonesy ever fired his weapon on the job?"

"That's not so unusual."

"You're right about that. But let me tell you two things that aren't in that report. One, did you notice that the guy who almost got his ticket punched by James Pope—the victim so to speak—wasn't listed in the report?"

"Yeah, I did notice that. Who was it?"

Rosencrantz turned his back to Miles for a moment and looked up at the apartment where the crime scene techs were working. When he turned back he said, "Someone with enough juice to get their name pulled from the paperwork. Know anyone like that?" Before Miles could answer, Rosie said something else that made Ron wonder if someone he thought he could trust hadn't already played him for a fool. "That apartment behind us? The one with all the blood? It belonged to a guy named Nicholas Pope. He was only five or six years old when Jonesy shot his old man to death. He and his twin sister were there, at the shooting. They saw the whole thing.

Now it looks like there's another dead Pope. Might be a coincidence though."

Miles rubbed his temples with his right hand, then squinted through one eye at Rosencrantz. "Who did Jonesy save that day when he shot James Pope?"

"It's not in the report, but it's not exactly a secret, either. The man he saved was Bradley Pearson." Then, as if to hammer home his point, he added, "Out of curiosity, when they hired you, who approached you first? Was it Cora, or Pearson?"

Miles let out a sigh. "It was Pearson."

Rosencrantz raised an eyebrow at him. "Might want to think about that. Or hell, maybe not. You might be right. What do I know? Maybe this one will be different."

———

NICHOLAS POPE'S APARTMENT COMPLEX HAD BEEN converted from an old-style traveler's motel. The conversion process had gone like this: The original owner of the motel went broke, which is something that will happen when you don't pay your income taxes. The new owner picked up the building at the subsequent tax sale, fired the housekeeping crew, then erected a sign that said, 'Studio Apartments For Rent - No References Required.' The only actual requirement for occupancy was cash in advance every Friday by five or your personal belongings were tossed out on the lot and the locks were changed faster than you could get to the payday advance loan sharks and back. The building was a two-story, L-shaped structure with units on both the front and the rear. Nicholas Pope's unit was in the back on the second floor, about midpoint in the short section of the L. The building was old and its occupants generally fit into one of three categories: Poor, transient, or illegal. Most, Ron thought as he looked around the backside of the building, probably fit nicely into all three.

"You going to suit up, take a look?" Rosencrantz asked him.

"No. I think I'll get with the uniforms and coordinate with the background."

"Start with the woman in the unit right below Pope's. She's the one who made the call."

"She hear or see anything?"

"Not really. But one of the city uniforms said the blood dripped through her ceiling and landed right on a little statue of the Virgin Mary she keeps on her living room coffee table. She thought it was a miracle."

Miles shook his head. "Ah, Christ."

Rosencrantz winced. "Don't say that around her. She'll take your head off."

"How long before she figured it wasn't divine intervention?"

Rosencrantz thought for a few seconds. "You know, I'm not sure. Probably at least a half-day, based on what Mimi is telling us."

Then, as Miles was about to go talk to the woman, a car turned the corner around the backside of the building going much too fast, its tires squealing in protest. The driver slammed on the brakes and locked up the wheels, but it was too late. The car slid into the side of Miles' brand new squad car with the sickening sound of crumpled sheet metal and broken glass. The driver jumped from her vehicle and half ran, half stumbled toward the stairs that led to Nicholas Pope's apartment. She began to scream, "My brother, my brother. Where's my brother?"

One of the uniforms caught her by the arm, but Nichole Pope was a little faster and a little stronger than the cop expected and when she tried to pull free, they got tangled up in each other and ended up on the ground in a heap.

Rosencrantz looked at Miles, then at his car, then back at Miles. "Probably shouldn't have parked there. My car is out front, across the street. Welcome to the MCU, Ron."

CHAPTER FIVE

VIRGIL LEFT CORA AND BRADLEY, AND CARRIED HIS broken fishing pole and medical supplies back toward the house. When he walked inside he heard Sandy as she moved about between the bedroom and the bathroom. He set the pole on the countertop that separated the kitchen from the living room then placed the medical supplies into the refrigerator. When Sandy came around the corner her blonde hair was still wet from the shower, slicked back across her head. She walked over and got up on her toes and kissed Virgil.

"I was getting ready to come out and sit with you, but then I saw Cora and Pearson pull in. What did they want?"

Sandy was employed by the Indiana Law Enforcement Academy as their Director of Training. Before that, she worked for Virgil as a field investigator for the MCU. She transferred to her current position after Cora discovered they were dating. She would have taken the job anyway, but the way it was handled still rubbed Virgil wrong when he thought about it. He pulled out two stools from under the counter and sat down. "Can we talk for a minute?"

"Sure. Don't want to be late for your appointment, though."

"We'll be okay."

Sandy sat down next to him. "What is it? What did Cora have to say?"

"Plenty."

"What do you mean?"

Virgil removed his hat, set it on the counter, and ran his fingers through his hair. "Cora came for my badge, Sandy. She brought Pearson as her witness."

Virgil watched Sandy's lips start to move, but she didn't speak. Her face turned red, and after a few seconds she stood and looked out the front window toward the drive. "I'll be right back."

"Sandy, wait. Don't do anything. There's more I need to tell—"

But she'd already stopped listening. She cinched her robe tight and walked barefoot out the front door. By the time Virgil made it to the porch she was halfway down the front drive waving her arms at Cora and Pearson as they backed out toward the road. They were far enough down the drive that Virgil couldn't make out what she was saying, but he didn't need to. Sandy was bent forward from her waist and was leaning almost all the way into the car, her finger pointed directly at Cora. The glare at the top of the windshield prevented Virgil from seeing the look on Cora's face, but he could see her hands on the steering wheel and it looked like if she gripped it any tighter it might snap in half with the same ease as the cane pole after Pearson's misstep. When Sandy stepped back from the car, she pointed to the road, then stood with her fists on her hips until Cora backed the rest of the way out and drove away.

When she stepped up onto the front porch the bathrobe slipped open enough to expose the swell of her breasts and the light sprinkle of freckles across her chest. They went back inside and all Virgil really wanted to do was take her to the bedroom and make love to her…to tell her of his conversation with his dead father…to ask her to help pull him up from the depths of a place in which he sank a little lower with the passage of every waking hour. But none of that happened. "I wish you hadn't done that," he said.

"What? Why on earth not?"

Before he could answer, Sandy noticed the cane pole in pieces on the counter. "Oh, Virgil. What happened?"

"Pearson broke it. It was an accident, I'm sure. You're the best, baby. You know that, don't you?"

He'd hoped to make her smile, to somehow lighten the load he had managed to put them under, but it didn't work. "What are we going to do, Virgil?"

Good question. "About what?" Virgil said with feigned indifference. Even as he said it, he knew his cavalier, drug–induced attitude had broken the moment. He watched the hurt, frustration, and embarrassment as it played across Sandy's face. Then, without saying a word she walked into the bedroom and closed the door, leaving him alone in the kitchen with a bottle of pills, a busted fishing pole, and a ruined career.

———————

AN HOUR LATER, THEY RODE TO THE HOSPITAL IN complete silence. When they pulled to a stop in the parking lot, Virgil shut the engine off and turned toward Sandy. She wore a lightweight dress that matched her blue eyes, along with square-toed, short-heeled cowboy boots. The dress hung above her knees, the fabric tight across her breasts and loose around her hips. It was a perfected look and it had a tendency to turn a few heads. Virgil wore jeans with a hole in one knee, a cartoon T-shirt, and flip-flops. That turned a few heads as well, though for entirely different reasons. "What did you say to Cora?"

"Nothing that she didn't already know," Sandy said.

"I'm not sure I know what that means."

Sandy huffed. "It means you think she walks on water but I've always thought she's a typical administrator who watches out for herself above all others. Look what happened when she found out we were dating."

"It seems to have all worked out."

Sandy shook her head. "Has it? I changed jobs, a change that I'd be the first to admit was something I'd been thinking about anyway, but it ended up being something I was forced into so you and I could get on with our lives. Except you were almost killed and now you're hooked on pain medicine. How is that 'working out,' exactly?"

Virgil ignored her remark about the pills. "You still haven't answered me. What did you say to her?"

"When I was venting or trying to communicate?"

"Aren't they the same thing?"

"No. They're not. When I was venting I'm pretty sure I referenced the size of her ass."

"I see. And after that?"

"I told her that she lost the best thing that's ever happened to her."

Virgil reached over and took hold of Sandy's hand. "Thank you. I'm sorry. I didn't mean to upset you or cause you any embarrassment."

She pulled her hand away and waved it in the air. "It's not that. That's not what upsets me. God, Jonesy, where is your head?"

"Then what is it?"

She turned and looked out the passenger window as she spoke. "It's what she said back to me. I told her she'd lost the best thing that's ever happened to her and she looks me straight in the eye and says if I don't get you off those pills then she and I will have more in common than either of us wants. I'm scared, Virgil. I've never been this scared in my entire life."

———————

VIRGIL THOUGHT IT ODD THAT THE DOCTOR HAD ORDERED the removal of the PICC line at the hospital instead of the office until he discovered that the doctor would not be the one removing the line. They had been waiting for almost half an hour when a nurse came into the room. She wore plain green scrubs with white tennis shoes, had a stethoscope around her neck and her hospital ID badge clipped low on a side pocket. Virgil guessed her age to be about twenty years younger than he was which would put her somewhere in her early twenties. Her hair was short and choppy and looked like she spent a considerable amount of time making it look like she'd recently rolled out of bed. Her eyes were clear and brown and her teeth were perfect. When she saw Virgil sitting on the hospital bed she stopped in her tracks and when she did, her shoes made a little double squeak on the floor. The sum total of her greeting went like this: "You're supposed to be wearing a gown." She sounded bored; her voice dull and flat like a butter knife at the back of the drawer…if a butter knife could sound dull and flat, that is.

When Virgil didn't immediately reply, she shrugged her shoulders and pulled a gown from the cabinet next to the bed. "Slip into this. I'll be back in a minute." She looked at Sandy, pointed an index finger her way, and said, "No funny business."

After she left the room Sandy said, "Maybe she was here last time we were."

Virgil smiled at her then changed into the gown after the nurse left...then they waited another half hour. When the nurse came back in Virgil made the mistake of asking her if a doctor might be available to handle the removal of the line. She rolled her eyes, put her hands on her hips, and spent the next five minutes explaining her qualifications and training. When she finished, she looked at him and said, "So, okay if I pull the line now?"

Virgil may have been half stoned on morphine, but he wasn't an idiot. "Absolutely," he said.

The nurse pulled the tape from the entry point—a little harder than necessary—then cleaned the area with rubbing alcohol. She told him to hold still even though he wasn't moving and slowly began to extract the line. It was an unusual sensation. Not painful, but he could feel the line snake away from his heart and through his chest. The tube was longer than he thought it would be. She pulled it out with one slow and steady motion and by the time it was all the way out her arm was almost fully extended.

After she cleaned the entry point again, she put a bandage over the area and told him to keep it dry for a couple of days. Virgil said he would, then asked, "Is that it then? Can we go?"

"Not yet," the nurse said. "I've got to do the paper and ask you a couple of questions. Are you currently on any medication?"

Virgil kept his head still, but his eyes slid over toward Sandy. "Yeah, I'm on some pain medication."

"Still hurts, huh?"

"You could say that."

"I know *I* could say that," the nurse said, "but what would *you* say? Where do you rate your pain on a scale of one to ten?"

"I thought we were going to pull the line and then I could go."

She stared at him without answering. Sandy stood from her chair and said, "I'm going to wait outside. Can I have the keys to the truck?"

"Sure," Virgil said. "They're in the pocket of my jeans. I think we're almost done here though. Why don't you wait for me?"

Sandy pulled the keys from the pocket of his pants as if she hadn't heard him, then said, "See you outside."

The nurse looked at Virgil. "So, as I was saying, on a scale of one to ten…"

———

Sandy was waiting for him in the parking lot. They got in the truck and as Virgil was about to start the engine, she reached over and took hold of his hand. He let the keys dangle in the ignition and looked at her. "What?"

She dropped her head a little and looked over the top of her sunglasses. "You're going to make me say it?"

"Say what?"

"Tell me what's going on."

"What do you mean?"

"I mean there's something that you're not telling me."

Virgil gave her his best 'everything is all right' smile, but it had no effect. "Okay. Here it is. You're going to think I'm crazy, but I had an interesting conversation this morning."

"You mean with Pearson and Cora?"

"Not exactly. It was before they showed up."

"Someone else came over?"

"You could say that." He took a deep breath and let it out. "I spoke with my dad today, Sandy. He was standing under the willow tree. I looked over and he was…there."

"*What?*"

"Hear me out, will you? I feel like I'm losing my mind. I've got this buzzing in my head…I don't know how to explain it. I was sitting there with a line in the pond, letting the Vanco run through me and when I looked over at the willow tree, he was standing there. He was sort of hidden behind a few of the branches and when he saw me, or when he noticed that I saw him, he moved over so I could see him clearly. He was *there*. I don't know what it means, but the buzzing in my head was gone while we spoke to each other."

Sandy leaned forward, put her elbows on her thighs, and her face in her hands. After a few seconds, she raised her head and looked at Virgil like he was a stranger. "I can't do this, Virgil. You've got to stop. Do you hear me? You have to stop. I just can't do it."

———————

IF THE RIDE TO THE HOSPITAL WAS ONE OF STRAINED silence—and it was—the ride back was like a vacuum. When they pulled into the drive and parked by the house, Sandy looked at him and said, "What are you going to do?"

Before Mason died, he and Virgil owned a downtown Jamaican-themed tavern called Jonesy's, one of the most popular bars in the city, if not the state. When Virgil spoke, he did so with little care or forethought. "I've got to go down to the bar."

Sandy gave him a deliberate look. "That's not what I meant. And you know what else? I think you know it." She hung her head and let it sway back and forth. "What I meant, Virgil, is what are you going to do about *you*? God, Jonesy, where are you? Where is the man I fell in love with? I'll tell you something…he's not here right now. In fact, I haven't seen him for weeks."

"Hey, Sandy, come on now. That's not exactly fair. I'm right—"

Sandy opened her door and got out of the truck. When she turned back her face was red and the wind blew her hair across the corners of her mouth. "Don't you say it. Don't you dare try to tell me you're right here, because you're not. Your body is here, but your mind? Your spirit and your soul? They're someplace else. I think they're living in that pill bottle you carry round in your pocket. I don't fit in a bottle, Virgil. I never thought you did, either." She slammed the door of the truck and started to walk away, but then she turned around and yanked the door back open. "I'll never leave you, Virgil. Never. Not after what we've been through. But let me ask you something. How do you think it feels to know that right now, right this very minute, of the two of us, I'm the only one who can honestly say that?"

When Virgil didn't answer she let the door of the truck hang open and walked away. Virgil thought of about twenty different things he should have done right then, but he did none of them. Instead, he dropped the truck into gear and drove away, the door slamming shut against the frame, gravel pinging at the underside of the wheel wells.

SANDY'S WORDS AND THE MANNER IN WHICH SHE SPOKE left little doubt in Virgil's mind about the state of their relationship and what he needed to do. His addiction to the pills was driving a wedge between them, a situation that was unacceptable, especially after what they'd been through together. Sandy was not only his girlfriend and lover, she was Virgil's entire life. Their future had been sealed by fate long ago when her father died while saving Virgil's life. His name was Andrew Small and he was the station chief for the fire department that served the neighborhood where Virgil lived when he was a young boy. When the house caught fire and burned he was trapped inside, buried beneath a pile of rubble that collapsed over his head as he tried to escape. Chief Small and another fireman went in to rescue him, but Sandy's dad perished in a secondary explosion before he made it out of the house. So Virgil grew up happy and healthy, but it came at the expense of Sandy's lifelong sorrow. Yet fate had intertwined their lives and left them beautifully connected, but with a level of expectation that amazed and often frightened him.

He made it about halfway to the bar before he turned the truck around and drove back to their house. He hadn't been gone very long, but by the time he returned, Sandy's car was not in the drive or the garage and when Virgil went inside he discovered she was no longer home.

CHAPTER SIX

NICHOLE POPE HAD HER ARMS CROSSED, THE LOOK ON HER face a mixture of disbelief, anger, and fear. Mostly anger. She jabbed her finger at Miles. "What do you mean there's no body? Let me tell you something, that's wrong on about ten different levels, but the main thing is, when you use the word 'body' it implies that my brother is dead. Are you saying my brother is dead, Detective?"

"Ms. Pope, we don't really know what's going on yet, other than the blood in your brother's apartment and the apparent lack of a victim."

"So in other words you don't know anything, do you, *Detective*?"

Miles was still more than a little hot himself about the side of his new car and he wasn't about to be pushed around, grieving sibling or not. "I'll tell you what we know for sure. We know you're a lousy driver and you wrecked my new car." Jabbing his finger right back now. "That's what we know for sure."

"Your car? *Your car?* You're dancing around the fact that you've got blood all over my brother's apartment, buckets of blood in fact, no witnesses, no body—your words, not mine—and you're worried about your car? Let me tell you something, Detective, and hear me when I say this: *Fuck your car.*"

———————

MIMI WALKED OVER, INTRODUCED HERSELF TO NICHOLE, and said, "Ms. Pope, if you'd be willing to let us take a sample of your blood we'd be able to get a definitive answer as to whom the blood belonged to much faster than we normally could. It will still have to be processed through the lab and all that, but they could begin with random samples and we'd have a conclusive answer much quicker."

Nichole gave Miles a parting glare before she turned her attention to Mimi. "How much faster?"

"We'd be looking at hours instead of days."

"Then, yes, of course. Let's do that. What do I have to do?"

Mimi took her by the arm. "Come with me. We'll get you all set up. It should only take a few minutes."

"If that's my brother's blood in there, is there any chance that he'd still be alive?"

Mimi shook her head. "I'm not going to dance around it, sweetie. With that amount of blood…"

––––––––––––

ROSENCRANTZ INTRODUCED MILES TO LOLA IBARRA, THE tenant who lived in the apartment directly below Nicholas Pope. She was on the far side of middle-aged, but not too far, Ron thought. She wore a flowered housedress that matched the flowered scarf in her hair, the flowered sandals on her feet, and the flowered bracelets on her wrists. The apartment was, Ron discovered, surprisingly well kept and clean. It smelled of pine-scented cleaner, incense, and coffee. But it was the artwork and absurdity of Lola Ibarra's decorative choices that caused Ron to bite the inside of his cheek.

The walls were covered with paintings of Jesus, all on black velvet. They were markedly similar to the Elvis on velvet series, or the dogs playing poker on velvet series, except of course, these all pictured Jesus. Elvis had apparently left the building, took the dogs, and left Jesus behind to fend for Himself.

"Mrs. Ibarra, I'd like to walk through the sequence of events with you. Would you tell me what happened, please?"

"I have already talked with the other man. I cannot remember his name. Detective, um, Happenstance?"

"That would be Rosencrantz."

"Yes, of course. Rosencrantz." Ibarra tugged at her scarf until it was arranged just so, then pointed to the coffee table in the center of the small living room. "I woke up and sat down on the sofa to wait for the coffee. I boil it on the stove instead of using one of the drippy machines, so it takes a little longer. That is when I saw my statue of the Holy Mother. It had blood on it. I thought it was a miracle." She crossed herself when she said miracle and it gave Miles the impression that it was a 'just-in-case' crossing, like perhaps it really was divine intervention and not something quite so simple as evidence from a crime scene.

"I see. And how long did it take you to figure out that it wasn't a miracle?"

"Hmm. I am not sure. I began to pray right away of course. I got down on my knees and prayed as I have never prayed before, I can tell you that. But then I could smell my coffee starting to burn—I had prayed so long that the pot boiled dry—so I had to clean that up. When I came back I was going to pray some more—which I did —and then I went in the bathroom to shower and get cleaned up. I wanted to look nice for Father Peralta, my priest."

"And did Father Peralta come by?"

"Yes. He was the one who told me it was not a miracle after all and that we needed to call the authorities."

"And how did he determine that, Mrs. Ibarra?"

She pointed at her ceiling directly above the statue. A

dark stain covered the thin plaster. "He look at the ceiling."

"So…no miracle I guess."

Ibarra shrugged her shoulders and then crossed herself again. "Who is to say?"

I am, Ron thought. "I'm afraid we're going to have to confiscate your statue as evidence in an ongoing investigation. It will be returned but we're going to have to take it for now."

Ibarra waved her hand in the air. "This is not a problem for me. I have a whole box full of them in storage. I sell them on the E-bay."

"I'll have one of our crime scene technicians come over and get it. In the meantime, please don't touch it."

"Yes, yes."

"A few more questions then, Mrs. Ibarra. Did you hear anything last night or yesterday either outside or in the apartment above you that seemed out of the ordinary?"

"No, I hear nothing. Nothing at all."

"No loud bangs, or thumps, or shouting? Nothing like that?"

"Si. Nothing."

"Huh."

"What is this, huh?"

"Well, I don't mean to alarm you Mrs. Ibarra, but whatever happened up there, it had to have been violent. I'm surprised you didn't hear anything."

"I did not hear anything because I was not at home."

Miles audibly exhaled and then scratched the back of his head. "I see. And what time did you get home?"

"Hmm, I would say it was well after midnight."

"Sort of late, then."

"Si, very late for me. It was bingo night at the church. It was my turn to be the caller."

"What do you know about Mr. Pope? Did you ever speak with him? Was he friendly with you?"

"Oh yes. My little Nicky, he was very friendly. A very nice man. Most of the people around here do not like to give you the time of day and to tell you the truth, you would not want it if they did, comprende?"

"Yes, I comprende. But you and Mr. Pope were friendly?"

"Yes. He always fix my computer for me whenever I have a problem. I think the E-bay messes it up somehow."

"When was the last time you saw him?"

Ibarra looked up at the ceiling, either trying to remember, or looking for a sign from Jesus, Ron couldn't tell for sure. "Three days ago. He carried my garbage to the container for me."

"Is there anything you could tell me about Mr. Pope that would help me find his killer, Mrs. Ibarra? Anything at all?"

Ibarra waved her hands in front of herself. "No, there is nothing. Nicky, he is a nice young man who helped me out sometimes. He said I reminded him of his mother. He had a good job and he worked for the lottery people. He used to tease me and say he knew the secret to winning and that one day he would tell me how to pick the numbers and I would become wealthy."

Miles handed her his business card. "If there's anything else you can think of, call me right away. Keep your doors locked. We don't know why Mr. Pope was killed, only that he was."

"Yes. I will lock my door. There is only the one."

"Windows too, Mrs. Ibarra."

"Yes. I have only the one window too, but I will lock it."

Miles thanked her and began to leave, but Ibarra had one more thing. "Señor Detective?"

"Yes?"

"Nicky, he such a nice boy like I said…"

"But?"

"He had some bad friends, I think."

"Bad how?"

"They like their checkers. I smell the stink right through the window."

"Checkers?"

Ibarra laughed. "It is a Mexican term for low-grade marijuana. What you would call ditch weed."

"Checkers?"

"Si, checkers."

"Huh. I've never heard of that. What do you call high-grade marijuana?"

"Chess." Then she lowered her voice and leaned in

closer to Miles. "Is also sometimes called 'good shit.'"
Crossed herself again when she said it.

———

Miles walked outside and found Mimi and
Rosencrantz standing together next to the stairs that led to
Pope's apartment. He nodded at Mimi and then looked at
Rosencrantz. "What do you know about Checkers and
Chess?"

Rosencrantz didn't hesitate. "Always go with Chess.
Checkers will destroy your lungs. Tastes like shit too.
Now Chess, true Chess if you can find it, that's some
really good shit, even though that statement itself is
slightly redundant. Why do you ask?"

"Never mind," Miles said. "I think I'm getting old."

———

"Might want to take a look at this picture," Mimi
said, and at the sound of her voice, Miles forgot all about
his age. "It's a Polaroid. We'll have other pictures with
better resolution later today when we get the digital prints,
but you should see this." She handed the photo to Miles.

Ron looked at the photo but he couldn't tell what it
was. "I don't get it. What am I looking at here?"

Mimi positioned herself next to Miles and that gave
him a little thrum. "It's what we in the business of crime

scene investigations often refer to as a *clue*." She made little air quotes with her fingers when she said 'clue.' "Specifically, it's the floor underneath the front of Pope's sofa, behind the dust ruffle. Is that what they're called? Dust ruffles? You know, the flap part that hangs down at the bottom? If you lift it up you can see under the couch? Anyway, my guys found this when they moved the sofa. It's some sort of code."

Once Mimi explained it, Miles could see it right away. It was a long series of numbers. The sequence read: 102120103157123 "Is it written in blood?"

"It sure is," Mimi said. "Looks like your victim was trying to tell you something."

Rosencrantz stepped closer and took another look at the photo. "Trying to tell us what?"

Mimi let her eyes do a little half roll before they landed on Rosencrantz. "Me and my crew? We process the scene. You guys are supposed to be the crack investigators. My guess is your victim was trying to tell you who let him bleed out all over the floor. It'd take some balls to write a message in your own blood."

When Mimi said the word 'balls' Rosencrantz and Miles made a point not to look at each other. "I'll want a copy of that as soon as you can get it to me," Miles said.

Mimi handed him the photo. "You can have this one now. I'll email the digital ones to you when they're ready."

Miles took the Polaroid from Mimi. "Do that," he

said. "I've got to figure out what to do about my car." He stuck the photo in his pocket and walked away.

Rosencrantz and Mimi stood there and watched him go. "What was that bit about Checkers and Chess?"

"Apparently, it's Mexican slang for pot," Rosie said. "I'd never heard of it until I spoke with Mrs. Ibarra." He winked at her before he walked away.

CHAPTER SEVEN

SHORTLY AFTER HIS FATHER PASSED, VIRGIL'S FAMILY attorney called and informed him his father's will stipulated that if his mother preceded him in death—which she did—most all of his possessions were to be bequeathed solely to Virgil, save two. He left the majority of his half of the bar in various percentages to three people. Of them, two were employees; Delroy Rouche, their bar manager, and Robert Whyte, their chef. Delroy and Robert were Jamaicans who had been working for Virgil and Mason almost as long as they had been in business. Virgil met them both by chance several years ago while on vacation in their hometown of Lucea, a small town about halfway between the tourist destinations of Montego Bay and Negril. They ran a roadside stand that served Red Stripe beer and homemade Jerk chicken to tourists like Virgil. He'd picked up a nail in the road and the tire went flat almost immediately. When he pulled into their lot to change it out for the spare, Delroy and Robert fixed it for him while he ate their chicken and drank their beer. A friendship developed and when they came to the states to work for Virgil and Mason they transformed what would have been a regular downtown bar into a one-of-a-kind Jamaican experience for anyone who walked through the door. Mason's will stipulated that Delroy and Robert were to each receive fifteen percent ownership in the bar, while nineteen percent went to Murton, who had been a part of Virgil's family since childhood. The remaining one percent went to Virgil.

When Virgil walked through the back door of the bar and into the kitchen, Robert handed him a plate of chicken pulled from the bone and covered with his homemade Jerk sauce. "Hey, look who here. It part-time. Good to see you, you. Eat dat chicken. Heal you right up, mon."

Virgil carried his plate from the kitchen and sat down at the end of the bar. Delroy was doing what had become known as the Jamaican shuffle. He was mixing two different types of drinks in separate blenders, pulling a pitcher of Red Stripe from the tap as he washed dirty glasses in the sink, all as he flirted with two female customers who hung on his every word.

Delroy finished the blended drinks for the women then insisted he receive a kiss on the cheek from both before he would allow them to return to their table. The ladies obliged him as if the idea were their own. Then he reached into the cooler, opened a bottle of Mountain Dew, and slid it across the length of the bar where it stopped right next to Virgil's plate. When he walked over, they bumped fists. "Good to see you," he said. "How dat leg, mon?"

Before Virgil could answer, a man walked over and began tapping his empty pitcher on the bar top. "Little service be nice." He was overweight, dressed like a biker wannabe, and spoke louder than necessary. "When you're ready, that is. I wouldn't want to interrupt a management meeting or anything like that."

Delroy turned, the smile never leaving his face, and said, "Be right there...two Jamaican minutes, mon." The man grumbled something unintelligible and leaned on his elbows, his back against the bar. Delroy turned his attention back to Virgil and raised his eyebrows into a question.

"I'm doing okay. Still hurts quite a bit. The pills knock it down though."

"Yeah, mon, I bet day do," he said. Virgil felt the probe of Delroy's eyes into his own. "When you coming back?"

"Pretty soon, I hope. Have you seen Murton?"

"Yeah, mon, he upstairs on the phone."

Murton had converted the upstairs storage room of the bar into a workspace for his private investigations office. Virgil was getting ready to tell Delroy he'd be right back when the biker wannabe got tired of waiting for their conversation to conclude. He slid his pitcher down the bar and Delroy reached out and grabbed it without ever turning his head. He picked it off the bar and set it underneath the counter.

"Just how long is two Jamaican minutes anyway?" the man said.

Delroy turned and smiled at him. "A week from next Tuesday. Maybe we see you then, mon."

The man turned and faced the bar, his cheeks and neck flush with color. "Now wait a fucking minute," he said, his finger pointed at Delroy. "Where's that respect you're always talking about?"

"Ha. You get what you give, mon. See you next time. Don't make me repeat myself."

The man pushed himself off the bar and started to approach, but Murton caught him from behind and clamped his hand on top of the man's shoulder. "Time to boogie on down the avenue, Bub."

"Who the hell are you, dickweed?" the man said.

Murton had a merry look on his face. "I, along with these two gentlemen here, are three of the four owners of this fine establishment. And if you were paying any attention at all, you might notice about half the people in here are off-duty cops." Murton spun the man around. "See, you can tell who they are because they're the ones watching us right now. I can spot them a mile away, but maybe that's because I used to be one. So what's it going to be big boy? You want to walk out of here on your own, or do you want us to carry you out?"

The wannabe tried to pull free from Murton's grasp, but when he was unable to do so Virgil finally saw his body relax. "That's what I thought," Murton said. "Come on, I'll walk you out." Murton let go and walked with him to the door.

Delroy looked at Virgil and said, "Eat dat chicken, you. Heal you right up, mon." Then he laughed his big Jamaican laugh and went back to work.

———————

MURTON WORE A PAIR OF DESERT ARMY FATIGUES CUT OFF at the knees, a multi-colored Hawaiian shirt, and a battered Panama Jack hat set jauntily to one side. He pulled out a chair, winked at Delroy, and waved Virgil over. "What's shakin' bacon? Sandy give you the old heave-ho?"

"Not yet," Virgil said. "But it's early. You never know."

"You never really do. Hey, love your shirt, man." Virgil was wearing a cream-colored, short-sleeved Underdog T-shirt from the old Saturday morning cartoons.

"Simpler times, huh?"

Murton picked up a piece of chicken from Virgil's plate and popped it into his mouth. "You think?"

The question gave Virgil pause. His childhood had been one of normalcy. He had food to eat, clean clothes to wear, a solid roof over his head, parents who loved him, and a grandfather who was the center of his young life. Murton, on the other hand, had not been quite as fortunate. His mother died when he was a young boy and his father— a binge-drinking alcoholic brakeman for the railroad— would show his love for his son in ways that would now have Child Protective Services knocking on the door with a court order. "We all play the hand we're dealt, Murt. I think you've done a fine job of it all." When he didn't respond Virgil asked him a question. "How are you and Delroy hitting it off?" Murton grinned and took a swig of Virgil's pop. "Would you like me to order you something?"

"No, thanks. I'm good. Delroy's great. We're doing well. He misses your old man. I do too. So, are you going to tell me what's going on with you or do I have to guess?"

Virgil took a bite of chicken and chewed as slow as possible. When he spoke, he thought his own voice sounded foreign. "I sort of wanted to talk to you about my dad."

"What about him?"

"Remember what Delroy told me the day you guys showed up at my place with that willow tree? After my dad died? You had his bloodied shirt and when we put it at the bottom of the hole he said something like, *The groundwater will soak through the paper and into that shirt. Your father's blood will flow through that tree, just like it does your own heart.* Do you remember that?"

"Of course I remember. We wanted you to feel better man, that's all."

"I do…or at least I did."

"What's that supposed to mean?"

"I saw him this morning. I actually…sort of spoke with him."

"Who?"

"My dad. He was standing under the willow tree." But Virgil couldn't look at him when he said the words, his gaze drifting around the room as he spoke. "He was dressed exactly the same way he was the day he got shot behind the bar. I'll tell you something else, Murt, he wasn't wearing a shirt. I think he wasn't wearing his shirt because it was at the bottom of that hole where we put it before planting that tree."

Murton turned his attention to the bar as well and a long time passed before he spoke, but when he did, his eyes were focused directly on Virgil. "You talked to him?"

"Yes, I did."

"Did he talk back?"

Virgil let his eyelids droop a fraction. "Yeah, Murt, he did."

"What did he say?"

"He said I was hitting the pills a little too hard."

"Are you?"

"Don't change the subject."

"I'm not, Jonesy. Are you hitting the pills too hard?"

Virgil took a drink of his soda, which gave him a few seconds before he had to answer. "I don't know, okay? I know my leg hurts like hell unless I take the medication." Then he said something else, something that surprised him, as if the words were not his own even as they spilled across his lips. "I like the way they make me feel, Murt. They make me feel alive. They make me feel well and normal and happy and able to do almost anything I want. They make me feel like I have no regrets about anyone I've ever had or known or lost in my life, even though deep down I know that I do. Have regrets, I mean. But when I feel the meds starting to wear off, I tell myself I know they're wearing off because I can feel my leg start to hurt. But I think that's backward. I think my leg starts to hurt so I'll go ahead and take the pills. I think the pills are making my leg hurt. Does that make any sense to you? I'm not in control of it anymore."

"You have them with you?"

"What?"

"The pills."

"Yeah…why?"

"Let me see the bottle."

"Why?"

"Show me the damn bottle, will you? I'm not going to take them from you."

Virgil reached into his pocket and pulled the bottle out and set it on the table. Murton picked it up and studied the label, counted the number of pills, did the math in his head, then replaced the lid before he handed it back. "Looks like you're only taking what's been prescribed."

"Yeah, I'm mostly staying on schedule. But it's getting harder and harder. I've called the doc twice in the last two weeks alone and had them up the dosage. They've gone along so far, but that ship is getting ready to sail, if you know what I mean."

"One day at a time, brother. One day at a time. When it's time to quit, you won't question it. You'll know for sure. You might not want to admit it to anyone, maybe not even yourself, but you'll know. Somewhere deep down inside in that part of you that's safe from everything and everyone else in the entire world, that part of you will tell you to stop. All you have to do is listen."

"It's that easy, huh?"

"Hell no. It's a bitch with a capital B. But it's a ride you've got to take or we'll be planting a tree for you on the other side of that pond sooner than you'd like."

"We?"

"Yeah, asshole. Me and Sandy." Then he smiled, wiggled his eyebrows and said, "I think she's sort of hot for me lately."

"Fuck you."

"Yeah, fuck me," Murton said, and they both laughed like they were young boys again.

After a few minutes of silence, Murton looked at Virgil and said, "So...heard you got sacked this morning.

Who gets fired on a Saturday, anyway?" Then before Virgil could answer, he said, "Sit tight, Jonesy. I've got to get a cup of Blue." Virgil watched him walk behind the bar and pour a cup of Jamaican Blue Mountain coffee. A minute or so later he sat back down, cocked his head slightly, and let his face form a question.

The more he thought about it, the more Virgil realized that most of the cops in the department probably knew about his termination before he ever walked through the back door of his own bar. "I guess some news travels faster than others."

"Every badge in this room has got your back, brother," Murton said. "I guarantee it. Hell, probably every badge in the city."

Virgil wasn't up for anyone's shame or pity. "I appreciate it, Murt, I really do, but could we talk about it some other time?"

Murton had his hands wrapped around the sides of his coffee cup, pushing it around the table in small circles. "You're gonna dick around and burn yourself," Virgil said.

He smiled. "You sound like your mom."

"My mom didn't swear."

"Sure she did," Murton said. "Just not in front of us."

Virgil let a few seconds tick by, then looked across the table at his friend. He was someone who had almost gotten him killed during their time together in Iraq, but had also managed to save his life…more than once. The thought clicked in the back of Virgil's mind if maybe he was somehow asking Murton to save him yet again, only this time from himself. "Ever wish you could go back?"

Murton thought about the question for a minute before he answered. When he did, what he said reminded Virgil why they considered themselves not only friends, but brothers. "Go back to what, Jonesy? Back to sand-land to kill more innocent Iraqis? Back to my old man beating the shit out of me when he was drunk? Back to watch your mom suffer and die all over again? Or how about this? Back to your first day riding solo? What would you do? Shoot Pope in the leg this time? Get out of your own head, Virg. We might be shaped by our past, but the future is wide open and we get to define it. The choices we make? The ones we think about right here, in the moment? A year from now they'll be gone and good or bad, we can't go back. No one ever gets to turn the lights back on and replay the last inning. Is that what you're looking for?"

Virgil didn't answer. Instead, he said, "You got a little time to spare?"

Murton looked at his watch. "Maybe. How much time are we talking about?"

"Probably an hour or so. I've got something to show you."

But Murton had never been the kind of guy to let someone get the drop on him. "You know what I was thinking about?"

"What?"

"Those Underdog cartoons we used to watch when we were kids. Do you remember what Underdog did right before he chased down the bad guys?" He was smiling when he asked the question. It took Virgil a minute to remember, but when he did, he smiled as well. "That's right, Jonesy. He popped a pill. It's what gave him his power." He took a drink of his coffee, stood from the table, and said, "So, where we going?"

CHAPTER EIGHT

THE GOVERNOR'S CHIEF OF STAFF, BRADLEY PEARSON, and executive director of the state's lottery, Abigail Monroe, sat across from each other in the living room of Monroe's condo. Their conversation had deteriorated to the point where they were hissing at each other like a couple of alley cats. Pearson pointed his finger at her. "Let's not forget who got you this job, Abby."

"How could I, Bradley? You remind me every time you want to get laid."

Two years ago, the position of executive director opened up when the then-current director—Abigail Monroe's soon-to-be ex-husband, Lee, opened up one too many bottles of scotch before taking his car out for a midnight spin. He drove the car—a sporty little Mini Cooper—right off the road and through two backyards before he stopped. Unfortunately for Lee Monroe, what stopped him was the in-ground pool in the third yard. The Mini slid right into the deep end of the pool at three-thirty in the a.m. and sank slightly slower than a lead balloon. As any good drunk driver would tell you, the formula for survival in that type of situation was simply one of time divided by lung capacity. Regrettably, Monroe, a two-pack-a-day bureaucrat, was short on both and the math didn't work to his advantage. He was dead before the pool owner crawled out of bed and dialed the third digit of 911.

Over the course of the two days that followed Lee Monroe's accident, he was buried and properly mourned by Abigail. The mourning itself took the better part of two full minutes and even that was about a minute and a half longer than she would have liked. With that accomplished, Abigail set her sights on her dead husband's job. She used every tool in her bag—ample tools that they were—to secure the position. Besides, who could possibly object to the grieving widow coming to the aid of the state, not to mention its people in their time of need? She might not have been the best candidate for the job, but Abigail knew someone who could help her with that.

It didn't take long before she had her hooks in Bradley Pearson, who, to his discredit, melted just a tad slower than a candy bar on the sidewalk in the middle of July at high noon. Pearson lobbied for Monroe's appointment long and hard with the governor, the investigation into Lee Monroe's death was quietly set aside—a drunk is a drunk after all—and at the end of the process, the appointment was hers.

The end of the process also meant the end of her romantic involvement with Pearson. Monroe had what she wanted and Pearson wasn't it, not that he ever had been. Unfortunately for Pearson, he'd been a little too busy to notice. After Monroe got the job, Pearson had quietly called in every single political favor he was owed and had the state's legislature attach a provision on to a highway expansion bill that steered unclaimed lottery winnings into a fund designed to help pay for the completion of the state's first private prison in neighboring Hendricks County. Monroe didn't care in the slightest. Her job was to take the money in. What the state did with it wasn't her concern.

What was her concern though was the bomb Pearson had dropped on her, said bomb being that her head programmer, a young man by the name of Nicholas Pope had been murdered. "It's too much scrutiny, Abby. The police, not to mention the press are going to be all over this."

Abby shook her head. "Try to get a grip on yourself, Bradley. We have no involvement in Pope's murder. Besides, he was a pot hound, a doper. I overlooked it as much as I possibly could because of his talents, but in the end, he got himself killed over it. Another drug deal gone bad."

"Oh come on, Abby, nobody gets killed over a little

weed. Even I know that and I know the cops know it too. I'll tell you what's going to happen…the police are going to look at this and when they do they'll discover that not only was I present when Jones shot James Pope, they'll discover my connection to his son, Nicholas, through you. Some hard questions are going to be asked and if we don't get in front of this the consequences will be serious. We need to get on the same page here, Abby. We need some damage control."

"We are on the same page, Bradley. What else can we do? It really is one big coincidence."

Pearson stood up. "I don't believe in coincidence. I'm managing this thing on my end. What I need you to do is to not make any moves unless you run them by me. Can you do that for me, Abby? Both our careers are on the line here."

"How are you managing it?"

"That doesn't concern you."

"You're asking for my cooperation, but you're not willing to tell me what you're doing?"

"It's not that deep."

"Then tell me."

Pearson sighed. "I knew the Major Crimes Unit would be investigating this mess. I've had the governor relieve Jones of his position. It wasn't that hard. He's got a little drug problem of his own. I can control the new guy."

"You're sure?"

Pearson tugged at an earlobe and wiggled it back and

forth. "He's already on the hook. I've been doing this a long time, Abby. There isn't much that gets by me. Maybe you should remember that."

Monroe stood from the sofa, walked to her front door, and held it open. When Pearson moved through, she brushed her hand lightly across the back of his neck. "I got by you though, didn't I?"

He turned to say something, but Abby closed the door on him.

CHAPTER NINE

VIRGIL LET MURTON DRIVE AND GAVE HIM TURN-BY-TURN directions. When they turned the last corner Murton pulled his car to a stop in front of Mason's house, the same house where they'd both grown up. They sat for a few minutes before Murton glanced over with a 'what gives?' look on his face. "Let's go inside," Virgil said.

They got out of the car and made their way up the front walk. The house was a small three-bedroom bungalow with a detached garage and wood siding that Mason had always kept meticulously white with regular coats of paint every other year. When they stepped onto the porch Virgil watched as Murton ran his hands across the railing next to one of the support beams. He looked out at the front yard and Virgil knew, or at the very least suspected what he was thinking about.

IT HAD BEEN THE YEAR THEY REDID THE FRONT LAWN... the very next summer after the fire. Virgil and Murton had only been friends for a year or so, but the foundation of a lifelong bond had been poured and they both knew it.

Virgil's father had recently been elected as Marion County Sheriff, and to say that he was a busy man was an understatement. His days were long and his nights held an unpredictability that only a mainline gambler could appreciate. As a result of his hectic schedule, he'd let the front lawn go without fertilizer that spring. By the time the heat and humidity of the summer arrived, the crabgrass had taken hold so wide and deep that he could barely push the lawnmower through it without stalling the engine. When he'd finally had enough and decided it was time to address his own disregard, he did so with a vengeance.

He began with a rented sod cutter and ripped out the entire front lawn right down to the dirt. Murton and Virgil —both of them only seven years old at the time—helped him carry the heavy pieces of cut weed to the end of the drive. It was a dirty, laborious job that took most of the entire weekend. On Sunday, with freshly raked dirt in place and leveled just so, they began to plant the new seed. The seed had to be sown by hand, then raked into the soil. They were almost finished when Virgil saw Murton's father, Ralph Wheeler, walking down the middle of the street, right toward them. He wore his work clothes

—a dingy T-shirt beneath blue and white striped overalls, the fingers of his work gloves sticking out of a side pocket. He walked across the freshly raked front yard as if Mason's efforts of the past two days or their intended results meant nothing to him. Virgil and Murton were at the other end of the yard so they couldn't hear what was said between their fathers, but Virgil had an impression that something was terribly wrong, the first indication when Mason extended his hand to Murton's dad, then slowly let it drop to his side when his greeting was not accepted. Instead, Murton's dad covered his face with both his hands, let out a sob, then fell to his knees in the dirt.

Virgil's mother had walked out onto the porch carrying a tray that held a glass pitcher of lemonade and plastic cups. When she saw Murton's dad go to the ground and heard his sobs, she dropped the tray and ran, not to the men, but to the boys. She had no idea what was happening, but she knew in the moment her job was to protect the children from whatever sort of drama was playing out before them. Virgil and Murton watched over their shoulders as Virgil's mom ushered them up the porch steps and past the broken glass of the lemonade pitcher, their fathers still in the front yard, out by the street. Murton's dad was on his knees and he was bent forward from his waist, his forehead pressed firmly into the dirt. He was wailing and sobbing and when he raised his head from the ground his face was covered with dirt and grass seed that had mixed in with the spittle that ran from the corner of his mouth. What he said next was something no young child should ever have to hear.

By the time they made it inside, Murton was already crying.

———————

ALMOST A FULL WEEK WENT BY BEFORE VIRGIL SAW HIS friend again. The funeral was simple, attended by only a handful of mourners. Afterward, when Virgil tried to speak with him, Murton turned and ran away without saying a word, his sense of loss and anger pointed in the only direction that felt safe. This went on for over a month. The very next night Virgil found out what kind of people his parents were.

Shortly after dinner the three of them walked a few blocks over to the city park where Ralph Wheeler coached Murton's soccer team. The team played twice a week but this would be the first time that Murton played since the passing of his mother. It was the first time his father would return to coach as well.

The night was mild, filled with the promise of sportsmanship and laughter, and regardless of the tragedy Murton had been forced to endure, Virgil remained hopeful that the night might be a turning point in his friend's life, a frame of reference he might one day be able to look back on and recognize when his healing began. As it turned out that is exactly what happened, except not in a way anyone expected.

Virgil's mother carried a blanket so they could all sit in the grass to watch the game and his father carried a picnic basket filled with fresh fruit and a jug of ice water and white plastic cups. The lights were on at the corners and midpoints of the field, the moths and other winged creatures already starting their dance around the lights as the three of them settled in to watch the game.

Murton stood at the side of the field, his father towering over him. They were deep in conversation about something, the opposing team waiting patiently at midfield. Ralph Wheeler was saying something to Murton who was shaking his head back and forth so hard it looked as if he were trying to remove a bee that had gotten tangled in his hair. Wheeler grabbed his son first by one arm, then the other. He held him so hard and tight that Murton was forced to stand on his tiptoes. Virgil's mom started to rise, but Mason placed his hand gently on her thigh and dipped his chin just so. The message was clear. The Jones family would not get involved with the Wheeler's grief.

It was clear that Murton did not want to play soccer, but his father was not having it. He pushed Murton onto the field past the sideline and then pushed him again to send him further out. When Murton turned around to walk off, his father grabbed him by the scruff of his neck, dragged him to the bench and forcefully sat him down.

Ralph Wheeler turned to walk away and then something else happened, something that turned out to be a catalyst of change that would forever alter not only Murton's life, but Virgil's family as well.

Murton said something to his father.

No one heard what was said, but whatever it was, Murton's dad was not in the mood nor the proper state of mind to hear it. He spun around and leaned into his son's face and began to yell at him, his words thoughtless and cruel. Spittle flew from his lips and landed on Murton's face, but to his credit, Murton never looked away in fear or shame. Mason stood and began to make his way over behind Ralph, any thoughts of remaining uninvolved in another family's grief quickly forgotten. But even as he approached it was clear that Ralph Wheeler was losing steam, his words now focused more on himself than his only child. At last he sat down at the far end of the bench, away from Murton, his head hung low. The coach of the opposing team walked over and said something to Ralph Wheeler that went unacknowledged before he gathered his team and left the field.

Virgil was disappointed about the game and embarrassed for his friend. When he called out to him, Murton turned away as if he hadn't heard and left the field. Virgil stood there for a few minutes and watched him go, then helped his mom fold the blanket and gather their belongings.

Everyone mistakenly thought the evening was over.

THEY HADN'T BEEN HOME MORE THAN AN HOUR. MASON was tinkering with something out in the garage while Virgil helped his mother wash the dinner dishes they'd set aside for later, after the game. As Virgil set the last dish into the rack, he and his mother heard a loud crash at the front of the house. They ran into the living room and discovered the large plate glass window that fronted the porch had been shattered. Glass was everywhere and a softball-sized rock sat in the middle of the room. When Virgil looked out through the hole where the window used to be, Murton was in the front yard, his small body illuminated by the mercury street lamps that hummed overhead at the edge of the sidewalk. He was on his hands and knees and he swept his arms back and forth and kicked and scuffed his feet across the seeded lawn in an attempt to do as much damage as he possibly could.

Later in life it would become obvious to Virgil that Murton wasn't only mad because he'd lost his mother, he was mad at his best friend because of what Virgil had…two parents who loved him and a future that was both bright and secure. Virgil and his mom went out on the front porch as Mason came running around the corner of the house. Murton's hands and face were covered with a mixture of dirt and snot and tears and Virgil watched as his father sat down on the ground next to him, wrapped Murton in his arms, and held him on his lap until he cried himself out. They stayed out there for a long time, deep in conversation, until finally Mason walked him inside, his massive arm around Murton's shoulders. Murton's face was red, his lower lip was split open and he had the beginnings of a shiner on his left eye. They all stood there for a beat looking at each other before Virgil's mom took Murton by the hand, and said, "Come on honey, let's get you a bath. We'll put some antiseptic cream on your lip, and get you an ice pack for your eye. Hey, I've got an idea. You can wear a pair of Virgil's pajamas and spend the night with us. How does that sound?"

Murton followed her upstairs without answering and when Virgil looked at his father he saw the muscles of his jaw flex with tension. "I'll be right back," Mason said. An hour later he walked through the door carrying a small canvas-sided suitcase. The knuckles of both his hands were bloody and swollen, but other than that he didn't have a scratch on him. "Murt will be staying with us for a while," he said. "What do you think of that, Son?"

Virgil didn't remember if he answered his father or not, but he remembered hugging him, his face buried in his shirt, his boney arms wrapped around Mason's massive body, Murton's little suitcase banging against his side as he did.

Two days later Ralph Wheeler bonded out of county lock-up, hopped a Southern Freight boxcar, and was never heard from again. Murton lived with Virgil and his parents until they were both grown and left for the army.

MURTON HAD YET TO TURN AROUND. VIRGIL PUT THE KEY into the lock, opened the door then walked over to the porch railing and stood next to his friend. "What are you thinking?"

Murton turned, his eyes dark. The look on his face caused Virgil to take a half step back. "Simpler times my ass," he said. "That's what I'm thinking." But then he removed his hat, wiped the sweat ring inside the band with his index finger, and placed it carefully back on his head. He winked at Virgil and smiled as if he didn't have a care in the world. "So, why are we here?"

"I'VE GOT SOMETHING FOR YOU," VIRGIL SAID.

"Why didn't you bring it to the bar?"

"How about we go inside?" They walked through the front door with Murton leading the way. They were only a few steps inside when he stopped and turned around. "What gives, Jonesy? I thought you said you had something for me. The place is empty. Where's all your dad's stuff?"

"I had the mover's put it in storage. You can have anything you want, Murt. Just let me know and I'll get you the key. I had everything stored because I thought maybe you might want your own stuff here. You know, a way to sort of make the place your own."

Murton visibly swallowed and opened his mouth to say something, then closed it almost as quick. He looked around the front room, walked into the kitchen, then back out again. "What are you saying? You're giving me your old man's house?"

Virgil smiled at him. "I wish I could take the credit, but I can't." He pulled the deed from his pocket and handed it to Murton. "I'm not giving you his house, Murt. My dad is. He left it to you in his will."

───────

THEY RODE BACK TO THE BAR WITH LITTLE CONVERSATION. After pulling into the rear lot, Murton turned and looked at Virgil.

"What?" Virgil said.

"I'm not sure I know what to say. His house? It's too much, man. I'm not going to take his house."

"Well, not to put too fine a point on it, Murt, but it's already yours. He left it to you, no different than your percentage of the bar. You own it, free and clear."

"I don't believe it."

"What's not to believe? He wanted *you specifically* to have it."

"Why?"

For reasons Virgil could not readily explain, he found

himself irritated. "Why? What do you mean why?" he said, his voice louder than necessary. "Christ, Murt, that is a hell of a thing for you to say to me after everything we've been through." He laughed without humor. "And people are questioning my judgment lately?" But when Virgil saw the effect his words had on his friend he wanted to try again, except Murton cut him off.

"I'm going inside. Thanks for the trip down memory lane. What time is it anyway? You sound like you might be ready for your medicine." He slammed the door and walked away.

How much damage can one guy do in a single day? Virgil thought.

CHAPTER TEN

SANDY WAS ALREADY ASLEEP WHEN HE GOT HOME. VIRGIL thought about waking her so he could apologize and explain his feelings in a way that might put them back on track, but in the end, he simply let her sleep. He went into the kitchen and poured a glass of ice water, but when he raised it to his lips his hand shook so badly he had to set the glass back down. He pulled out his pills and set them on the counter, then reached into the silverware drawer for a straw. And that's when it happened. He took a pair of kitchen shears and cut the straw down to half its original length, then put both of the pain pills between two spoons and ground them together until they were a fine blue powder. He dumped the powder into a little pile and used the handle of the spoon to draw out two lines then bent over and snorted the medication through the straw, one line for each nostril.

The rush hit him at once, the warmth and lightheadedness something like a surprise meeting of a long-lost friend or lover. When he stood and turned from the counter he saw that Sandy was standing behind him, her blonde hair askew, sleep lines etched across one side of her face, her naked body warm and inviting. The look she gave Virgil was one he would not soon forget, if ever. She covered her breasts and pubic area with her arms and hands and ran back to the bedroom. When she snapped the lock on the knob, the finality of the noise reminded him of the sound a jail cell door makes when it clangs shut.

He stood there, a cut-down straw in his hand, the buzzing in his head as loud as a gas-powered leaf blower, blood pounding through the dark rivers of his heart. But when he picked up the glass of water, his hand was rock steady.

———

HE KNOCKED ON THE BEDROOM DOOR BUT SANDY REFUSED to acknowledge his presence, so he walked outside and sat down in a lawn chair near the edge of the pond and stared across the black water. The moon was out and full, the night sky cloudless and when he looked up and cupped his hands around his eyes and blocked out the ambient light it felt like he could see halfway across the galaxy. Tree frogs and crickets sang in the darkness and Virgil thought were it not for his addiction and the people he continued to abuse with his own selfishness and indignation, the night might have been perfect.

A sense of calm floated over him as he stared upward into the night sky. At some point he fell asleep for a while and a few seconds after he woke and without warning, the tree frogs and crickets stopped their nocturnal calls and the buzzing in his head went quiet. He closed his eyes again and folded his hands into his lap. A soft breeze blew across the pond and tickled his face. When he spoke, he thought he sounded like a fool. "I'm not doing very well, am I?"

"No, Son, I don't think you are."

Virgil opened his eyes and looked at his father's willow tree. Mason stood there like before, visible behind the hanging branches. "Lately I'm having some difficulty distinguishing reality from fantasy, Dad."

"I'm not surprised. When you flood your system with mind-altering chemicals, you're not foolish enough to believe that they won't have any ill effects, are you?"

Virgil didn't ignore the question, but he didn't answer it, either. "I don't know what to do."

"The answer is right in front of you, Virgil. It has been all along. You *do* know what to do, you simply refuse to do it."

"You may as well ask me to stop my own heart from beating. That's how much control I have over it."

"That's a bullshit cop-out, Virg and you know it."

"They let you swear in heaven?"

Mason smiled and the lines on his face looked like a familiar road map one might consult out of ritual rather than necessity before taking a well-known cross-country journey. "One of the first things you learn when you come back home is this: There isn't anything you can do that is ever wrong."

"So it's not like it is here, huh?"

Mason laughed. "No, Virg, it sure isn't. But you already know that. You simply can't remember it. But you will, when your time comes."

Virgil looked away from his father for a long time…so long in fact, that he thought his dad might be gone when he looked back. But he was still there, now seated at the base of the tree, his fingers interlaced behind his head, his legs crossed at the ankles.

"I feel like my time might be right around the corner."

"It's not hard to understand why you might feel that way."

"Are you real?"

"We're talking aren't we?"

Virgil nodded at him. "Yeah, we are. But I don't think that answers my question. Are you chained to that tree or can you move around?"

He stood up and dusted off the seat of his pants with his hands, an act that Virgil found odd. "You're asking all the wrong questions, Son."

"Am I, Dad? Never mind. Don't answer that. Answer this instead: Am I doing anything right?"

Virgil wasn't very surprised that his father refused to play the part of an enabler when it came to his own self-victimization. "Have you already forgotten what I told you earlier? You've got people in your life who are going to need you."

"Everyone seems to be doing fine."

"Your thoughts are deluded, Son. Everyone is not doing fine. Sandy lied to you today. When was the last time that ever happened?"

"*What?* It's never happened," Virgil said, his voice louder than necessary. "Ever."

"You're mistaken, Bud. She lied to you today, only she doesn't know it yet."

"How about we can the mysticism? Will you please come out with it, already? It's almost time for—"

"Almost time for what? To snort some more Oxy?"

"So you're not tied to that tree after all."

"I never said I was. Do you remember what I told you that afternoon at the bar, the day my body was killed? We were talking about Sandy, right before Amanda Pate came in."

"Yeah, I remember. What about Amanda, by the way? Is she there?"

Mason smiled in a way Virgil did not expect. "She sure is. In fact, we're on something of a journey together."

"What does that mean?"

"Answer my question, Virgil. What did I say to you that day?"

"I said I remember, Dad."

"Then tell me what I said."

"You said, 'that's one you don't let get away, Son.' What about it?"

"The intricacies of free will are really something. Absolutely amazing. I wish I had the words to describe it to you. I almost think I could spend the rest of eternity studying nothing else."

Virgil rubbed the heels of both hands into his eyes. "You're losing me, Dad."

"That might be the most accurate thing you've said all night. Sandy told you she'd never leave you, but she was wrong. You're losing her, Son."

Virgil stood from the chair and pointed at him. "You're wrong. Do you hear me, you're wrong. She'd never leave me." Then, as if he had to make his point to an apparition whose existence was questionable at best, he added, "You're not even real."

"Virgil? Who are you talking to?"

The sound of Sandy's voice made Virgil jump and he lost his footing in the wet grass and ended up flat on his back. She walked over and ran her fingers through Virgil's hair. She wore an oversized sweatshirt that hung down below her waist and a pair of lime green rubber garden boots embellished with images of multi-colored daisies.

"Who's wrong? And why are you yelling?"

"Will you help me up please?" Virgil asked.

The night was warm and the sky was clear and instead

of helping him up, Sandy laid down next to him in the grass and placed her head on his chest. They stayed there like that for a few minutes, neither of them speaking, then she lifted her head and began to kiss him, her tongue probing desperately inside his mouth. She swung one of her legs over his body and sat on top of him before peeling the sweatshirt over her head.

But Virgil was having some difficulty with the sequence of events as they unfolded around him and he grabbed her arms and gently pushed her back. "Sandy, I don't think I can. I want to, but the medicine—"

Even in the dark of night he could see the embarrassment of his rejection play across her face. She grabbed the sweatshirt from the ground and then, almost as an afterthought, dropped it on his chest. She stood over him, her mouth moving as if to speak, but if she said anything at all Virgil never heard it over the buzzing in his head. He watched her walk back to the house, her daisy-laden garden boots leaving dew tracks across the lawn. She looked, Virgil thought, like a little girl.

When he looked back at the willow tree, his father was gone.

CHAPTER ELEVEN

VIRGIL AND SANDY HAD A QUIET SUNDAY TO themselves, both taking a mental break and pretending that Virgil did not have a drug problem and the events of the previous night hadn't happened. They spoke of nothing of consequence, were together yet separate and when they made love in the evening Virgil felt a sense of urgency and a longing for normalcy that seemed to exist without boundaries. She fell asleep in his arms that night and Virgil began to understand what his father had said, the truth of his words. He *was* losing her. The woman he loved more than anything else was drifting away, yet he felt powerless to do anything about it. Ultimately he would have to make a decision, one that would not come easily. He wanted to talk to Sandy about how he felt with the hope that it was not too late, that they could put the past few months behind them and look forward to a future free from the relentless grasp of the pills and the damage they'd done. Those were the thoughts going through his head as he fell asleep, but by the time he woke on Monday, Sandy had already left for work.

In truth, he felt a little relieved.

VIRGIL KILLED THE MORNING AND MOST OF THE afternoon taking care of household chores. He paid some bills, mowed the lawn, and generally kept himself busy, even though he knew what he was really doing was nothing more than delaying the inevitable. It was time to go to the office and collect his belongings, sign the necessary forms for his discharge, and participate in an exit interview, something he thought absurd. Someone gets fired from their job and the H.R. people want to interview them? What did that look like? *Tell us, Mr. Jones, would you characterize your time spent here as a productive part of your professional life and career as a whole? Would you recommend the state of Indiana as a viable and worthwhile employment opportunity to someone if they were to ask you? Do you promise not to sue the everlasting bejesus out of us for firing you after you were nearly killed in the line of duty?*

He crushed a couple of pills, snorted them back, and made it downtown in record time.

WHEN HE GOT TO HIS OFFICE—WHICH NOW BELONGED TO
Ron Miles—he walked in only to discover that somebody
had been kind enough, or, depending on one's generosity
of thought, cruel enough to box up his belongings for him.
The cardboard box sat on one of the two chairs that
fronted his old desk. The box itself was old, had notched
out ovals for handholds and the words, *Produce: Handle
With Care* printed on the side. Virgil rifled through the
contents to make sure everything was there, and in doing
so discovered the contents were of little value to him
anymore. Most of it was old police procedural manuals
that he'd picked up over the years, a certificate of perfect
marksmanship from a handgun competition, a distinguished service award, and a few photographs. Virgil put
everything back in the box with the photos on top. He was
about to carry it out to his truck when Ron Miles walked
in. The look on his face was an odd mixture of embarrassment and shame. He walked behind the desk and sat
down, let out a sigh, and motioned Virgil into the empty
chair next to his box of belongings. Virgil remained
standing.

"I'm not exactly sure what I should say here, Jonesy."

Virgil had always liked Ron. He was a fine investigator, a streetwise cop with one of the best homicide closure
rates in the state and despite his age and time on the job,
he was still one of the most energetic, loyal and honest

law enforcement officials Virgil had ever met. None of that could suppress the feelings he had at that moment, though, and as irrational as it was, Virgil felt like knocking Ron's teeth down his throat. "Then maybe you shouldn't say anything."

"I was going to come down to the bar and talk to you tonight."

"Were you?"

"Look, I didn't ask for this, I didn't want this, I didn't know anything about this and I sure as hell didn't know what they were going to do to you."

"You must be relieved as hell then, Ron," Virgil said, his voice thick with sarcasm. "I can't imagine the level of stress my situation must have caused you. I hope you can find it in your heart to forgive me."

"Hey, that's not fair."

"Fair? You want *fair*? Let me tell you something, Ron. I haven't seen fair in so long I'm not sure I'd recognize it if I did. Fair can kiss my ass. As a matter of fact, so can you."

Virgil grabbed the cardboard box by the handles and turned to leave, but his dramatic exit was not to be. The box was weak and overloaded and when he pulled it from the chair the contents spilled out the bottom and landed in a pile at his feet. The glass shattered on the picture frames and the distinguished service award broke into pieces with much the same sound as Virgil's cane pole after Pearson cracked it in half.

Ron came around the side of the desk and gently took the ruined box from Virgil's hands. "Hey, come on now, Jonesy. I'm sorry, man. I really am. Look, why don't you wait here and I'll go get another box. Just sit tight, okay? Will you do that?"

After Ron walked out, Virgil picked up the photos and removed them from the damaged frames, slipped them into his pocket, and left the building.

———————

VIRGIL WAS DUE AT THE BAR BUT INSTEAD OF GOING straight there he drove a few miles in the opposite direction and stopped at a city park situated between the suburbs and downtown. He walked across the grassy knolls and tree-lined trails before sitting down on one of the benches. Sunlight glimmered through the tree limbs and shadows danced across the trail in the afternoon breeze.

Virgil heard a rustling noise behind him and when he turned he saw a small child—a boy, no more than four or five years of age. He held a packaged toy fishing pole in his hands, the kind with a superhero screen-printed on the plastic spinner reel. The boy's hair was light and fair but more than anything it was the colors of his eyes that caught Virgil off guard and left him momentarily unable to ask even the simplest of questions, like why he was alone in a public park or where his parents might be. His left eye was a deep crystal blue and his right was as green as the ocean waters of Montego Bay. He wore a white T-shirt with an American Flag across the front, blue dress shorts that hung to his knees, and white tennis shoes. The boy stared at Virgil for a few seconds, then smiled and darted across the trail and up the hill. Virgil stood and shouted for him to wait, but he ran up the hill without stopping or turning back.

Virgil began to climb the hill, conscious of the fact that he was a middle-aged man chasing a young boy through a deserted park. Nevertheless, this child was alone in a place where he shouldn't be and no matter what anyone might have thought, Virgil felt like it was his responsibility to help the boy find his parents or guardian. He shouted to him again. "Wait, let me help you. Where are your parents?"

At the mention of his parents, the boy stopped and turned. Virgil had narrowed the gap between them and they stood only a few yards apart, halfway up the hill. When Virgil asked him again about his parents, he simply shrugged his shoulders, his smile still in place. Virgil squatted down and kept his voice calm and peaceful. "My name is Virgil. What's yours?"

"Wyatt."

Virgil smiled at him. "Hey, that's a great name. We'd make a good team, wouldn't we? Virgil and Wyatt."

He gave a funny look and when he did Virgil realized

he was referencing something the boy would have no knowledge of.

"What about your mommy? Is she around here somewhere?"

He tilted his head to the side and stared at Virgil's face. Virgil had a scar that ran along his jawline, the result of an injury he sustained when pulled from the rubble during the house fire. It had faded over the years, but it remained visible, especially when he smiled and his skin stretched tight. Wyatt reached out with his hand and ran his fingers across the scar. His touch was soft and warm as the tips of his tiny fingers traveled along the side of Virgil's face.

"Say, that's a pretty fancy fishing pole you've got there," Virgil said. "Did your daddy get that for you?"

Wyatt looked at the fishing pole in his hand as if he were only then aware of its presence. He nodded at Virgil, then dropped the pole in the grass. "He was gonna teach me to fish."

"Going to? You mean he didn't?"

He shook his head. "No. He went away."

"Where did he go?"

"I don't know where it's called. Can't 'member."

"What about your mommy?"

He didn't answer and instead turned and looked up at the top of the hill.

Virgil wasn't quite sure what to do. He couldn't leave this

young boy alone in the park, yet at the same time, Wyatt wasn't being very helpful or forthcoming about his mother or father. Virgil was about to suggest that he go with him back to the MCU. Once there, he'd be able to leave him in the hands of one of the detectives who could locate his parents. But what happened next defied almost anything Virgil had ever witnessed. The air had suddenly gone still and the birds and other wildlife went quiet as if they were suddenly nonexistent. The little boy leaned in close and ran his hand along Virgil's scar once again then looked him straight in the eye and said, "Keep taking those pills and you're going to die."

His words were like a slap in the face, and Virgil grabbed him by the arms. "What did you say?"

Wyatt slipped away and ran a few steps up the incline and pointed at the top of the hill. "I said, keep walking up the hill and you can touch the sky!" Before Virgil could process what had happened, Wyatt crested the hill and started down the far side.

By the time Virgil got to the top, Wyatt was nowhere in sight.

———

VIRGIL SPENT THE NEXT HALF HOUR LOOKING FOR THE little boy named Wyatt, but never found him. When he returned to the spot on the hill where they were before he ran off, Virgil noticed the toy fishing pole still lying in the grass. He picked it up, carried it to his truck, and drove back to the MCU headquarters. He signed all the necessary forms for the state's human resources department, answered a few questions that seemed to constitute something of an exit interview, then headed toward Ron's office to offer an apology.

He'd realize later that he should have simply gone home or to the bar.

Unfortunately, he did neither.

———

WHEN VIRGIL WALKED INTO RON'S OFFICE HE FOUND Miles wasn't there, but Bradley Pearson was. He was talking on his cell while looking through Virgil's personal belongings Ron had re-boxed. When Pearson realized someone was behind him he turned around. When he saw who it was, he ended his conversation in mid-sentence and slipped the phone into his pocket. His face lit up with a huge grin, something that happened about as often as a solar eclipse.

"Jonesy," he said, as he reached out and offered his hand. Virgil shook his hand out of instinct, but what happened next was not one of his better moments. "Did you get your new fishing pole? I sent it via special delivery. I know it's probably not as nice as the one I broke at your house—" And that's as far as he got. Virgil still had Pearson's hand in his own—they were only mid-shake—when he mistakenly concluded that the boy in the park had been part of a cruel hoax initiated by Pearson.

Virgil slapped him full in the face, a humiliating blow that snapped Pearson's head sideways and caused his eyes to water. Then Virgil pushed him into one of the chairs, picked up his box of personal belongings, dumped it in his lap, and smashed the open container bottom-down over his head. By the time he was finished, Pearson looked like a Jack-in-the-Box with a bad set of springs. Virgil stared at him for a moment and then walked out the door.

———

HE WAS ABOUT TO GET IN HIS TRUCK WHEN HE SAW MILES turn into the lot and get out of his rental car. He walked over and said, "Hey, Ron. Listen…I was out of line. Everything seems to be happening sort of all at once for me and well, I don't know…I guess I lost my shit for a minute. I'm sorry."

Miles puffed out his cheeks. "Forget about it. And I'm sorry too. I mean, your job, Jonesy. Jesus."

"Ah, it's not like I need the money. I simply liked doing what I do." Virgil looked down at the rental car sticker. "You having car trouble?"

"Something like that. Listen, Jonesy, I've got to run. I'm late for a meeting with Pearson."

"Yeah, he's waiting for you in your office."

"Great. What's he doing in there?"

"Oh, you know…he's doing what he does best."

"What's that?"

"He's thinking inside the box. See you around, Ron."

———————

THIRTY MINUTES LATER WHEN VIRGIL WALKED INTO THE bar, Delroy motioned him over. "Those two Red Stripes at the other end of da bar, mon, they say they need to talk to you. What you do, you?"

Jamaicans use the term Red Stripe for two things. One is their beer. The other is a slang term for police officers. "Probably something I shouldn't have."

That earned Virgil a sideways look. "Yeah, mon. There's a lot of dat going around lately."

Virgil glanced at the other end of the bar. Two uniformed city police officers were sitting very still and watching him through the mirror. The older of the two let out a heavy sigh before they both got up and made their way over to where he stood with Delroy. Virgil couldn't recall the name of the older cop, but had seen him in the bar any number of times. He'd never seen the younger one at all.

"We'd rather not cuff you up, if you promise you won't give us any grief," the younger of the two said.

Virgil shook his head and fixed his gaze on the veteran. "Who's the boot?"

"What did you call me?" the young cop said.

"What dis about, now?" Delroy said.

The rookie turned and looked at Delroy. "This is about baldheaded island jerk-waters like you knowing your place. If that's too complicated for you, let me put it this way: butt the fuck out."

Delroy started to respond, but Virgil beat him to it. "You're in our place of business. You'll show some respect, or you'll be shown to the door, badge or not. If you think I'm not serious, say something else to him or me and see what happens."

The rookie took a step forward and the veteran cop drew his nightstick from the chrome loop on his belt. But instead of using the stick on Virgil he laid the tip across the edge of the bar and blocked the path of his trainee. "The man's right. Show some respect. Do you know who you're talking to here?"

The rookie cop suddenly looked very unsure of himself. "Isn't this the guy we're supposed to bring in? I thought you said this was him."

The veteran looked at Virgil and then shook his head before he spoke to his partner. "Go wait out by the squad. I'll be out in a minute. Don't touch any of the buttons on the radio." Then to Virgil and Delroy: "On behalf of the city of Indianapolis and the Indianapolis City Police Department, I'd like to apologize for my trainee's behavior." He scratched his forehead, then said, "I don't know where they get these guys anymore. I really don't. This kid's a perfect example. He'll be fired, or he'll quit, or he'll be dead on the job inside of a year. I guarantee it. No one knows how to do this work anymore." Then, almost as an afterthought he said, "Your old man knew how though."

"He sure did," Virgil said. "Did they cut a warrant?"

The cop shook his head. "No. I don't think they will either."

"Look, uh…" Virgil glanced at the cop's nameplate on his uniform. He still couldn't remember his first name. "Officer Nagy…"

"Jim."

"Ah, that's right. Jim. Sorry. So let me ask you something, Jim. Pearson is the governor's chief of staff. Why does he want the city to roll on this instead of the state?"

"Pearson? What are you talking about? I have no idea. I got the call on my cell phone, straight from central dispatch. It was Cora LaRue. She's the one who wanted us to pick you up."

Delroy looked at Virgil, then the cop. "You say Bradley Pearson? Ha. Delroy almost forget." He walked behind the bar, bent down, and gently set a brand new cane pole in front of Virgil. "He had it sent special delivery. It arrived 'bout an hour ago, mon. Dat's some nice pole, no?"

"Look, Jim, I know we don't know each other all that well, but if I said that you have always known me to be an honest and straightforward cop, or at the very least a man of my word, would you be inclined to agree with that statement?"

Officer Nagy didn't hesitate. "Absolutely."

"Then I want you to know I mean you and your department no insult or disrespect whatsoever when I say this: No warrant, no ride downtown."

Nagy thought about that for a second, then took out his phone and made a call. "No dice," was all he said to the person on the other end before he closed the phone. He twirled his nightstick between his fingers with the precision and dexterity of a gunslinger before he slid the baton back into the chrome loop on his belt. Then he smiled at Delroy and sat down at the bar. "I've never been to Jamaica, but every time I come in here you make me feel like I'm right at home. Got any more of that chicken cooking back there?"

"Yeah mon, you bet we do." Delroy turned to go get Nagy a plate of jerk chicken, but then he stopped and said something that surprised Virgil. "Don't you give up on dat rookie of yours."

Nagy cocked his head to the side. "Why's that?"

"Because it the ones we don't give up on that make it in the end. Anyting less and you not only fail them, but worse, you disrespect yourself, you."

When Virgil's cell phone rang, the caller ID said WORK. It was Cora.

———————

WHEN VIRGIL ANSWERED THE PHONE SHE WAS ALREADY speaking. "...listen to me, Jonesy and you listen good. There is no excuse for what you did today. Do you hear me? None."

"Cora—"

"Don't interrupt me. I'm not done. I wanted to have this conversation in person, but I guess we'll do it your way. In case you haven't noticed, your life is spinning out of control. I'd like to know what on earth makes you think that it is even remotely acceptable that you can come into a state office, assault an official of the state and then walk out as if nothing happened. Would you care to explain that to me?"

"I don't think I can. It obviously wasn't one of my better moments."

"That might be the understatement of the decade. I've somehow persuaded Pearson not to file assault charges against you. I hope that wasn't a mistake on my part."

"Thank you."

"Shut up. I've tried to be kind. I've tried to be compassionate. I've even tried to be your friend. Now I'm going to try the truth. You know what the difference between a victim and a martyr is? They both eventually go down in flames, except a martyr deludes himself into thinking that he's done it on his own terms. By the way, I've got your final paycheck in my desk drawer. You'll get it when you fish your badge out of that pond of yours. My God, you infuriate the hell out of me."

She hung up before Virgil could respond.

CHAPTER TWELVE

AUGUSTUS PATE WAS MAD ENOUGH THAT HE WAS HAVING trouble maintaining his composure. He'd met Pearson in a parking lot not far from his office and now the two of them were seated in the back of Pate's limo, along with Pate's assistant. The assistant was large, like a pro linebacker. Pearson had never seen him before. "Who are you?"

"That's Hector," Pate said. "He's my assistant. Never mind him. We've got some things to discuss. I told you I wanted his head on a stick. Why hasn't that happened yet?"

Pearson was seated in the rearward-facing seat, right behind the tinted glass partition that separated the men from the driver. "I'm not sure I'm comfortable talking about any of this in front of someone I don't know."

"Hector is well versed in all of my business dealings, Bradley. All of them."

"Still, as I said, I'm not—"

Hector leaned forward in his seat. "Answer the man's question please, Mr. Pearson."

Pearson saw the look in Hector's eyes and decided to answer. "I got him fired, didn't I?"

"Fired? You think I need you to get someone fired? I could have handled that without getting out of bed. I'm not talking about his career you idiot. I'm talking about finishing him. Do I have to spell it out for you?"

"Don't get your ball sack in a bunch, Gus. If it weren't for that degenerate son of yours, we wouldn't be in this mess. You said you wanted Jones taken care of, so that's what I did."

Augustus Pate, the late Samuel Pate's father held Virgil responsible for the death of his son. Virgil's most recent case—he'd been looking into the death of Franklin Dugan, one of the city's more prominent citizens—had focused almost exclusively on Samuel Pate as the suspect. Pate had been the senior pastor of Pate Ministries, and Dugan's bank had loaned Pate five million dollars when Dugan turned up dead. Virgil began digging into Pate's background where he uncovered, among other things, the junior Pate's bloodlust for child pornography. When it became obvious that he was about to go down for his crimes—the kiddie porn was only part of it—Pate confessed his sins to hundreds of thousands of faithful viewers on live television. Then he put a gun in his mouth and blew the back of his head off. That was on TV too.

"Jones is responsible for Samuel's death. What part of that don't you understand, Bradley?"

"Let me tell you something, Gus. I understand exactly what you're saying and now I want you to understand me. First, it wasn't my fault that your kid took the chicken-shit express to hell. That's on him, not me. As far as Jones goes, the man is wrecked. He's been relieved of duty, fired from the department and he's hooked to the gills on prescription pain meds. That's just for starters. I'm hearing rumors that he's walking around having conversations with his dead father. A father, I might add, that your son's wife shot to death. He's gone from one of the most powerful cops in the state to the co-owner of a corner tavern. He is without question coming apart at the seams. All in all, from my perspective, that's about as good as you're going to get."

"Sounds to me like you're still playing in the minor leagues, Bradley. I would have thought you could do better than that."

"Think what you want, Gus. If you want the man 'finished' as you say and make no mistake, I completely understand what you mean by that, you'll have to do it yourself. That was not part of our deal."

Pate waved his words away like the annoyance that they were. "What about the funding? Where are we with that? The union people are breathing down my neck and the investors are starting to get jumpy."

"There's been no change. The legislature passed the bill. The rest of it is on autopilot."

The passage of the bill had cost Pearson dearly, politically speaking, but the payoff had the potential to be massive. Pearson had set up a blind trust and the trust had then made an investment in Pate's corporation, Augustus Pate International. API was nothing more than a holding company, but its holdings were substantial. Among them, a multimillion-dollar company called Pri-Max, a construction firm that built state-of-the-art prison facilities all over the world. Pearson's blind trust held stock options that if exercised would net him millions of dollars. But his options could only be exercised if certain conditions were met, chief among them, the passage of a house bill which stipulated that unclaimed lottery winnings would be appropriated into a fund designed to match—dollar for dollar—the completion of the state's first private prison. The unclaimed funds were starting to trickle in, but the big one, the three hundred million dollar unclaimed prize was the one they were after, and the time frame for anyone to claim that prize was about to expire. Once it did, the funds would revert back to the state. After that, the bill would kick in and the money would be distributed into a discretionary fund, a fund that was by its very nature, discretionary.

Pate wouldn't get the money directly. That would be

completely illegal, but Pri-Max would. They'd get subsidized by the state—dollar for dollar in matching funds—to not only build, but also run the prison. Pri-Max would turn the money over to API and from there it would get shuffled, rounded, disbursed, then eventually distributed back to Pri-Max to cover cost overruns on the operational side, and as dividends to their primary shareholders.

Of course, Pri-Max had inflated their numbers almost beyond belief when it came to construction costs, ongoing maintenance, staffing, and direct operating expense projections. So with the inflated numbers—just shy of twenty-million dollars—and the state's generous matching program, Pate was looking at a massive influx of capital that was his to spend as he saw fit, and Pearson, or more specifically, Pearson's trust, would walk away with almost twenty percent of the take.

"What about Monroe?" Pate asked. "At least tell me you've got her in line."

"Of course she's in line. Abby does what I tell her."

"Your use of Ms. Monroe's given name in the abbreviate suggests a certain level of familiarity that might extend itself beyond the normal boundaries of a working relationship. Is there something I should know, Bradley?"

"Gee, that's a lot of fancy words, Gus. I'm having a little trouble keeping up. If you're asking me if I'm romantically involved with her, I can honestly say, no, I am not."

"Good. See that it stays that way. What the hell is going on with this Pope kid? Was that your doing?"

"I wasn't anywhere near that. The police are clueless as well."

"Good. Do whatever you have to do to make sure it stays that way. We don't need any more complications." Pate pressed a button on the center console next to his seat. When he did, the limo pulled to a stop and the doors unlocked automatically. "I'll be in touch, Bradley. Be sure to contact me immediately if anything else arises. And if I were you, I'd distance myself from Jones."

"As I indicated, I already have. But let me give you a bit of advice, Gus. You're not the first guy to come along and try to take him out. If you're not careful, you won't be the last."

Pate had already lost interest in Pearson's words of warning, his gaze directed at nothing outside the limo's tinted window. When he didn't respond, Pearson got out and walked away.

Hector stared at his boss until he was sure he had his attention. "He is going to become a liability."

Pate didn't answer. He pushed another button on the center console and the limo pulled out into traffic.

CHAPTER THIRTEEN

MURTON SHOWED UP AT THE BAR LATE IN THE AFTERNOON, and Virgil poured two cups of Blue Mountain coffee and carried them over to the same table where they'd been sitting before. "If we keep sitting at the same table all the time we're going to end up looking like a couple of goombahs or something."

Murton ignored his attempt at levity. "I shouldn't have said what I did the other day. Any of it. I'm sorry."

"Ah, me too. Forget about it." They were both quiet for a beat before Virgil went on. "Look Murt, you had a rough go of it for a while a long time ago. You might have drawn a shitty hand, but I've never seen anyone walk away from the table with their head held higher. I'm proud of you, brother."

Murton chewed at his bottom lip before he spoke. "I don't really remember my parents. Isn't that something?

It's almost like I don't have any memories before that summer. Boy, I'll tell you, after I busted that window at your house I thought your old man was going to take me to the woodshed. Instead, he and your mom gave me my life back. The way they took me in? The way they raised me like I was their own? Who does that? It was foreign to me. In many ways it still is. I guess that's why I sort of freaked out there for a second. They gave me more than I ever deserved and now, even though they're both gone, the only real parents I ever had, they're still giving to me."

"Who says you didn't deserve it? They loved you, Murt. You were every bit as much their boy as I was."

Murton grinned, then shook his head.

"What are you thinking?" Virgil asked.

"I'm thinking it *is* a pretty nice house. Say, will you help me move?"

"Hmm. I can't."

"Why not? Isn't that what friends do for each other?"

"Yeah. But the doctor told me no strenuous activity for another two weeks, so…"

———————

VIRGIL TOOK THE PILL BOTTLE FROM HIS POCKET AND downed another dose of Oxycontin. After he swallowed the pills, even after he felt the euphoric rush of the chemical bombardment, he had to admit that his father—or the part of his brain that manifested his apparition—was right.

He was hitting the pills too damn hard. But he also felt like he was past the point of no return. He simply didn't know if he could stop. He didn't even know if he wanted to try. And if he did, could he do it? It was a question he was not prepared to answer in the moment. As it turned out, someone else answered for him, just not in the way he expected.

During the course of the rest of the evening, Virgil noticed that his partners seemed to take some sort of pity on him. Robert brought him a plate of food, Murton worked doubly hard behind the bar, Delroy seemed to sing just a bit louder along with whatever song was playing on the jukebox, and all in all, with the exception of Sandy not being present, Virgil found himself having a great time.

But things have a way of coming around as his grandfather used to say and when they came around for Virgil, he wondered at the state of his being, the people he loved, and the events of his life that had yet to take place. He could feel a dull throb deep inside his leg and right as he reached into his pocket to retrieve his pain pills, Delroy walked over and stood next to his chair.

"Hey, Delroy. What's happening?" Virgil said.

"Ha. Plenty. Too bad you're not noticing."

"Pardon?"

He pulled out a chair and sat down. "What you tink you know about Jamaican people, you?"

"I'm not sure I understand the question, Delroy."

Virgil began to twist the top from the bottle of pain pills when Delroy's hand clamped down around his wrist.

"Your leg? It hurts, no?"

"Yeah, it does. Plus, it's time for the medicine anyway. If I get behind…"

He waved Virgil's words away like a fly that hovered over a bowl of soup. "Yeah, yeah. Delroy heard it all before, mon. Mostly from you. You get behind on da medicine and it start to eat you up. You tell Delroy this one ting: What I ever ask of you before?"

The look on his face was one Virgil had never seen. "I'm not sure I understand what you're asking me, Delroy."

"Don't you insult me, you. When I walk into our bar and everyone shouts, 'Yeah Mon!' you tink I don't know what dat is? It respect, mon, plain and simple. How many conversations we have about your grandfather, you and me? Delroy know somewhere deep down you tink in some way he live inside me. I tell you someting else, mon…maybe he do, but it not for me to say. *If* he do though, it up to you to honor and respect what come your way. Now, you tell me I'm wrong."

Virgil looked at the bottle of pills in his hand and then did something he thought himself not capable of ever doing. He tried to hand Delroy the bottle of pills. But Delroy sat back in his chair and crossed his arms over his chest. "Those pills, day don't belong to me, mon. Problem is, day don't belong to you, either."

"So what should I do?"

Delroy laughed. "Come on. Let's take a little ride, you and me."

"Where?"

"Don't you worry about it, mon. I introduce you to someone. You tank me later."

VIRGIL LET DELROY DRIVE, AND IF ASKED, WOULD HAVE admitted it might not have been one of his better decisions. They left the city and took the loop north, which took them about an hour out of the way, though Virgil didn't know it at the time. Jamaicans were odd drivers. They use the horn as much as the gas and the brake pedals and to sit in the passenger seat of a vehicle driven around the city of Indianapolis by someone from a small island nation is somewhat akin to taking a flight in a hot air balloon with a student pilot. In other words, things will probably be all right, but in the end, you never really know. An hour later they finally turned into Virgil's driveway and parked the car. Delroy looked over at him and said, "Whew. Dat's some traffic, no?"

Virgil swallowed instead of answering. They got out of the car and walked up toward the front porch, but instead of going inside Delroy pulled Virgil by his arm and led him around to the back of the house. When they turned the corner Virgil saw something that made his heart skip. Tiki torches had been erected around the perimeter of the pond, their flames reflecting across the water. Sandy stood next to the willow tree dressed in a long white gown that flowed with the evening breeze. Murton and Robert were there as well. Robert walked over and placed his hand on Virgil's chest before he spoke. "It time to come home now, mon."

Sandy came from under the willow tree and kissed Virgil hard on the mouth and didn't say anything. Murton put his arm around Virgil's shoulders and said, "Welcome home, brother."

Everyone in Virgil's life was there at that moment. When he looked at the willow tree, he saw his father. His arms were crossed over his chest, his head tilted to one side, the look on his face an odd combination of sorrow and hopefulness. For a moment Virgil felt so dizzy and lightheaded he thought he might pass out. It was deathly quiet for an indeterminate amount of time before anyone spoke. When someone finally did, it was Delroy.

"You hear me now…there is nothing wrong with your leg. The doctor say it healed and he right. It not your leg that hurts, mon. It your heart. They don't make no pill for dat, no. What you do right now, right this very moment, Virgil Jones, it define the rest of your life." Then he swept his arms wide and said, "Maybe ours too. So, what you do, you?"

Virgil looked at Sandy and walked toward her, but he was so heavily focused on the vision of his father under the tree that he almost walked right past her. She held out her hand and stopped him.

"He's here, isn't he? Your dad."

"Yeah, he is."

"I believe you, Virgil, I do. But the rest of us? We're here for you too. We love you and we're not ready to let you go. You're killing yourself with those pills, baby. Do you hear me? You are literally killing yourself. You don't need them anymore. Delroy's right. Your leg is healed, Virgil. It's your heart that's broken."

Virgil opened his mouth to say something…he wasn't sure what, but closed it again before he said anything that might cause more hurt or damage to the woman he loved and the three men who stood by her side. Then something odd and beautiful happened. Robert walked away from the rest of the group and over to the pond. He removed his shirt, his brown skin taut with muscle, his shoulders almost twice as wide as his waist. He dropped his shirt in the grass and waded hip-deep into the pond. He cupped the water in his hands then raised them above his head and let the water trickle down each arm. As he did, he began to chant something, his Jamaican accent so thick and strong Virgil could not make out his words.

Delroy looked at Virgil and said, "He pray for you."

Murton stepped up close and cupped his hand on the back of Virgil's neck. "I'll do anything in the world for you, brother, except continue to look the other way." Then, as if he hadn't made his point, or perhaps to make sure he had Virgil's full attention he added, "Stop jerking me around. You're the only family I've got left." He sounded pissed. Then he walked over and picked up Robert's shirt and held it open for him as he came out of the water.

When Virgil turned back to Sandy it was clear to him how much damage he'd managed to inflict on the people he loved. "I'm afraid if I stop, I'll never see him again. He died for me."

"He died for us, Virgil. You remember what he did right before he passed? The way he put your hand on top of mine? The way he looked at me until he was gone? You said something to me the day we planted this tree. You said he was telling you he loved you…that he didn't say those exact words, but that was what he meant. I'm telling you, baby, in that moment behind the bar, when he put your hand on top of mine and looked at me until he passed, he was telling me that he trusted me to take care of his boy. So that's what I'm doing. That's what we're *all* doing."

"What if I stop and I don't ever see him again?"

"Then he was never really there, was he?" Sandy took his hand and led Virgil away from the weeping willow and closer to the edge of the pond. When Virgil looked back over his shoulder, he could still see his dad under the tree, but Mason seemed focused on someone else. It was then that Virgil reached into his pocket and grabbed the bottle of pills. He twisted the lid open, poured them out in his hand, and threw them into the water. When he did, two things happened almost simultaneously.

Murton laughed and said, "Wow, those are going to be some fucked up fish for a while."

Robert moved away from the water and over to Virgil's side. His shirt was damp, his pants clung to his legs and his shoes made little squishing noises when he walked. "Maybe you lend me some clothes?"

"You bet," Virgil said.

But it was what he said next that caused Virgil's throat to constrict and his heart to skip a beat. "Your father...he look happy. Everyting gonna be irie, mon. You wait. You see."

―――――――――

THEY ALL WALKED UP TO THE HOUSE AND WHEN THEY GOT inside, Virgil wasn't surprised to find his family physician, Dr. Bell, waiting in the kitchen. He was dressed casually, his black bag in one hand, a glass of water in the other. "You've been better, I understand?" he asked.

Virgil looked at Sandy, Murton, Delroy, and Robert. "I wouldn't be too sure about that. How'd they get you here?"

Bell began pulling supplies out of his bag. 'Ah, I bought a Porsche a few months ago…"

―――――――

"So…a little trouble with the pedals?" Virgil said.

Bell nodded. "Only the one in the middle. Can't seem to get to it quick enough when the radar detector goes off. Sandy and I made a little deal."

"Do I want to know?"

"Let me just say it wasn't the deal I would have liked."

Sandy said, "Bell!"

He laughed and then looked at Virgil. "Sandy has agreed to take care of the next ticket, that's all." He pulled out a chair and sat down and as he did, the smile left his face. "I'd have been here anyway. Surely you know that."

Virgil tipped his head. "I know, Bell. Thank you."

"Come on and sit down. Let me have a listen." He took Virgil's pulse, blood pressure, listened to his heart and lungs, checked his reflexes, looked inside his ears, nose, and throat, and generally gave him a complete physical. When he finished the exam, he started on the questions. How long had he been on the narcotics? What dosage? Had he been taking any extra? Did he really want to stop? And on and on...

"Any more pain meds in the house?" he asked.

Virgil hesitated, but in the end he told the truth. "Top shelf of the kitchen pantry, behind the noodles."

Murton shook his head, reached into the cabinet, and rooted around until he found the bottle. "At least you're finally using your noodle," he said.

Doctor Bell looked at the bottle and then put it in his pocket. "Don't throw any more pills of any kind in the pond. Your fish will be all fucked up." He pulled three vials of drugs from his bag, lined them up on the table, then began to fit needles on the ends of three syringes that looked big enough to put down a horse with a broken leg. "I have to tell you, Virgil, you appear healthy enough."

"Healthy enough for what?" Virgil said as he looked at the syringes on the table.

"There are two ways to deal with this kind of thing," Bell said. "Three if you're one of those twelve-steppers."

"I don't need a twelve-step program," Virgil said.

"All right then. Two ways. First, you wean yourself from the medication little by little over the course of a month or two, gradually reducing your dosage and frequency until you're off the meds completely. Quite a lot of people have had success with that particular method, though I'd be the first to admit, it often doesn't work. It's too easy to cheat."

Virgil looked at Sandy, who was already shaking her

head. Bell noticed too. "All right then, the other is what we are going to do here, starting right now, tonight."

"Which is what, exactly?" asked Murton.

"We are going to bring him off all at once. I believe you are healthy enough and still young enough that you can handle it, Virgil. But I have to emphasize, it *is* a strain on your system. Your heart most of all."

"My heart is fine," Virgil said.

Delroy huffed a little. Bell didn't notice, or if he did, he didn't let on. "There are three things I want to give you. The first is a massive dose of vitamins. The second is a non-narcotic anti-anxiety medication that will help take the edge off."

"And the third?"

"The third is the one you'll thank me for," Bell said. "It'll knock you out cold as soon as I give you the shot. It's similar to Jackson juice, but safer. You'll sleep for at least the next twenty-four to thirty-six hours, which should get you through the worst of the withdrawal and anxiety. But make no mistake, you're in for a rough couple of days."

Virgil looked at Sandy. "I can do it."

"I know you can, baby."

Bell seemed to take note of everyone in the room for the first time. He looked at Delroy and Robert. "I don't believe I've had the pleasure, gentlemen. I'm Doctor Robert Bell."

Robert sort of sniffed. "Good name, you."

Delroy just smiled.

———————

SANDY, BELL, AND VIRGIL LEFT MURTON, DELROY, AND Robert in the kitchen. They went into the bedroom and Bell pulled some paperwork from his bag and attached it to a clipboard. "I'd like to go ahead and give you the vitamin and anti-anxiety shots now. Do I have your permission to do that?"

Virgil nodded at him.

"I have to hear you say yes, Virgil."

"Yes, yes. Let's get on with it."

Bell raised his eyebrows. "Maybe we'll start with the anti-anxiety shot."

"Sorry," Virgil said. He sat quietly as Bell gave him the shots, though he didn't know in what order they were administered. "If I'm asleep, why do I need the anxiety meds?"

"Because without them you won't sleep for long and when you wake, you'll want to unzip your skin and leave it behind like a snake in the grass." Then, "Relax, Jonesy. It sucks, but you can do it. The trick is to get in front of it. That's what we're doing here." He finished with the first two shots, then handed Virgil the clipboard with the paperwork. "Read this and then sign at the bottom. Don't forget to date it as well."

"What is it?"

"Standard medical release. Informed consent and all that. Gives me permission to treat you and take any and all necessary measures to ensure your health and well-being while under my care or the care of those I designate, who, having been properly trained in the administration of, etcetera, etcetera and so on and so forth. Just sign and date at the bottom."

Bell handed him a pen. Virgil noticed the form contained a considerable amount of fine print. In addition, Bell kept speaking, which made any concentration difficult.

"I want you to eat nothing but fruit and raw or steamed vegetables during the day. You can have any different combination of vegetables that you'd like for dinner, but try to stay away from any type of starch and nothing except fruit after eight p.m. Also, no sugar or salt of any kind except what you find naturally in your fruits and vegetables. No other artificial sweeteners, either. And I know you're going to think this is odd, but no water, and I mean none at all for at least a week."

"No water?" Sandy said. "How can that be?"

Virgil chimed in as well. "Look, Bell, I trust you and all, but what the hell am I supposed to drink if I don't have water?"

"I've got a brand new juicer for you. I brought it with me. It's top of the line. Don't thank me because I'm adding it to your bill. When you're up and around you're going to drink thirteen glasses of fresh juice a day—a combination of both fruit and vegetable—for at least a week."

Virgil could tell that the anti-anxiety medication was starting to take hold because he was having trouble concentrating on what Bell was saying. He finally gave up on reading the form, signed and dated it, then handed it back to the doctor.

"Okay Jonesy, off with your clothes, then get in your bed here. You can leave your skivvies on if you like."

Virgil got undressed and laid down on his back. Bell uncapped the final syringe and injected the medication into his arm.

"I'll give the rest of the instructions to Sandy. You won't remember them."

Virgil thought Bell might have said 'sleep well,' or something to that effect, but either way, he was out before Bell was finished with the shot.

CHAPTER FOURTEEN

ABIGAIL MONROE FINALLY FINISHED ONE OF THE MOST stressful days at her job that she could recall. She'd spent most of the day with the programmers, listening to them drone on and on about how difficult it had been to sort through the code to ensure that Nicholas Pope hadn't buried anything in the system. Every time one of them would come into her office and say they were ready, they had to take the entire system off-line to run the diagnostics. That involved notification of all retail outlets, a nightmare in and of itself. And they couldn't take the system off-line without her approval, so she was stuck in her office for the entire day. The programmers ended up going through the entire process nine times before they were sure they'd covered everything.

In the end, they assured her the system was clean. If pressed, however, Abigail thought they didn't sound completely sure. Maybe ninety-five percent, but not one hundred. They said they were positive, but they didn't *sound* positive. That was troublesome. For now though, the system was functioning perfectly, the security measures were in place and everything seemed normal enough. It was the 'seemed' that bothered her. When you were the executive director in charge of oversight on an entity that brought in and gave out hundreds of millions of dollars, *seemed* didn't cut it.

Plus, she'd had to sell her own story to the programmers about how she knew—*suspected* was the word she'd used with them—that there remained a real possibility that something might be amiss in the system. Everyone knew Pope had been killed, after all. And not only killed, it looked like he'd been tortured to death. It was the 'who' and the 'why' that had Abigail stressed. Maybe someone had tried to extract some information from Pope as a way to gain access to the system. Had anyone thought of that? Or perhaps he'd been involved with someone and together they were going to try to cheat the security measures that the lottery had in place. Either way, something was going on. "Get in there and find it," she'd told them.

She thought her performance was acceptable. Maybe not Oscar-worthy, but good enough to fool a few office nerds that sat at their consoles and stared at computer code all day. She'd certainly dressed for the occasion, wearing a tight, mid-length black skirt that looked like body paint, open-toe high heels that showed off her feet—

she'd been told by more than a handful of men that she had great feet—and a sheer white blouse with a skimpy lace bra. It worked. The programmers were drooling like lapdogs by the time they left her office and it seemed like almost every one of them came back in at fifteen-minute intervals with this question or that. If she'd taken a poll, she thought not a single one of them could have told her the color of her eyes.

Still, the stress. And she'd brought it on herself. She'd made a mistake and a massive one at that. My God, what had she been thinking? *Well, greedy bitch, you knew exactly what you'd been thinking. You'd been thinking wouldn't it be great to be sitting on the beach, sipping an umbrella drink and calculating the interest.* Looking back though, it was one of the stupidest things she'd ever done...getting into bed with Nicky Pope. And what was it that Bradley had told her the other night? They needed to manage this thing on their end? Something like that. Well, that's exactly what she was doing now, wasn't she? And what about Bradley? Had he been the one who killed her Nicky? He found out they had been dating and he was pissed, but murder? Abigail didn't think he had it in him. Still...Nicky...gone.

He'd told her they were going to be rich. *Stupid rich* was how he'd put it. Except now that he'd been murdered —Abigail shuddered at that thought—she was right back where she'd started.

Abby kicked off her heels, walked into her kitchen,

and poured herself a glass of red wine. She took a long swallow, refilled the glass, then picked up her iPad and walked into her study. That's when the doorbell rang.

She tucked the iPad under her arm, walked down the hall, and opened the door with her free hand. When she saw the man standing there, the thought that inflated inside her brain was: *Cop.*

———————

THE LOTTERY OFFICE WAS LOCATED IN A NONDESCRIPT, brown-bricked, three-story building on Meridian Street about a mile north of the city's center. A small sign hung above the door—a banner, really—that said Lottery Office. Other than that, the building looked like an office supply store or maybe an H & R Block tax center. Ron Miles had driven by the building or through the area about a thousand times over his career, but he'd never been inside. Miles had no real reason to drive by it now except for the fact that it was on the way to his destination, the home of the executive director of the state's lottery, Abigail Monroe.

It would have been more convenient to conduct the interview at her office, but Miles knew that if he did that, she'd have the upper hand. Home turf and all. It might not be important with Monroe—she wasn't a suspect after all —but she had been Nicholas Pope's boss, so he had some amount of hope that an informal chat in her home would create a more comfortable environment, one where she might be a bit more forthcoming with any information that could help in the investigation.

Miles rang the bell and when Monroe answered the door she was still dressed in her work clothes, minus her shoes. It was the first thing Ron noticed. Her feet, specifically her toenails, were perfect. She held a glass of red wine in her hand and had an iPad tucked under her arm. When he looked up from her feet, Miles got the impression that he'd startled her. Caught her off guard or…something. He could see it behind her eyes.

"Hello. May I help you?"

"I'm Detective Ron Miles, Indianapolis Metro Homicide. Are you Abigail Monroe?"

"Yes."

"Ms. Monroe, our office has been charged with the investigation into the death of Nicholas Pope. I understand he worked for you?"

"Yes, he was one of our programmers."

"I have a few questions I'd like to ask you. May I come in?"

Miles got the impression that she had to contemplate her answer, but after a brief pause, she said, "Of course" and opened the door for him to enter.

"I was about to go sit out on the veranda and relax. I allow myself an evening cocktail. Would you care for something?"

"No, thank you," Ron said as he followed her through

the living room and then the sliding glass door that gave way to her back porch.

"No drinking on the job, I suppose?"

"That's right." Miles made a show of reaching for his pen and notebook. He kept a dummy set of keys in his pocket and he pulled those out and then set them on the table. Once they were seated: "Would you tell me what you know about Mr. Pope?"

"Well," Abigail began, "I'm almost embarrassed to say that I don't know very much at all."

"And why is that?"

"Nicky was one of many programmers that we employ. As you might imagine, given what we do it takes quite a few people to maintain our type of system. Plus we have different levels—they're actually separate departments, so maybe I shouldn't say levels—anyway, different levels of programmers for different functions. Some handle basic functions like ongoing system maintenance, some take care of security, while others are responsible for writing new code for different types of games."

"What level or department did Mr. Pope work in?"

Monroe crossed her legs, then reached down and massaged her left foot. "Let's see, Nicky was, um, security I believe. Yes, security. I'm sure that's correct. To tell you the truth, Detective, the programmers? They all sort of blend together in my mind. We have quite a few of them and frankly, they're all a little peculiar. They work odd hours, they're about the least sociable people you'd ever want to meet and, well…there's no diplomatic way to put this I suppose, other than to simply say it: They sort of look down on everyone else in the organization..like they're better than the rest of us."

"I see. So if I understand you correctly, you personally did not know Mr. Pope any better than the rest of the programmers who work for the lottery, is that correct?"

"Detective, uh, Niles, is it?"

"Miles."

"Yes, of course. Detective Miles, my title is Executive Director of the lottery. I report to the lottery's board of directors. While I'm sure there are other organizations whose directors take a more hands-on approach with their employees, that simply isn't my style. Not only that, but my position is one of development as opposed to straight managerial."

"Development?"

"I am the face of the lottery, I guess you could say."

"I see. But you still didn't answer my question, Ms. Monroe. Did you know Mr. Pope any better than the rest of the programmers who work for the lottery?"

Abigail took a long deliberate sip of her wine. "I'm not sure I understand the nature of your question, Detective."

I think you do, Ron thought, *otherwise you would have answered me by now.* He tried a different tactic. "Would you give me the names of your programmers please?"

Monroe blinked at him. "All of them?"

"Yes, please." Miles had his pen and notebook ready.

Monroe set her wine glass down on the table with great care. Ron thought it looked like a practiced maneuver. "That would have to come from our Human Resources department. I'm afraid I don't know. I mean, I know a few of their first names, but…"

"But Mr. Pope, Nicky, as you called him. No trouble remembering him?"

"What exactly are you implying, Detective?"

Time to dial it back. "I'm sorry Ms. Monroe. I think sometimes I've been doing this type of work too long. I need to practice my people skills or something. No implication whatsoever. Boy oh boy, if you knew the type of people I have to interview day in and day out…the way they lie right to my face."

"I can only imagine."

Miles made a show of checking his watch. "You know what? I think I might go ahead and bend the rules a bit. I'm supposed to be off the clock right now as it is anyway. If your offer of that glass of wine is still good…" He glanced at her feet and smiled.

———

NEVER TALK TO THE COPS. *EVER.* THAT'S WHAT ABIGAIL'S husband, Lee, had always told her. Once you open your mouth and start down that road, they'll back you into a corner, with no way out. And that's exactly what she'd done. She opened the door, invited him in and now after only a few questions she felt like he knew she was lying. Had to get him out of the house. Had to think. She'd offered him a glass of wine? What, they were on a date now?

"Yes, of course. In fact, why don't we go back inside? These chairs are wonderful to look at, but they're hell on my back."

They went inside and Ron followed her into the kitchen. "Forgive me, Detective. Where are my manners? Please, have a seat on the sofa and I'll bring you a glass of wine."

"Oh, I'm fine right here, Ms. Monroe. In fact, I'm sort of a kitchen kind of guy."

Great. Plan A was to tell him she was out of wine. Now what? Plan B, that's what. Abigail pulled the cork from the bottle and when she made a show of reaching for another glass, she knocked the bottle to the floor and it shattered at their feet. "Oh, damn."

The glass was everywhere and the white tiled floor was now covered with red wine. Miles jumped back, the glass crunching under his feet, wine splashing across the bottom of his pants. "Whoa. Don't move Ms. Monroe. Are you cut? Is that wine or blood on your leg there?"

Abigail looked down. "No, no, I don't think so. It's only the wine."

"Where are your shoes? I'll get them for you. If you take a step you'll slice your feet up."

"Um, right over by the front door, I think."

"Okay, stay right there." Miles went and got her shoes and brought them into the kitchen. Monroe slipped them on and together they crunched their way past the glass and naturally, right back to the front door.

"Detective, I'm wondering…well…to tell you the truth, I've had a particularly stressful day at work today. Could we finish another time? Perhaps tomorrow at my office? I can make sure the HR people are there. Most of the programmers should be present as well. I think it might be more productive that way."

Miles didn't hesitate. "Yes, of course. I'd be happy to help you clean up the mess in the kitchen though. I feel like it was my fault."

"That's quite all right, Detective. I'm sure I can manage and I'm equally sure that's not in your job description." Monroe opened the front door.

Miles started to step through the door, then stopped. "Out of curiosity, Ms. Monroe, how long have you been with the lottery?"

———————

SHE CLEARLY WANTS ME OUT OF THE HOUSE, RON thought. Knocking the wine bottle from the counter couldn't have been more obvious. But why? And why was she lying?

"Almost two years exactly. I took over for my

husband Lee after his unfortunate automobile accident."
Monroe glanced back toward the kitchen. "I'm sorry,
Detective, but that wine…I'm afraid it will stain the tiles
if I don't get it cleaned up."

"You bet. How about nine tomorrow then, at your
office?"

"Tell you what. Call me at nine and we'll figure something out. That will give me a chance to check my
schedule and make sure all the appropriate department
heads can be there as well."

"If we could firm something up right now, that would
probably be best." Monroe pinched her lips together in a
line and looked down at the floor. Ron saw the look and
backed off a little more. "You know what? You're right. I
shouldn't waste my time coming to your office if the
appropriate people aren't going to be there. And who
knows? You might have an important meeting with the
governor or something."

Monroe let out a little laugh, thought, *Thank God, he's
leaving,* then made another mistake.

───────────

"OH, THE GOVERNOR IS MUCH TOO BUSY TO SEE ME, I
assure you, Detective. In fact, most of my political dealings are with Bradley Pearson, the governor's chief of
staff."

Miles laughed with her and said, "Huh."

"What?"

"Oh nothing, really. Most of my dealings are with Pearson as well."

Shit. Stop lying. It's not necessary. "How do you know Bradley Pearson? I thought you said you were with the Indianapolis Police."

Ron put the flat of his hand against his forehead. "Did I? Boy, I've got to get a handle on that. I'm sorry. I *was* with the Indianapolis Metro Homicide Unit. In fact, I was with them for over twenty years. But my new job is Lead Detective for the state's Major Crimes Unit. Pearson hired me. I guess we practically work for the same guy. Anyhow, sorry for the mix-up. I'll call you tomorrow."

Monroe watched the cop walk down the sidewalk and around the corner before she shut the door and picked up the phone.

———————

MILES WALKED AWAY CASUALLY, TURNED THE CORNER and once he was out of sight he picked up his pace and jogged to his car. He took out his cell and punched in the number for their unit's researcher, a smart, sassy young woman named Becky Taylor, who, Ron had heard, could find anything on anybody.

"I was getting ready to go home, Ron."

"I'll authorize the overtime."

"Don't need it."

"Really? That practically makes you a suspect."

"A suspect for what?"

"For being mean. Who doesn't need overtime?"

"I guess I should have said want. As in I don't want it. Not tonight." When Ron didn't say anything he heard her eyes roll on the other end of the line. "Okay, what?"

"Okay you'll do it, or okay you want to know?"

"I'm hanging up now."

"Okay, okay. You don't have to do it tonight, but first thing tomorrow I want you working on this."

"Donatti has me working the gang thing."

"Too bad. This comes first. It's one of the perks of being the boss. Maybe the only one."

"Okay. What is it?"

"I want everything you can get me on a woman named Abigail Monroe."

"Monroe. Abigail. Got it. Good-bye."

"You sound a little irritated."

"I'm not. But I'm about to be. Anything else?"

"Nope. Have a great evening."

———

"HE ONLY LEFT A FEW SECONDS AGO," MONROE SAID INTO the phone. "I need you to get over here. We've got some things to talk about."

"What did you tell him, Abby?"

"Bradley, we have to talk. You're the one who said we

needed to get on the same page. I'm saying let's do that. I'm suggesting right now. In fact, I'm insisting on it."

"Okay, I'm close anyway. I'll be there in five minutes."

Monroe ended the call and sat down on the couch, then remembered the mess in the kitchen. She got a broom and dustpan, swept the larger pieces of glass into the pan, then ran a damp mop over the floor. By the time she was done, Pearson was at the door. She'd have to be careful here. *Think.*

———

MILES SAT IN HIS CAR AROUND THE CORNER FROM Monroe's condo. He was willing to bet twenty genuine United States dollars—though he had no one with whom to bet—that one of two things would happen within the next thirty minutes. Either Monroe would leave and go somewhere, or someone would come to her. He wouldn't have thought it at all, except for the fact that the entire time they'd been speaking she was lying her pretty little head off. He didn't know why, but he was determined to find out, even if he had to hold her feet to the fire to do it.

Well, maybe not her feet…

———

He would have won the genuine twenty United States dollars but would have lost his ass had someone offered him a secondary wager that said the person who would come to Monroe would be Bradley Pearson. Miles crept forward in his car and watched as Pearson parked right in front of Monroe's condo and walked to the door. Miles checked the time, waited an agonizing five minutes, then got out of his car and headed up the walk. On the way, he thought about doubling down on his imaginary bet. Would Pearson show himself? He couldn't decide.

Miles rang the bell and waited.

The alley cats, at it again. "Christ, Abby. Cleaning up after you is a little like following an incontinent Alzheimer's patient around the bus depot. Why did you lie to him?"

"I don't know. I panicked a little."

"A little? You stupid bitch, you're—"

"Don't you call me that. Don't you dare. You want to know why I lied? I'll tell you. I was protecting you."

"Protecting me? From what?"

"You killed him, didn't you? You're the one who killed my Nicky."

"Abby, that is absolutely wrong. I don't have any idea what happened to Pope."

"You're lying. You knew I was sleeping with him and

you couldn't handle it. Maybe I should tell that to the cops. How about that, hotshot?"

"I'll tell you something, Abby, I wish I'd never—" The doorbell cut him off. "Who is that? Are you expecting anyone?"

"No."

"Check the window."

Monroe peeked out the window closest to the door and her heart very nearly skipped three beats. "It's him," she hissed at Pearson.

"Who? Miles?"

"Yes, Miles, you idiot. Who else? Go back and wait in the kitchen."

"I am not going to hide from someone who—"

"I said go." The look on her face told Pearson he didn't have a choice, at least in the moment.

"Okay. Don't say anything."

Monroe waited until Pearson was out of sight before she answered the door. Then, with an exasperated look on her face, she pulled the door open. "Detective, I thought I made it clear that I've had an extremely stressful day at the office. I'm not up for this. I'm really not. I was under the impression that we would continue our discussion another time."

"I'm sorry to bother you, Ms. Monroe. The parking around here is nonexistent. I'm almost two blocks away."

"If you have a point, Detective, it's lost on me."

"I can't find my keys. I think they might be on the table on your back porch. Would you mind?"

Monroe huffed and said, "Wait here." She closed the door on him and then was back in less than a minute. "They were on the table," she said.

Miles nodded. "That's what I thought. Sorry to be a bother."

"That's fine, Detective. Is there anything else?"

"No, no," Miles said as he jiggled the keys at her. "Just needed these."

"Very well then. Good evening."

"And to you, Ms. Monroe."

The door was almost shut, but it wasn't Ron's first day on the job. "Oh, Ms. Monroe? Like I said, I had to park quite a ways down the street. I couldn't help notice as I was walking back that someone was at your door. Was that Bradley Pearson I saw?"

Monroe looked at Miles for a beat and then said something in the moment that altered her future, though she never knew it. "No, it certainly was not. I have a gentleman caller. And let me say, Detective, the Columbo routine is getting to be something of a bore. I'm not sure what it is you're after, but you're barking up the wrong tree." She slammed the door in his face.

And Ron thought, *Gotcha*.

———————

Pearson came around the corner from the kitchen stripping off his jacket as he did. He got right up in Monroe's face. "What the hell was that? What's the matter with you? Didn't we already have a conversation about this? Were you listening? You never lie to the cops, Abby. Never."

She took a step back. "What was I supposed to do?"

Pearson shook his head and moved to the front door. "Wait here. Do not come outside. I'll be back in a minute."

"What are you going to do?"

Pearson pointed his finger at her. "I said wait here." He loosened his tie, undid the top button of his shirt, then walked out the front door. He looked both directions down the sidewalk and saw Miles as he was about to turn the corner. "Ron! Hey, Ron, hold on a second."

Miles turned, saw Pearson, and began walking back. They met at the midpoint between the corner of the intersection and the walkway that led to Monroe's condo.

"Ron, Abby told me what happened. There's been a hell of a misunderstanding here."

Miles stared at him but didn't speak. It was Cop 101. If you've got someone circling the line, eventually they'll take the bait and set their own hook. "I think Abby might have been a little intimidated back there."

Miles stayed quiet.

"Okay, look. Abby and I, well, we're sort of seeing each other."

"As in your eyes are functioning properly, or the two of you are dating?"

Even Pearson grinned at that. "I don't know if dating is the right word for it. We're sleeping together. I mean, we're not sleeping together right now…she sort of broke it off, which is a hell of a shame because let me tell you…" Buddies now.

Miles wasn't having it. "Here's the thing, Bradley: I'm investigating the murder of Nicholas Pope. Murder is considered a capital crime in the state of Indiana. For some reason or another, Monroe was lying to me back there, or at the very least, being extremely evasive. My questions couldn't have been any more basic. Withholding information relative to a capital crime in our state makes someone an accessory after the fact."

"Look, Ron, you're making this into something it's not. Look at me for Christ's sake. I'm not exactly what any woman would call a good catch. I'm short, round, and getting rounder. When I saw a chance with Abby I took it, but she's not too proud of herself over it."

"Why's that?"

"Because the only reason she slept with me in the first place was so that I would help her get the job of executive director at the lottery."

"So why lie to me about Pope?"

Pearson gave Miles a little grimace. "That might actually be my fault. After Pope turned up dead, Abby and I talked about it…the coincidence of the whole thing…how

Jones shot and killed James Pope twenty years ago, how that saved my life and now his son, Nicholas turns up dead *and* he happens to be employed by the woman I talked into the sack so she could get the job she wanted? The entire thing really is one big coincidence."

"Then why not get right out in front of it?"

Pearson took a breath. "That's exactly what I'm doing right now, Ron. Neither Abby nor I have anything to hide regarding the Pope matter. She was simply trying to protect her reputation, her place in the community. I don't blame her. If word got out that she was hired after I pulled the right strings and in return, she slept with me as a form of recompense, she'd be ruined. The governor wouldn't be too happy with me, either. It's not that complicated. Surely you can see that, can't you, Ron?"

Nice try. "You bet, Bradley. Offer my apologies to Ms. Monroe, will you?"

CHAPTER FIFTEEN

WHEN VIRGIL WOKE HE EXPERIENCED A CLARITY OF thought that he'd not recognized for quite some time. He felt refreshed, but he was surprised and even a little disappointed when he noticed that only about eight hours had passed instead of the twenty-four to thirty-six that Bell had mentioned. The sun was out and the bedside clock said it was a little after eight in the morning. His bladder said he had to pee.

He stood from the edge of the bed and while his back felt a little stiff from sleep, Virgil noticed his leg didn't hurt at all. He went into the bathroom, took care of business and by the time he returned to the bedroom, Sandy was there, a look of apprehension dancing around the corners of her eyes. She kissed him, then stepped back and asked how he felt.

"You know what? I feel pretty well. My leg doesn't hurt, Sandy. Not one bit."

She smiled, then handed him a tall glass of fruit juice. "Drink this. All of it. After you do I'll get you a bowl of fruit. After the fruit, Bell wants you to take some more vitamins and he has some anti-anxiety pills for you too, but he doesn't want you to take them unless it's absolutely necessary. You've got a lot of juice to drink over the next week or so. Nothing to eat except organic fruits and veggies for the same amount of time either."

Virgil scratched the back of his head and realized he could smell himself. "Listen, do you think all of that is really necessary? I mean, I've always liked Doc Bell and all, but he said that I'd be out for twenty-four hours. Hell, it hasn't even been eight. Maybe nine, I guess. I don't remember exactly what time it was when he put me under."

Sandy had her back to him as she removed the sheets from the bed. When she didn't answer, Virgil said, "I'm going to open the windows. It's sort of stale in here or something."

"You can say that again."

Virgil noticed for the first time that he had a small clear bandage on the back of his hand. "Say, what the heck is this?"

Sandy had the sheets balled up and tossed them on the floor by the foot of the bed. "What?"

"This bandage." He waved his hand at her. "Did I cut

myself or something last night? How would that have happened? And listen, not to be too crude or anything, but my ass is kind of sore. I'm thinking maybe we need a new mattress or something."

Sandy sat down on the bed and patted the mattress as an indication for him to sit next to her. "You didn't cut your hand. You were sound asleep all night last night."

"So what gives?"

"Come on, sit down with me for a minute."

———————

"IT'S FROM THE IV LINE," SANDY SAID. "BELL PUT IT IN after you were out. The catheter too."

"Catheter?" Virgil looked down at his groin. It took him a few seconds, but he finally got it. "This isn't Tuesday morning, is it?"

Sandy shook her head.

"It's been more than a few hours, then?"

"You could say that."

"How long?"

Sandy rubbed the bottom of her nose with the back of her index finger. "Bell wanted you out for the worst of it, Virgil. He said if you'd been awake it would take twice as long and be twice as hard. He's been here the entire time. He's downstairs right now. So are Murton and Delroy. They hardly left your side the whole time."

"How long?"

"Bell put you on a very mild IV sedation that kept you under for the most part. Hydrated too. Also, the vitamins were an essential part of—"

He was starting to get irritated. "Sandy, how long?"

"Let's see, tonight is fish Thursday at the bar, so…"

———————

"WHAT? THREE DAYS?" VIRGIL COULDN'T BELIEVE IT. "He kept me under for three days?"

"It was really only two and a half."

"Sandy, he told me it was going to be twenty-four hours tops."

She shook her head. "No, he said it'd be *at least* twenty-four to thirty-six hours."

Virgil's hands were trembling slightly. Adrenaline, he thought. He also heard a loud grinding noise coming from the other room. "What the hell is that? It sounds like someone is running a wood chipper in the kitchen."

"It's probably Delroy. He's fascinated with our new juicer."

"I have to tell you Sandy, I feel sort of violated or something."

"How else do you feel though?"

"Kind of pissed, actually."

"That's not what I meant."

When he didn't say anything else, Sandy kissed him on the cheek, patted his thigh and stood from the bed.

"Take a shower, Virgil. And you're welcome. I'll be in the kitchen. You might want to think about keeping that beard going too. I kind of like it."

She closed the door softly behind her.

———————

VIRGIL TOOK HIS TIME IN THE SHOWER. HE ALSO SHAVED. *Three days?*

———————

WHEN HE WALKED INTO THE KITCHEN, DELROY AND Murton were speaking with Sandy and Bell. The four of them all had evil grins on their faces. It didn't take long though before Virgil was grinning right along with them. Sandy handed him about a hundred vitamins, which he took with another glass of juice. Delroy was leaning against the counter, munching on a raw carrot. Sandy walked over and stood next to him and when she did, he leaned close and whispered something in her ear. Then he smiled, pointed the end of his half-eaten carrot at Virgil, and said, "How you do, you?"

Virgil set the empty juice glass down on the table and thought for a moment before he said anything. "This is later, isn't it?"

Delroy tilted his head, turned the corners of his mouth

down and nodded just so. "Dat up to more of you than more of me, but, yeah, mon, it might be."

"Thank you, Delroy."

Delroy threw his head back and laughed his big, loud Jamaican laugh. "Respect, mon, respect." Then he set about chopping up more fruits and vegetables. "You know what Delroy tink?" He pointed a carrot at Virgil again. "Delroy tink we should get some of these juicers for the bar. We could open up earlier in da morning and sell fresh juice. Five bucks a cup. I tell you something else, mon. If we start using fresh juice in our mixed drinks instead of dat pre-made mix we always buy, they be knocking down the door for more. You wait and see."

He was completely serious. Virgil looked at Murton, who simply shrugged. "Whatever you think Delroy. You manage the bar."

"Good. Delroy get some then. Maybe a new sign too. We call it Jonesy's Rastabarian. How 'bout dat, mon?"

"How about one thing at a time and we'll see?"

Delroy laughed his big Jamaican laugh again. "Yeah, mon. One ting at a time. Nothing wrong with dat, no." Then he looked at Murton and pointed his finger at him, the change in his expression quick and serious. "Keep him out of trouble. It on you." Then he walked over to the back door. "Delroy have to get to work now. It fish Thursday."

After the door was closed Virgil looked at Sandy. "What did he say to you?"

Sandy looked like she was trying to decide whether or not to say anything, but she finally did. She tucked her chin into her chest before she spoke. "He said, 'I know dat man like he my own child. You watch, you. He going to say tank you to Delroy.'"

"Holy smokes, Small," Murton said. "I love you and all, but that might be the worst attempt at a Jamaican accent I've ever heard."

Sandy picked up a dishrag and threw it at Murton. It hit him square in the face, but did little to muffle his laughter...or Virgil's.

They all stood there laughing and Virgil could feel the relief, like a weight had been lifted from his soul and the thought crossed his mind that the people in his life had once again saved him. He was free.

Or so he thought.

THE DOC GOT HIM SEATED AT THE KITCHEN TABLE AND gave Virgil another exam. Then he started in with more questions.

"Tell me how you're feeling."

Still a little pissed that you kept me under for three days. "I feel pretty damn good, Doc. I guess I needed the rest, huh?"

"You could say that. The type of strain your system has been under for the last few months is not to be taken lightly, Virgil. You've stressed yourself physically—not to mention emotionally—to the breaking point. That's not an exaggeration. If you were ten years older, based on what I've seen, you wouldn't have made it."

Virgil tried not to let his skepticism show. "Bell, that seems a little…dramatic. I feel fine."

"Of course you do. Now. And if you continue to do what I say, you'll continue to get better. But your body has to heal."

"Okay. I get it. I'll keep taking the vitamins and all that."

Bell bit into his lower lip. "You sound sort of irritated, Virgil."

"Well, if I'm being honest with you, Bell, I guess I'm sort of pissed that you had me out for so long."

"It was the best way to control you, medically speaking. Think of it as a medical procedure, one where you had to be sedated, because that's exactly what it was."

"Yeah, except you didn't tell me ahead of time."

Bell reached into his bag and pulled out a clipboard with some paperwork attached and set it on the table. "Is that your signature on the bottom there?"

Virgil refused to look at the paper. "I didn't get a chance to read it."

"Did you read any of it?"

"Yes. I started to read it, but then you were talking and Sandy…"

Bell was still taking notes, as if the nature of their

conversation was of little importance. He spoke without looking up from his notepad. "What does the first line say right there at the top? It's the part that's in big bold red letters. Never mind, I'll tell you what it says. It says 'Read this document in its entirety before signing.' If I'm not mistaken—and I'm not—it goes on to say that failure to read the entire document before signing does not invalidate your signature or your consent to treatment. Always read the fine print, Jonesy. The bold print too."

"Yeah, yeah." Fucking doctors.

Bell put the paperwork away. "Listen, you and I, we've known each other a long time. You know damn well that anything I do to you is going to be with your best interest in mind."

"I know, Bell. Except when I was in the hospital after...well, after I got my ass kicked, when I realized how long I'd been under, it sort of freaked me out. This kind of feels the same way. It's almost sort of claustrophobic after the fact. Maybe it shouldn't bother me, but it does."

"That's understandable, Virgil, but hear me when I say this: You are not out of the woods yet."

"I thought you said this would do the trick."

"If by 'this' you mean the little nap you took and the intravenous fluids and vitamins I gave you, then no. That was the part that helped you from an emotional and physiological standpoint. What I'm talking about is healing the damage you've done to your body. We've got to draw the toxins out of your liver and let your body repair itself."

That sounded reasonable. "Okay. How do we do that?" Sandy was standing at the stove, stirring something in a pot and Virgil could smell the aroma of fresh ground coffee. Before Bell had a chance to answer, Virgil looked at Sandy and said, "Is something wrong with our coffee maker?"

"No, but this is the best way to do this."

"It sure smells good." Virgil looked back at Bell. "I can have coffee, right?"

"Oh yeah. You can have coffee. As a matter of fact, that's how we're going to get the toxins out of your liver."

"Hey, no argument here." Virgil smiled. Things were suddenly looking up. "You sure won't need me to sign a release for this part of the treatment, I can tell you that. I love coffee."

"Jonesy, I want you to give me your word," he pointed his finger at Virgil as he spoke, "which I've never known you to break, that you'll take this coffee as often as I tell you for as long as I tell you."

"Sure, Bell. That's no problem."

"I mean it, Virgil. Give me your word." He put his hand out to shake.

Virgil grasped his hand and they shook on it. "I give you my word, Bell. Whatever you say goes."

"Great. Sandy, Murton? You guys heard him. You're my witnesses."

Sandy and Murton both agreed with Bell. When Virgil glanced at Murton he saw him chewing on the inside of his lip.

"Fine. That's just fine, then," Bell said.

"In fact," Virgil said, "if it's all the same to you, I think I'll have a cup right now. Can I get you one?"

Murton began laughing so hard his eyes started to water.

"What's so funny?"

"Nothing, Jonesy. Nothing at all. Say, I'm going to head down to the bar. Maybe I'll see you later, okay?" He kissed Sandy on the cheek, gave Bell a pat on the shoulder and walked out the back door. Virgil thought he heard him say 'oh boy' under his breath.

"Will one of you guys please tell me what's going on here?"

Bell looked at Sandy, then over to Virgil. "Ever heard of the Gerson Therapy?"

―――――――――――――

"YOU WANT ME TO DO WHAT?"

"It's the only way, Virgil," Bell said. "The toxins you've been putting into your body have to be drawn out. That's what your liver does. The liver is the second largest organ in your body. Its main job is to filter the blood coming from the digestive tract before passing it to the rest of your system. In other words, it detoxifies chemicals and metabolizes drugs. You know what really fascinates me? It does so at the rate of almost fifteen-hundred liters of blood per day."

"Can't I just drink the coffee?"

Bell shook his head. "It's not the same. It doesn't work that way. If you drink the coffee, by the time it goes through your stomach and the digestive process, the benefits of the chemical compounds are lost. You've got to get the coffee directly to the liver."

Virgil had heard of coffee enemas before, but had always suspected that they were the product of quackery, a deception perpetrated on the uneducated or the uninsured as a last-ditch effort to maintain some semblance of health and well being. "How long would I have to do this?"

"Twice a day, morning and night, but only for another two days," Bell said.

"What do you mean by *another* two days?"

"You've had them now for three days. You know, while you were under…"

Virgil looked at Sandy, then put his elbows on the table and his head in his hands.

CHAPTER SIXTEEN

LATER IN THE DAY, AFTER ASSURANCES TO BOTH SANDY and Bell that he would stay on his schedule, Virgil went down to the bar. Murton was seated at one of the tables and Delroy was busy rearranging things to make room for the two new juicers he'd purchased. Virgil sat down with Murton and suddenly realized, other than boredom, he had no real reason to be at the bar. They were fully staffed, he wasn't on the schedule, and Delroy and Robert had a handle on the day-to-day operations. For the first time in his adult life, Virgil felt like he didn't quite belong... anywhere.

"I'm not really sure what I should be doing," he told Murton. "I mean, this is my bar, but it has always been sort of a backup plan for me. You know, something to do when I'm retired."

"Aren't you retired now?" Murton asked.

"Yeah. Aren't you?"

Murton kept glancing at the clock behind the bar. "You know what I think you should do?"

"I'm afraid to ask."

"I think you should go into business with me. I could use a partner and you're the best investigator I've ever met. We'd be unstoppable."

Virgil tried to keep his face neutral. "Ah, Murt. I don't know…"

"No, no, think about it for a second, will you? Here's the way I see it." He started ticking points off on his fingers. "One, we know everything there is to know about each other, so in that regard, we'd work well together. Hell, we already *are* working together right here at the bar. Two, if you were to examine the situation, you'd discover you are in the unfortunate position of what most anyone at all would refer to as limited employment opportunities. Three, I don't have a drug policy…"

"Hey…"

"Relax, Jonesy, I'm just messing with you. I actually do have a drug policy. Anyway, four, a PI badge is bigger and shinier than that little state badge you used to carry around. So what do you say? Wheeler and Jones Investigations. Has a nice ring to it, don't you think?"

"I don't think so, Murt. Thanks all the same, but I think I'll take a pass."

"What? How can you turn down an offer like that?

We'd have this city cleaned up in no time." He was serious.

"Oh yeah? How exactly would that work? Hold on, let me guess. We sit around here and wait for clients to walk through the door who want to hire a couple of bartenders?"

He wagged his finger back and forth. "Wrong. Not bartenders. Bar *owners*. Bar owners who used to be *cops*. We'd have them lined up and waiting."

Virgil chuckled for a few seconds. "Let me ask you this, how many clients do you have lined up and waiting?"

Murton sort of shrugged. "Hell Jonesy, I'm just getting started. But once the word gets out we'll have to beat them back with a stick."

"How many?" he asked again.

"You mean right now, at this very moment?"

"Yes, I mean right now, Murt, at this very moment."

As an answer to Virgil's question, Murton did two things at once. He pushed one of the chairs out from under the table with his leg, then picked up his mug of coffee and blew the steam away from the top of the cup. As he did, an attractive young woman walked up to their table and sat down in the chair. She addressed her question to Murton, who to his credit—or perhaps his salesmanship— never took his eyes off of Virgil.

"Are you Murton Wheeler?" the young lady asked. "That nice Jamaican man behind the bar said you were. My name is Nichole Pope. I need your help."

Virgil looked at Nichole Pope, the grown daughter of the man he'd shot and killed over twenty years ago, then looked back at Murton. "Are there benefits?"

"Nope. And the pay sucks too. In fact, after expenses, there probably won't be anything left over at all."

"Then I'll take it." Virgil looked at Nichole Pope then pointed across the table. "He's Murton Wheeler. I'm his partner. How may we help you, young lady?"

———————

HENDRICKS COUNTY IS HOME TO THE INDIANA LAW Enforcement Academy, where Sandy worked. Over the years as a state cop, first as a trooper, then an investigator, Virgil had built up any number of relationships with different county sheriffs and patrol officers, particularly in the counties closest to Indianapolis. Nichole Pope hadn't even answered his question when Virgil noticed Hendricks County Sheriff Jerry Powell walk into the bar. He was in uniform, so Virgil knew he wasn't there to eat or drink. "Excuse me for a moment," Virgil said to Murton and Nichole. He walked away from the table and met Sheriff Powell in the middle of the room. "Jerry, what is it? Is Sandy okay?"

Powell looked at him in confusion before he put it together. "Ah, Jonesy, I'm sorry. Didn't mean to scare you. I should have called first. Sandy's fine. Haven't seen her in quite some time, now that you mention it. How's she doing, anyway? Hey no disrespect, but if I were twenty years younger…"

Virgil exhaled noticeably. "Come on, Jerry, have a seat at the bar with me for a minute."

Powell slid onto a barstool, his gun belt squeaking in protest as he did. He removed his Smokey the Bear hat, set it crown down on the bar top, looked at Virgil, and said, "You okay? You look sort of pale."

"No, I'm fine," Virgil said, frowning at the contradiction of his own statement. "What's up?"

"I was going to call you at your office and put in an official request…"

"A request for what?"

"Got a little arson problem. Different spots, but we're mostly getting hit in Plainfield and Danville. Was sort of hoping you could take a peek and see what you could see."

Virgil watched in the mirror behind the bar as Nichole Pope stood from her seat and made her way to the restroom. He turned his attention back to the sheriff. "What's the state's arson inspector say?"

Sheriff Powell dropped his eyelids a fraction. "He says it's arson."

"Sounds like he knows what he's talking about then."

"Oh come on, Jonesy. You know those guys don't do anything except determine cause and half the time they're wrong about that. They all think they're Quincy or something but the truth is, they come in, sniff a few wires, cut a deal with the insurance company and call it a day. I need someone who can find these punks and put a stop to it."

"Quincy? How old are you, Jerry?"

"Still young enough to kick your butt."

"Hmm. You may be right about that. Look, Jerry, maybe you haven't heard, but—"

Powell's laugh cut him short. "Maybe I haven't heard? You're kidding right? Half the criminals in the state are celebrating as we speak. I said I was going to call you at your office, but I knew you wouldn't be there. That's why I came here. The county wants to hire you and Wheeler to catch these guys. Word is, you two have started your own shop. A retired fed and an ex-state investigator? When it comes to getting new clients you guys will be beating them back with a stick. I figured I better get you while the gettin's good." He put out his hand to shake. "If you can come over to my office tomorrow you can review the files and we'll work out the details and budget and so on and so forth. What do you say?"

Virgil shook his hand, but said, "Let me call you in the morning, if that's okay."

He nodded, picked up his hat and stood from his seat. "Fair enough. My best to Sandy. Talk to you tomorrow."

He started to walk away, but before he got too far, Virgil said, "Hey, Jerry?"

He turned back. "Yeah?"

"Which half?"

"Excuse me?"

"You said half the criminals in the state are celebrating. Which half?"

The sheriff set his hat squarely on his head and checked its placement in the bar mirror before he answered. "The smart ones," he said to his own reflection. "I'll be expecting your call, Jonesy."

When Virgil turned around, Murton was staring at him, the grin on his face as wide as ever.

NICHOLE POPE TOLD THEM ABOUT HER BROTHER, NICKY, and how the police had, in her opinion, all but given up on catching his killer. "I don't know if it's because they don't have a body, or if it's because they don't have any evidence, or if it's something else entirely. But I do know this, they've made exactly no progress and I'm tired of waiting."

"There's something you should know, Ms. Pope, before we go any further," Virgil said. He never got a chance to finish.

"I know who you are, Detective. It was a long time ago. You didn't kill my father. He got himself killed. The choices he made...I'm speaking of the choices in that moment...they were his own. He got a raw deal out of life and it ended badly, but the responsibility was on him. I don't see how anyone, especially you, Detective, could possibly see it any differently."

"Still, I'd like to apologize for what happened. And it's not 'detective' anymore. I'm no longer with the state police."

Virgil's revelation didn't seem to surprise her. "I accept your apology." Her eyes turned down for a few seconds, her thoughts somewhere else. When she looked back at him she said, "How about we leave it at that?"

Virgil knew full well the reason he was alive today was because of the sacrifice Sandy's father had made on his behalf. The costs associated with Chief Small's actions were enormous, not only for him, but for Sandy as well. Because of Virgil, Sandy grew up without a father.

Though Virgil had always done his best to rationalize that the death of James Pope was not his fault, the fact remained that he was the one who pulled the trigger. Could he have responded differently to that call? He simply didn't know. Further, he didn't know if anyone else would have either. Fate played a major role in the events of that day. Had Virgil been closer when the call came in it stood to reason that he would have gotten there sooner and prevented the escalation of events, thus saving Pope instead of killing him. Virgil did know however that the burden he carried over the death of Sandy's father was one that would remain with him forever. Was it not then reasonable to assume that the death of James Pope by Virgil's own hand could have been a portent of things yet to come? Were the consequences he would have to face as a result of his own actions some sort of destiny? He simply didn't know. "I took your father from you. You grew up…"

"Detective…I'm sorry, Mr. Jones…"

"Please, call me Jonesy."

"Very well then. Jonesy." She reached across the table and placed her hand on top of his and Virgil could feel a slight tremble in her touch. "His path was set the minute he got together with my mother. They weren't right for each other. She drove him crazy and I'm sure he did the same to her. They were wrong for each other and I'll tell you what else, they were wrong for us. My struggle for all these years has been to try to balance the fact that I am both of them together. I am half my mom and half my dad. I am in fact, the sum of two parts that never quite fit together. My parents weren't bad people, they were simply bad together. Do you know what that kind of thing does to your emotional state, especially as a young child?"

"I'm afraid I don't."

"Then I'm happy for you. I really am. But let me tell you something, no matter the struggles my brother and I had to endure, we made it. We somehow managed to survive and do well for ourselves. Our mother passed when we weren't yet legal adults but we have been taking care of each other ever since. If you hadn't shot…" She cut herself off, visibly swallowed, then started over. "Had my father not made the choices he made that terrible day, had Nicky and I not been there to see it…had he survived,

I think things would be very different for all of us, don't you?"

"Yes, I'm sure they would. But you have to understand, even as we sit here right now, for me, it's like time has stopped. You will always be that five-year-old girl who watched me shoot her father to death. I don't know how I could possibly put that aside to help you now."

"Maybe the way to do that, Jonesy, is to consider it a form of repayment. Let the death of my father go by helping me catch my brother's killer. Can you do that?"

"I had a very good man tell me not long ago that no one ever gets to turn the lights back on and replay the last inning. I think he's right."

"Would that man's name be Murton Wheeler?" she said.

Virgil looked over at Murton. Clearly Nichole Pope was not one to be underestimated.

"WHAT EXACTLY WOULD YOU LIKE US TO DO NICHOLE?" Murton asked.

"I'd like you to bring my brother's killer to justice."

"So even without a body, the police have told you your brother is dead?" Virgil asked.

Her lower lip trembled when she spoke. "Yes. They say there's no doubt. They've taken random samples of the blood from his apartment and matched it against my own. Every single sample they've taken is a perfect match. It's his blood. All of it. He's gone. I'll pay you whatever you require, but please, find whoever did this, will you? The police—I've been dealing with Detective Miles—are saying that without a body, no matter the amount of blood, there isn't anything they can really do. Quite honestly, I don't think they're trying all that hard. You've got to help me. Please."

Virgil started to say something, but Murton beat him to the punch. "What makes you think they're not trying very hard?"

"Maybe I shouldn't have put it that way. It's probably not a question of effort. In fact, I think they're trying extremely hard. I don't think they have any idea what's going on. I mean, how could they? I was closer to Nicky than anybody in the entire world and I don't have a clue."

"If you don't mind my asking, Nichole," Virgil said, "how did you happen to choose us?"

"It was Detective Miles. I had a very frank and honest discussion with him this morning during which I let him know that I wasn't satisfied with his results. He suggested that I contact you." Nichole seemed to think about what she'd said for a few seconds, then added, "Actually his suggestion was to contact Murton. He did say he thought the two of you might end up working together."

Virgil shot Murton a look. Murton pretended not to notice. "What do you do for a living, Nichole?"

"Is that relevant to your investigation?"

"I've been in law enforcement my entire adult life. If I've learned anything, it's this: Everything is relevant."

She looked around the room and then adjusted herself in the chair. "I'm a collector, of sorts. I acquire things that people want and I get paid well for what I do. Money is not an object. I can afford your fee, I assure you."

Virgil looked at Murton and said, "What is our fee, by the way?"

"So, I guess you guys are sort of new to this?" Nichole said.

"Only to the business. Not the work," Murton said.

Delroy walked over to our table with a tray that held three tall glasses of fresh juice. He set them down without speaking, but the look on his face was clear. It was time to drink up.

"You guys are juicing?"

"I am," Virgil said. "And if Delroy is right—Delroy here is our bar manager—I think you referred to him as 'that nice Jamaican man.' Anyway, if he's right, half the city will be in here wanting his juice."

Nichole looked up at Delroy. "I'll bet you're right. I love fresh organic juice." Then she turned her attention back to Virgil and Murton. "Say, have you guys ever heard of the Gerson Therapy?"

———

Virgil sidestepped the Gerson question by asking Nichole to tell them everything she could about her brother. She spent the next twenty minutes bringing them up to speed with her brother's life and background. It was his place of employment that caught their attention. "That seems like it must have been an interesting job, being a programmer for the lottery," Murton said.

"Boy, you wouldn't want to let Nicky hear you call him a programmer. It was sort of a sore spot with him."

"Why is that?"

"Hmm, pride I think. Nicky was a code guy. Real coders—I'm talking about the guys that go forty-eight hours or more at a keyboard—that was Nicky. When he got going on something, he wouldn't let up."

"Like what?" Virgil asked.

"I don't know…work stuff. He could go into work at the lottery on a Monday morning and sometimes I wouldn't see him until Wednesday night. He'd be wired up on Red Bull, smelled like one too—a bull—but he'd be done for the week with ten hours of overtime coming on his next check."

"So, dedicated," Virgil said.

"Obsessed, is more like it."

"Did he have any enemies?"

"Nicky? God, no." She reached into her purse and pulled out a picture of her brother. "I mean, look at him. He looks like a younger version of Brad Pitt. He was smart as a whip, kind to everyone he met and when he told one of his jokes people would literally wet themselves with laughter. That's not an exaggeration. I've seen it happen. Everybody loved him. People wanted to *be* him."

Murton took the photograph of Nicholas Pope. "But still," he said, "everybody usually has at least one person in their life who—"

Nichole was insistent. "Not Nicky, and you know what? Not me either. I think what you have to understand, is this…the kind of life Nicky and I had? After what we saw happen to our father, then losing our mother and being on our own? We learned to keep our heads down and our mouths shut. We went along to get along, if you know what I mean. It became a way of life for us. We lived it. We breathed it. Everyone loved him. No one would hurt my Nicky. We had plans. We were going to make it."

"I'm sure you would have," Murton said.

Virgil noticed that Nichole was consistently referring to her brother in the past tense. A small step toward acceptance. "You'll forgive me for saying so, Nichole, but you're wrong. Somebody wanted your brother dead." The words landed on her as if he'd slapped her in the face.

Murton reached across the table and took her hand, but he looked at Virgil when he spoke. "I think losing someone to violence is one of the most difficult things anyone has to endure. Most of the time there are no easy answers. Sometimes there are no answers at all."

Virgil watched as Nichole squeezed Murton's hand tight. She sort of bounced it on the table as she spoke. "But you'll try, won't you? You'll help bring justice to my family?" Then she sat back in her chair. "Listen to me... justice to my family. I don't have any family."

"You can count on us," Murton said. "Leave your contact information. Jonesy is close to the lead investigator handling your brother's murder. We'll talk with him and see what we can find out."

Virgil thought about how the last few days had gone so far, in particular his trips to the MCU headquarters and the conversations he'd had with Ron Miles and Bradley Pearson. "Well, maybe close isn't exactly the right word."

Murton shot him a look.

"You might not be entirely correct with your last statement, Jonesy," Nichole said as she dug through her purse. "I don't have anything to write on...wait never mind, I'll use this." She pulled out her rental car contract and wrote her name and cell number on the back, ripped it off, then set it on the table. "I want justice," she said, hissing it through her teeth. Then she got up and walked out of the bar.

A few seconds later Murton stood from the table. "Where are you going?" Virgil asked.

"I have to go find a bigger stick," he said.

———————

AFTER NICHOLE LEFT, VIRGIL THOUGHT ABOUT WHAT she'd said about her brother and his position at the lottery, wondering if his death was somehow connected to his employment. Then he remembered something else. He went upstairs and sat down at the ancient computer Murton had on his desk and typed PTEK into Google's search box. After paging through a number of results he eventually found the information he wanted. Not long ago, a company called PTEK had been hired to assume day-to-day administration of the state's lottery operations. The move by the state was one that in effect privatized the lottery and was highly criticized by left-leaning politicians and the media alike, but in the end, the passage of the bill was inevitable, mainly because PTEK promised the state close to two billion dollars in revenue over the first five years of their contract. Proponents of the bill noted that the lottery only took in an average of two hundred million per year and that PTEK would essentially be doubling that amount for a small percentage of sales as their fee.

Detractors voiced concerns that lottery earnings were supposed to go toward state-funded programs—chief among them, education—and anything that PTEK took would be coming out of those funds.

The proponents argued right back that any fee due to PTEK would be minuscule and, over and above what the lottery was currently earning. And so it went, on and on for weeks…

But two billion dollars is two billion dollars and the

individuals on the committee charged with putting the deal together assured the governor that it was doable, so the bill was passed, the governor signed and the deal was done. But the most interesting aspect was something not widely known. The individual that chaired the committee and pushed the bill through the state's legislative body was none other than Bradley Pearson.

Virgil also discovered that PTEK was a subsidiary of a holding company called API. A search on API turned up a number of different companies that used those initials; the American Petroleum Institute, American Professional Institute, and oddly enough, a now defunct Indiana company by the name of American Pet Insurance that had once sold veterinary medical insurance to pet owners. Virgil was about to abandon his search, but when he clicked on the next page of the results he found a listing near the bottom that identified a company with the API initials. When he clicked on the link he wasn't sure if he wanted to congratulate himself or pound his head on the desk.

He took out his phone and called Becky, the researcher at the Major Crimes Unit. "How would you like to have dinner at the most popular bar in the city tonight on my tab?"

"I don't think you can call it your tab if you own the bar. How's it going, Jonesy?"

"It's going well."

"How are you, uh, feeling?"

"I'm off the meds, if that's what you're asking, and I feel great. Listen, I'm serious about dinner."

"Uh-huh. What do you need?"

"Something that probably only you can give me."

"Jonesy…I thought you were happily involved with Small."

"I am. That's not what I meant. Are you done yanking my chain now?"

"Almost. What about Murton? Will he be there? He's yummy."

Murton? "Listen, Becky…"

"Okay, okay. What are you after? I might be able to help. The key word in that last sentence was *might*."

"I need everything you can get me on a company called API and its owner, a guy by the name of—"

"I already have it, Jonesy. API stands for Augustus Pate International. Ron had me look that up a couple of days ago."

"Can you send it to me?"

"Nope."

"Why not?"

"Because you are no longer an employee of the state and that would be a breach of protocol which would go entirely against my personal moral code of ethics and sense of civic responsibility."

"Huh."

"Don't 'huh' me. That only works with civilians. I'd

like to send it to you, but I can't. There'd be a record of the transmission. I don't think you'd want that."

"No, I guess I wouldn't."

"How about a printed copy?"

"Even better."

"Won't be until tomorrow, if that's okay."

"That's fine. Bring it by the bar. I might not be here, but Murton will."

"Mmm, Murton. Excellent."

RON MILES WALKED DOWN THE HALL, TURNED THE corner and stepped into Becky's office. She was on the phone, but had just hung up as he walked in. He heard her say, 'excellent.' He sat down and pulled one of the crime scene photos from a manila folder. "How are you with puzzles, Becky?"

"Hmm, not too good, really. Why?"

"I thought that was sort of your thing."

She rolled her eyes without trying to hide it. "I'm a researcher, Ron, not a mystery solver. That's more of your job, unless of course, you're trying to offer me a promotion. Are you?"

"Afraid not." He handed her the photo—the one with the series of numbers written in blood from Pope's apartment—and let her look at it a moment. "That's a copy of a photo from the crime scene. It looks like the victim was trying to tell somebody something. It's Pope's blood."

Becky looked at the photo for a few more seconds and shrugged before she held it back out to Ron.

"Keep it. I want you to spend some time with it. See if you can figure out what it means."

"How am I supposed to do that?"

"I don't know. Research it, I guess."

Becky thought about that for a minute. "You're positive that it's the victim's blood?"

"Yeah. Why?"

"I don't know. Just seems like a logical question. Here's something, though. If you don't have a body, how do you know that the victim was the one who wrote the message?"

"If you look closely at the photo, you can see that in a number of places in the message the victim's fingerprints are visible. We matched them to his other prints in the apartment. It's his blood and he was the one who wrote the message. But that's a good question, Becky. Maybe we *should* promote you."

"Could I have a raise instead?"

"No, but I can get you overtime if you get started on this right away."

"Excellent."

CHAPTER SEVENTEEN

The next morning Virgil slept late and by the time he was up, Sandy had already left for work. He felt good. The drugs were out of his system, the buzzing in his head was gone, his leg didn't hurt and his friends—including his girl—had once again overlooked his inadequacies and placed their love and affection for him over the hurt he had managed to inflict on them.

He made himself a glass of juice and then walked down the slope of the backyard and over to the pond. He sat in one of the chairs near the edge of the water and tried without success to focus on things other than the Pope family and how, like it or not, he remained connected to their grief beyond the boundaries of casual circumstance. It had been over twenty years since he'd shot and killed James Pope and no matter how often he thought back on that day, Virgil was always surprised at his own lack of recollection regarding the specifics of the only man he'd ever killed in the line of duty as a police officer. He could not remember what James Pope looked like, how tall he was, or even the color of his hair or eyes. While he knew the basic facts of that day, he didn't know what kind of man Pope was, what his childhood may have been like, or what events he may have endured in life that ultimately led to his death by Virgil's own hand.

The limitations regarding matters of recollection were not due to age or simple forgetfulness. They were due to a lack of concentration. Virgil had positioned his chair with purpose, near the water's edge, his back to the willow tree. The sky had turned cloudy and dark with the possibility of a summer rain shower and the longer he sat by the pond, his mood began to darken as well. He refused to look at the willow tree, not out of mulishness, but fear. He was afraid that the visions he'd experienced of his father and the conversations between them had not been real… nothing more than a product of his chemically altered imagination. He'd told Sandy that his fear of being free of the medication meant facing the possibility that he would never again see or speak with his father. The sagacity of her answer was something Virgil wasn't ready to address. Regardless, he had to ask himself, was she right? If he never saw or spoke to his dad again, did that mean he had never really been there at all? Or did it mean that he had always been there and the medication had somehow enabled him to communicate with his father outside the boundaries that define the laws of science and mortality? Neither answer seemed acceptable.

Virgil also had to consider that regardless of the answers he sought surrounding his father, he had participated in a tradeoff of sorts. Thanks to Dr. Bell and his treatment plan, the physical ill-effects and withdrawal symptoms normally associated with the complete and total cessation of the most powerful narcotics known to man were negligible. Virgil was not anxious or depressed or physically sick in any way. But he was disheartened. Was the disheartenment his cross to bear? He'd done what everyone—even his dead father—had asked. He was off the pills, but it seemed like the decision had come with a hefty price tag, one steeped with regret. Was this what addiction looked like?

No matter the questions or lack of any reasonable answers, Virgil ultimately decided that pretending like the willow tree was not behind him was a childish and disrespectful way to behave. The people he loved had planted the tree with his father's bloodied shirt at the bottom of the hole, not only for Virgil, but for Mason as well. Did the fact that Virgil could no longer communicate with him detract from any of that? Answer: No.

Virgil stood from his chair and moved over to the willow tree. He walked a complete circle around it, then stepped under the branches and wrapped his hands around the trunk. Delroy had told him that the blood of his father would flow through the tree just like it did his own heart.

Perhaps that was the answer. Maybe he hadn't been speaking with his father at all, but in a very real way, he'd been speaking with himself.

Yesterday Nichole Pope had said something that in the moment Virgil hadn't given much thought. She said that she was the sum of two parts that did not fit together. When she asked him if he knew what that was like, Virgil truthfully told her he did not. He was the sum of two parts that *had* fit well together…the sum of two people who had loved him more than anything. And even though they were both gone now, they still lived on because of his existence. Did he need a talking tree as a monument to their legacy? Virgil thought not, but he also realized that there might not be anything wrong with it either, so long as he didn't put too much stock in its meaning and managed to keep his priorities straight.

The struggle that he had forced Sandy to endure was almost unforgivable and something he wasn't proud of. He had an idea though, one that he thought might make up for everything he'd done wrong and prove once and for all that they were meant to be together forever.

Virgil still had his hands wrapped around the trunk of the tree. He leaned his forehead against the smooth green bark and closed his eyes. "Are you there?" he said, his voice soft and quiet. When the response didn't come, he walked away from the tree, got in his truck and drove downtown…but not to the bar.

LATE IN THE DAY, HE TURNED BACK INTO THE DRIVE. THE ring he'd picked out was elegant and tasteful, at least he thought so. It certainly had an elegant price tag. It was a one-and-a-half carat diamond solitaire, set in white gold. He had also stopped and bought a box of Sandy's favorite chocolates from the Fannie May store. He asked the clerk if she would gift-wrap his purchase, but before she did, Virgil removed a few pieces of candy and put the ring front and center inside the box. When the clerk saw what was going on she shouted to the other employees who all gathered round to help and fuss and make sure that the box looked its absolute best. They also peppered him with questions to the point where it felt like he was under interrogation. By the time they were finished Virgil had received three wishes of luck, two rather stern warnings about how easy it is to break a woman's heart and—interestingly enough—one offer of 'If she says no…'

Sandy's car was parked by the garage, so Virgil knew she was home. He had no real discernible plan of action, thinking it best to simply let the evening unfold naturally. He had the woman of his dreams alone with him in his house, an engagement ring hidden in a box of chocolates, and the most important question in the world on his mind. What could possibly go wrong?

As it turned out…plenty.

HE FOUND SANDY IN THE BEDROOM PACKING A SUITCASE. He set the box of chocolates on the dresser next to the bedroom door. "Hey. What's going on?"

"Hi, baby. Guess what?"

Virgil looked at the suitcase. "You've decided to update your status on Facebook?"

She laughed. "Fat chance, Mister. I'm going to Chicago."

"Chicago? What for?"

"The director of the academy was supposed to go up there with the governor. They're both giving speeches at the national law enforcement conference…well, they both were going to, anyway. My boss had some sort of family emergency and I got tapped to take his place. The governor is flying up on the state plane so I get to ride along. Pretty cool, huh?"

"Yeah," Virgil said, his voice dripping with sarcasm. "You and the guy who fired me flying to Chicago together. The epitome of cool."

"Virgil…"

"Ah, I'm sorry."

Sandy walked over and kissed him. "You miss me already, don't you?"

"I do. Listen, are you sure you're up to it? The travel? I know you haven't been feeling too well."

"I've been a little run down lately and I haven't been

sleeping very well either, but I'll be okay. Besides, I'm not going on a world tour. I'm fine."

"You are fine," he said and then kissed her back. "How long are you going to be gone?"

"A few days. I'll be back Sunday night. You could come with us, you know."

Virgil laughed. "No thanks. Don't think I'd be very welcome on the plane."

"We could always drive up together instead. Three hours from now we'd have a hotel room to ourselves and our imaginations to keep us busy."

"I don't need my imagination when I'm with you."

She smiled at him. "You're sweet. Hey, speaking of sweet, did you get me a box of candy?" She started to move toward the dresser but Virgil cut her off. He grabbed the box and held it behind his back.

"Yes, I did, but now I'm going to make you wait to eat them until you get back."

"Hey, that's not fair."

"That's the breaks."

"Come on, Virgil, come with me to Chicago. We can eat the chocolate in bed together." She gave him an eyebrow wiggle.

Maybe it wasn't a bad idea, Virgil thought. A couple of days in a different city and a marriage proposal in a hotel room. He bounced the idea back and forth for a few seconds, but in the end went with his gut.

"I really can't. Murton's got me working on something

with him. As a matter of fact, it looks like we're going to be working together."

"You mean besides the bar, don't you?"

"Yeah." He tried Murton's line on her. "Wheeler and Jones Investigations. Has a nice ring to it, don't you think?" Virgil thought he might have unintentionally overemphasized the word *ring*.

"Is that what you want to do?"

"I'd like to keep my hand in it…the work. It's interesting to me. It always has been. I love the bar, but day in and day out I think it'd drive me crazy."

"Your dad seemed happy doing it."

"He was. But he'd also put his time in as a cop. When we bought the bar he was ready for a change. I'm not sure I am. At least not yet. I don't feel like I should be done."

"What's the matter, Virgil?"

"Ah, nothing. Just feeling sort of sorry for myself, I guess. I was hoping for a nice romantic evening with you."

"How about a nice romantic ride to the airport?"

"You bet. When do you have to go?"

Sandy zipped the suitcase closed. "Now would be good."

Virgil set the box of chocolates back on the dresser. Sandy eyed it for a moment, but didn't say anything. "Hey, maybe we should have a party Sunday afternoon when you get back. Have everybody over. How does that sound?"

"Sure," Sandy said. "Would you carry my suitcase for me?" She walked out of the bedroom and never gave the box of chocolates a second look.

———————

VIRGIL STARTED THE TRUCK AND THEY WERE ABOUT halfway down the drive when Sandy said, "Oops. Back up. I almost forgot my purse."

He hit the brakes. "Wow. That wouldn't have been good." He backed up to the door and Sandy ran inside. When she came back out, she had her purse over her shoulder. She dropped it on the floor by her feet, buckled her belt, and said, "Okay. Let's roll."

"You know, when you get back, I feel like maybe we should talk some stuff through."

"Like what?"

Virgil spent the rest of the ride to the airport telling her what happened by the willow tree earlier in the day and more importantly, how he felt about it.

"I think what Delroy said is true, Virgil. It's not your leg that hurts. It's your heart. People die. I know how much you loved your father and based on all the stories you've told me, I know you feel the same way about your mom and your grandfather. Physically, they're gone, but like you said, they do live on through you. You should be proud of that."

He turned the truck into the parking lot of the airport's

Fixed Base Operations building. "I am. I simply miss them. Sometimes I think I miss them too much. Like it's not healthy or something…like I have trouble letting things go. I've been having conversations with my dead father and I'll tell you something, I still don't know if it was real or not."

"Maybe you should talk to Bell about it."

Virgil barked out a laugh. "Now there's an idea. He'd probably prescribe an extra week of coffee enemas. No thanks." A tall chain-link fence separated the parking lot from the tarmac, the state plane sitting on the ramp. One of the pilots stood next to the air-stair door as the other followed the governor out to the aircraft.

"We'll talk about it, Virgil. We will. But I think you're fine. Sometimes you worry too much. If you're feeling sad about your dad, go ahead and let yourself feel it. Keep it bottled up though and you'll never get past it." She picked up her purse and slung it over her shoulder. Virgil started to get out with her, but she pulled him over and kissed him long and hard. "I can get the bag. I think the pilots have to escort me out to the plane anyway. I love you, Virgil Jones. See you on Sunday."

Virgil thought about what was going to happen when Sandy came home, how they were going to take the first step of so many that were in front of them now. "I love you too, Small."

AFTER SANDY WENT INSIDE THE FBO BUILDING THAT gave access to the tarmac, Virgil turned the truck off and walked over toward the fence so he could wave good-bye to her. The state's plane was a small twin-engine jet— Virgil had no idea of the make or model because he knew nothing about aircraft—parked about forty yards away. The captain had already started the right engine, the noise a little louder than Virgil expected. The copilot walked Sandy over to the aircraft and then stood next to the steps, her bag in his hand as she climbed the stairs. What happened next was something so shocking Virgil was momentarily frozen in place and unable to respond.

When Sandy got to the top of the steps, she turned around to face him, then reached into her purse and pulled out the gift-wrapped box of chocolates. She held the box above her head the way a professional athlete would after scoring the winning points of a championship game. Then she gave Virgil an evil grin along with the thumbs-up sign and disappeared into the aircraft as the co-pilot shut the door behind them.

Virgil stood there with his jaw slack and his fingers interwoven through the small gaps in the fence as the blast from the aircraft's engines peppered him with grit, certain he held the sole distinction of being the only guy on the planet who was about to propose to his girlfriend without being present.

Way to go, Jonesy.

———————

SANDY SAID HELLO TO THE GOVERNOR, SET HER PURSE and the box of chocolates on one of the empty seats and buckled up. She looked out the window to wave at Virgil, but the aircraft had already turned and it was impossible to see him.

"How's he holding up?" McConnell asked, his voice louder than normal so he could be heard over the sound of the jet's engines.

Sandy pressed her lips together. "He's off the pills, Governor. That's the main thing. He's not too happy with you right now, if we're going to be honest with each other." Her tone held no animosity or bitterness, she simply threw the statement out there for what it was—a matter of fact.

"Wasn't an easy decision," the governor said, sans nastiness himself. "But we had to do something, Sandy, you know that. I can tell you this…it damn sure wasn't personal, no matter what he thinks and I sort of believe that he does think it was personal, but it wasn't. That business with my daughter from before? It was horrid, the entire thing. But it had nothing to do with my decision to name a new lead detective to the MCU. In fact, it wasn't even my idea. It was Pearson."

"He always seems to be the political scapegoat du

jour, doesn't he? How fortunate for you." Maybe a little nastiness now.

The governor held up his hands, palms out. "Sandy, I give you my word, if it were up to me—"

"That's just it, Governor. It is up to you."

They weren't even off the ground yet.

McConnell considered Sandy's statement for a moment. "Tell you what…can we table this for now? There are some changes coming down the line, things I won't talk about right now, not with you or anyone, but things are never quite as bad as they seem, are they?" He looked at the seat next to Sandy. "Say, are those Fannie May chocolates? They're my favorite."

The pilot's voice crackled over the intercom speakers. "Excuse me, Governor? Ms. Small? We're number one for takeoff. We'll be airborne in less than twenty-seconds. Make sure your seat-belts are fastened and until we're at altitude, turn your cell phones off if you would, please."

Sandy reached over and pulled her cell phone from her purse and turned it off. McConnell didn't bother. "I'll tell you something, Sandy, as a government official, I try to not only uphold the laws of our state and the nation, but as a citizen also follow them to the best of my ability, just like anyone else. But that whole 'turn your cell phone off or the plane will crash thing?' I'm telling you, it's pure, unadulterated bullshit."

Sandy grinned at the governor. "You're probably right. But why risk it?"

"Because there is no risk," the governor said. "Guarantee you. I never turn mine off. Not on this plane, anyway. The pilots...they always ask—I think it's required by federal law or something—but I have never done it. Not once. You have to if you're flying on the airlines. Now there's a bunch of genuine, grade-A, hardcore rule enforcers...most of your airline employees, if you ask me. You give some low-income sky waitress the complete and total backing of the United States Federal Government and watch out. They look for reasons to toss you off the plane these days." He paused for a moment. "So, how about that chocolate, hmm? Would you mind very much if I tried a piece? They're my favorite. Did I mention that?"

———

VIRGIL RAN TO HIS TRUCK AND GRABBED HIS CELL PHONE. When he punched in Sandy's number it went immediately to her voice mail. He ended the call without leaving a message.

———

SANDY FELT THE ACCELERATION OF THE JET AND WITHIN two or three minutes they were, according to the passenger flight display, passing through three thousand feet on a northerly heading. "I've got to use the restroom," she said to the governor. "Help yourself to the chocolate."

"I don't think we're supposed to leave our seats until the light goes out," the governor said.

"Yeah. This from the guy who makes his own rules about the cell phones."

The governor wagged a finger at her. "Executive privilege. Besides, that's a different deal. The cell phone thing is pure propaganda designed to instill fear so you'll follow the real rules."

"What's the rule on peeing your pants when there's a perfectly good bathroom less than fifteen feet away?"

"Good point. Hand me that box before you go though, will you? I don't want to unbuckle my belt yet."

She handed the box to the governor and then stood from her seat. "Save me some." It wasn't a request.

The governor turned the box over in his hands. "It's wrapped. Was this a gift?"

Sandy sighed. "Two things, Governor. Number one, Fannie May candy always comes gift-wrapped. It's part of their gig. I should know. I used to work in one of their stores back in the day. Two, if I don't go pee, and I mean right now, I'll probably never be invited to fly on this plane again."

The governor waved her away with the back of his

hand and began to unwrap the candy. He hoped they were Mint Melt-aways. Those really were absolutely delicious.

———————

VIRGIL WENT INSIDE THE FBO BUILDING AND SPOKE WITH the young man behind the counter. "How can I get in contact with the plane that just left?"

The young man looked up from his computer terminal. "You mean the state plane?"

"Yeah. My girlfriend got on there with the governor and I need to speak with her right away."

"Is it an emergency?"

"You could say that."

The young man stood from behind the desk and moved closer to the counter. "I could try to contact the pilots, but I've got to tell you, they're probably out of range and even if they're not, I doubt they'd be monitoring our frequency. We only talk to the pilots when they're inbound, you know, for rental cars or taxis or fuel requests, like that. What's the nature of your emergency?"

Good question. Virgil tried to explain the situation, but he knew it was hopeless.

"Let me see if I've got this straight," the young man said. "The hot-looking blond that got on the plane with the governor is your girlfriend. You were going to propose, but somehow didn't. Now the governor and your girl are headed to the windy city and you're stuck here by yourself. That doesn't sound like an emergency to me. That sounds like a chance to party like a rock star, dude. When are they coming back?"

For some unknown reason, Virgil answered him. "Sunday night."

"Man…that's like, two days from now. Go live a little."

Virgil walked out of the building.

———

THE GOVERNOR UNWRAPPED THE BOX, TOSSED THE PAPER on the floor by his feet and removed the lid. The candy was neatly arranged in the box, but it was what was in the center of the container that immediately got his attention. In the middle was a smaller, red-velvet box where most of the good chocolates were supposed to be. He turned around in his seat and looked back at the lavatory door. Still closed. The governor took the small red box from the center of the candy tray and opened the lid. When he did, he thought, *son of a bitch*. The governor—nobody's idiot —put it together in about a half-second. He slipped the ring box into his pocket and pulled out his cell phone.

———

WHEN VIRGIL'S PHONE RANG HE WAS CERTAIN IT WAS going to be Sandy. He didn't even bother to check the caller ID display before speaking. "Sandy…I'm so sorry. This is not how I wanted to do this."

"Lucky for you that you've got friends in all the right places," McConnell said.

"Governor?"

"You got it, Jonesy. So, gonna pop the question, huh?"

"Would you mind telling me what's going on up there?"

"Relax, tough guy. She's in the can. Boy, this is some ring. I'm guessing just shy of two carats. I'd say about what…eight grand, maybe?"

"Close enough. Has she seen it?"

"Of course not. I might be a lowly politician, but I'm not a fool. She *would* have seen it, but I opened the box while she was on the hopper. That part was pure luck. Boy, if she'd been sitting right there…whoops, here she comes. Gotta go."

The phone went dead in Virgil's hand.

———————

SANDY CAME OUT OF THE LAVATORY, SAT DOWN, AND fastened her seatbelt. She looked at the governor, extended her palm and wiggled her fingers in a 'hand it over' gesture.

McConnell handed her the box of candy. "Wow, that was good."

Sandy looked in the box. Everything in the center—

virtually half the box—was gone. "Boy, I guess you really do like this stuff, huh?"

"It's a weakness. You know what, I think I have to use the bathroom as well."

Sandy put a mocking tone in her voice. "You know…I don't think you're supposed to unbuckle your seatbelt until the pilots tell you to."

"Yeah, yeah, quit twisting my testicles. Christ, you're worse than some of the men I have to deal with. I hope you put the seat down when you were done peeing in there."

———————————

TWO MINUTES LATER VIRGIL'S PHONE RANG AGAIN. HE spoke without preamble. "If you mess this up for me, I will be pissed beyond belief. In fact, you can't begin to conceive how—"

"Hey, Jonesy, I'm trying to do the right thing here."

"Where are you?"

"Somewhere over Kokomo by now I would imagine."

"That's not what I meant."

"I'm in the can. Would you please dial it back a little? I'm trying to help you."

"Says the guy with a job."

"Look, Jonesy, now isn't the time, but you and I need to have a conversation. There's no denying that. Right now though, we need to figure out what to do about this situation."

Virgil wondered which situation the governor was referring to. "What are you proposing?"

"Hey, great choice of words," McConnell said. "How about this…I'll hold on to the ring. The pilots are going to spend the night here in Chicago. They can't come back until tomorrow…something about duty hours and flight time, I don't know. Anyway, I'll send the ring back with them. They can give it to Bradley and he'll bring it to you. How does that sound?"

"Do not disappoint me on this, Mac."

"Pearson will call you tomorrow. I promise…"

CHAPTER EIGHTEEN

VIRGIL WENT BACK TO THE BAR...OR THE OFFICE. IN truth, he didn't quite know how to define his workspace anymore. He wanted to coordinate with Murton exactly how they were going to work the Pope case, but when he walked in, he discovered that Murton wasn't there. Becky was though. She sat at the end of the bar, her hands wrapped around a tall glass of green juice. A manila file folder was on the stool next to her. She wore a frilly little sleeveless dress and when Virgil followed her legs down to her shoes, he noticed that she wore a pair of black platform flip-flops. Her bra strap peeked out at the edge of her shoulder. She looked good. He pulled out a stool and sat down next to her.

"I miss you, Jonesy. Working for Ron isn't the same."

"Is that the apple-asparagus?"

She took a sip, nodding as she did. "Yeah. It's great."

She picked up her glass and wiggled it at me. "This is a really good idea…the juice thing. Was it yours?"

"Not really. Delroy is behind that. So, about Ron…"

Becky shrugged. "I don't know…he's a fine cop, anyone would tell you that. But it's all business with him. Get me this, get me that, know what I mean?"

"I do. But I'll tell you something, Becks, he's really good at what he does."

"Better than you?"

"Maybe. In fact, I'd say yes. He's very…mmm… mechanical by nature when it comes to solving crime though. A leads to B leads to C and so on. I was never that way. I never have been. I notice things. I pay attention to the small stuff, the little things on the fringes that sometimes go unnoticed. When I do, things sort of become obvious to me. That's the way I've always worked and it has always worked for me."

"I don't get it."

"All right, look at it this way," Virgil said. "I just walked in, right?"

"Yeah."

"And we've been sitting here together, what? Two or three minutes tops, right?"

"Sure."

"Okay. Without looking, how many people are in the bar?" She moved to turn on her stool and Virgil touched her arm. "No, no. No looking."

"Okay. I don't know. Twelve?"

He smiled at her. "Look at me." When she did, Virgil closed his eyes. "There are exactly, at this very moment, thirty-one people in the bar and that includes you and me. Robert and his three sous chefs are in the kitchen. Delroy is behind the bar. You and I are sitting right here. The other twenty-four people are customers. Seventeen of them are men." He opened his eyes.

"How do you do that?"

"You know what? I really don't know. I notice things and they stick with me."

Becky laughed.

"What?"

"Nothing. Forget it."

"Come on, what?"

"I was thinking the next thing you're going to tell me is what color underwear I have on."

Careful, Virgil thought. Still, he couldn't quite resist. "Lime green. Matching bra and panties." The panty thing was a shot in the dark, but Virgil knew she was hoping to see Murton.

She punched him in the shoulder. Hard. "Shut up. How do you do that?"

Virgil smiled at her as he rubbed his shoulder. "So, what'd you bring me?"

Becky grabbed the file folder and placed it on the bar. "I feel like a spy."

"Nah. Too cute to be a spy. Besides, you said yourself you already had the information. How'd you get it?"

"Same way I always do. I don't know if you've heard or not, but Al Gore invented this neat little thing called the Internet. It magically goes right to the computer. It's pretty cool. All you have to do is sit down and type in—"

"Yeah, yeah." Fucking researchers.

———————

"Look, I don't want you to feel like you're doing anything illegal even though technically you are...sort of. Why don't you consider working for me and Murt? That way whatever you research would be on our time instead of the state."

"You mean, like, full-time?"

"Well, maybe not right away. You know, part-time to start, then we could see where it goes."

"I'm only part-time right now with the MCU. You know that. Plus, I've got these computer classes that I'm taking. Where would I fit everything in?"

"Nights and weekends?"

"Very funny, Jonesy. I do have a personal life, you know."

"How many hours are you working over there? At the shop."

"It depends. It's no different now than it was when you were there. If something major is happening I get a few more hours, but if nothing is really going on I barely get any. I guess I'm averaging about thirty a week."

"So quit. Murt and I could give you thirty hours, no problem. And here's something to consider…how many hours do you spend on your commute each week?"

Becky puffed out her cheeks. "Too damned many, that's for sure."

"Well, there you go."

"Well, there I go, what?"

"You could work from home. We'll pick up the cost of your Internet and cell phone, so you'd save a couple of hundred right there on utilities alone I bet, not to mention the gas. Listen, if you don't mind my asking, how do you live on thirty hours a week?"

She gave him a sideways look. "There's a little family money."

"Really?"

"Yep."

"So you don't need the money…"

She laughed. "Oh, I need it. I don't have access to my trust fund for another two years. All I get right now is a stipend."

"Huh."

"Look Jonesy, I didn't know this was going to be a job interview. Can I think about it?"

Virgil laughed. "I didn't either. And of course you can

think about it. But in the meantime, I don't want you feeling weird about giving me this." He tapped his finger on the folder.

"Can I share something sort of personal with you?"

"Sure."

"I hear things around the shop. People talk, you know? They screwed you over. Cutting you out like that? It wasn't necessary. It was all political."

"Ah, I already knew that, Becky, but I appreciate you saying so."

"To answer your question, I do feel a little weird about giving you this information. It's not something I could ever do again. I hope you understand that. I'm sure it's completely against the law."

"Yeah, me too. But it's a small law and it feels kind of good, doesn't it?"

Becky laughed. "It sort of does. Good thing you're not paying me for this stuff."

"Why?"

"Because it came out of the state's computer system. If you were paying me I'd not only feel like a spy, I'd feel a little like a slut."

"Says the girl in the platform shoes and matching underwear."

That got him another punch.

———————

"IF YOU KEEP PUNCHING ME I MAY RESCIND MY OFFER OF employment."

"I doubt it."

"Yeah…okay, but take it easy will you? You're stronger than you look. So what's in the folder?"

"Why don't you open it and find out?"

"Because technically neither one of us has broken any laws yet."

"So now you're Mr. Truth, Justice, and the American way?"

"Truth is largely subjective based on perception. There is no such thing as justice anymore and the American way is primarily centered around crony capitalism." They were both quiet for a beat. As much as he didn't want to, Virgil slid the folder back toward her. "I'm sorry, Becky, I shouldn't have put you in this position."

When Murton came through the back door, he walked over and sat down next to them at the bar. "Jonesy. Hey Becks. How's it going?"

Becky placed her hand briefly on Murton's forearm. "It's going well. Your partner here is trying to corrupt me."

Murton gave Virgil a dirty look, then reached into his pocket and pulled out a check and slid it over, face down.

"What's this?"

"It's a check for ten grand from Nichole Pope. It goes against our retainer. Now all we have to do is catch her brother's killer."

"Did you say ten grand?" Virgil turned the check over and looked at the front.

"Yep."

"I thought you said there wasn't any money in this business."

Murton flashed a fake grin. "I may have understated our prospects a little. Why are you looking at me like that? A guy's gotta eat. Hey, speaking of eating, I'm starved." Then he turned his attention to Becky. "So, you're a little corruptible, huh?"

Becky slid the folder back over to Virgil. "I've thought about it," she said. "I'll take the job. How long before I make partner?"

"Have I missed something?" Murton asked.

Becky looked him in the eye. "Yep, I'm your new researcher, assuming you go along with the idea."

"Sounds good." Murton looked at Virgil in the bar mirror and winked.

Becky smiled at both of them. "Excellent."

———

SATURDAY MORNING VIRGIL WAS UP AND OUT OF BED before sunrise. He made a tall pitcher of fresh organic juice, took care of the other business prescribed by Bell, then set about reviewing the information Becky had brought him the previous day. After a few hours, he felt well versed in all things related to Augustus Pate. One of

Pate's companies, Pri-Max, had been awarded a bid by the state to not only build, but operate and maintain the new prison in Plainfield. This fact by itself was not news. It also was not very remarkable that the state was funding the vast majority of the prison's construction via unclaimed lottery winnings. Somebody had to pay to erect the prison, after all. Unclaimed lottery winnings had always gone into the state's discretionary fund, no matter the amount. If the state wanted to use that money to build a new prison, no one could argue with them. Well, maybe the teacher's unions and the school administrators, but even they were mostly silent on the issue as the funding amounts allocated to them weren't dependent on unclaimed winnings. Their money came straight from ticket sales. In fact, political issues notwithstanding, the only remarkable thing about the Pri-Max prison deal was the amount Pate's company stood to gain from the state if no one claimed the prize.

Becky had also included information about the executive director of the lottery, Abigail Monroe. She had attached a handwritten note that indicated Ron had requested the information earlier in the week. While Becky's research into Monroe had turned up nothing out of the ordinary, the fact that Ron had requested it was noteworthy.

Clearly Pearson and Pate were working together on more than the prison funding. That was not a secret. Nor was it illegal. Pearson would double-cross his own mother if it worked into his agenda. Pate's other company, PTEK, had won the bid to manage the marketing and day-to-day operations of the lottery as a way to generate higher revenues. Again, Pearson was involved in that decision, but it wasn't illegal, unless you factored in the political favoritism and backroom deal-making. But all of that aside, it looked like Pate had positioned himself to make millions of dollars off the state and the people of Indiana, and while he had done it with the support of the governor's chief of staff and probably the governor as well, it didn't look like anyone had broken any laws. Virgil closed the file folder and tossed it on his desk.

Time for more juice.

He had trouble turning his mind away from the main issue. How did Nicholas Pope's death fit into the equation? Nicholas Pope's father, James, was linked to Pearson in an obvious way, but Nicholas was only five or six years old when Virgil had killed his father in order to save Pearson's life. No matter what he thought of Bradley Pearson, Virgil was having trouble imagining a scenario where Pearson would be responsible for the junior Pope's murder. Had there been some sort of attempt at revenge by Nicholas directed at Pearson? It seemed unlikely. Pearson had helped Monroe get the job as executive director of the lottery, which made her in effect, beholden to Pearson and by extension because he was the owner of PTEK, Augustus Pate as well. So it seemed likely Pope's death was in some way related to his employment at the lottery.

Was that why Ron had requested the information on Monroe? Did he suspect her of murdering Pope? That seemed unlikely as well.

Virgil picked up the phone and tried to call Ron in hopes that he might share his knowledge of the Pope case, but he didn't answer. He left a message for Ron to call him without explaining why, but after his behavior earlier in the week, Virgil wasn't too confident that he'd get a call back.

———————————

As it happened, Ron didn't call back, but he did knock on Virgil's front door a few minutes later. After they were inside, he said, "I'll tell you something, Jonesy, they're both lying…Monroe and Pearson."

"What about Pate?"

"Can't get past his lawyers."

"So walk me through Monroe and Pearson."

He told Virgil about his conversation with Monroe, and finished with, "What I can't figure out, is why lie about it?"

"This might be a little thin, but would you want anyone to know that you slept with Pearson as a way to get your job?"

Miles laughed without humor. "You know what? I wouldn't and let me tell you why: That's essentially what I did."

"I'm not sure I want to know what that means."

"I had my time in with the city. I was done. You didn't know that, did you? I had already turned in my papers. But then out of the blue Pearson comes along and tells me your job is mine if I want it. He said he could fix it so I'd keep my pension and everything. He dangled that little double salary issue in front of me like he knew I'd accept. You should have seen the look on his face."

"I have seen it, Ron. I've seen it plenty."

"You know what I figured out?"

"What?"

"I'll tell you something, Jonesy, I don't know if this is true or not…it's speculation on my part, but I *think* it's true and it's the reason I'm here talking to you. Rosie was the one who got me thinking about it. He said I should ask myself 'why me?'"

"What is it, Ron?"

"I'm in a little bit of a bind…financially speaking. A few years ago I knew I was getting close to retiring and the pension wouldn't be enough. I started thinking about what you and your dad did with the bar and I thought, you know what? I could do something like that. Not that exactly, but something. So I started buying some rental properties. I'm pretty good with the fix-it-up stuff anyway, plus I like doing it. I've solved more than a few cases simply thinking about them while I was hanging sheetrock. I wasn't making a profit but I wasn't losing anything either. Maybe a few bucks here or there but it came off my taxes anyway so it was all good."

"How many properties?"

"Eleven. The tenants make the mortgage payments and the rest goes to insurance and taxes. I figured ten years down the road I'd sell them all, take a little hit on the capital gains, put the money in the bank and go fishing."

"You said it 'was' good. What happened?"

"That's what I'd like to know. About a week before Pearson offered me the job, the common council held an unscheduled session and voted to raise taxes on single-family rental units. If I only had one or two units it wouldn't be a problem. But eleven? No way I could keep up."

"What if you sell them?"

"Ever try to unload a rental property that's behind on taxes? Every offer comes with a free bottle of lube."

"Seems like a bit of a stretch to put it on Pearson."

"Yeah, I know. But here's the kicker: When Pearson came to me he said he knew all about my tax problems and he could talk to some of the house representatives and persuade them to pass a state exemption for active-duty police officers. And you know what? He did. He fixed my problem all while making it perfectly clear that if I retired, I was sunk, but if I took the job the tax issue would go away and I'd be in the clear."

Virgil thought about it. Had Pearson gone to

extraordinary lengths to have him removed from his job and then maneuvered Ron into a position as his replacement? If so, why?

"The only thing that keeps me from doing anything about it," Ron said, "is the fact that I don't have any proof. And even if I did, what would it look like? I know you're off the meds, Jonesy, and with God as my witness, nothing could make me happier. But I'm going to be brutally honest here, so no disrespect intended, okay? You essentially showed yourself to the door…with the pills, I mean. I know that Cora and Pearson and even the governor himself could have stuck it out with you for a while longer, but if you put yourself in their shoes, where do you draw that line? Do you say, well, if he quits the medication tomorrow everything will be okay? I don't know the answer to that, but with what Rosie said to me the other day…the 'why me' part of the equation, it makes sense to ask—the medication issue notwithstanding—why put you out and me in?"

"Pearson wanted me out because he knew he couldn't control me or manipulate me. It might not be much deeper than that. He's an opportunist. I think he must have known that if he could get his hooks in you—and your tax troubles were a perfect way to do that—he'd have some sort of leverage if and when he needed it."

"Leverage for what?"

"I'm not entirely sure. At least not yet. But it must tie in with the Pope shooting, and with Pate."

Virgil could see Ron's wheels spinning. Then his phone rang.

———————

"Got a little problem," the governor said without preamble.

Virgil glanced at Ron, held up a 'wait a minute' finger and moved out of the kitchen. "That is not what I want to hear, Governor."

"I meant to emphasize the word 'little.'"

"Tell me."

"It seems there is some sort of mechanical issue with the aircraft. A fuel control unit. Boy, how's that for coincidence, huh?"

"I'm afraid I'm not following you."

"It'll come to you. In the meantime, the pilots are stuck here in Chicago, so you're not going to get your ring back today. Probably not tomorrow either."

Great. "I'm willing to entertain suggestions."

"The pilots say they'll have the part installed and the plane ready to go for our trip back on Sunday. I'll hold on to the ring and get it to you when we get back. How does that sound?"

"That sounds like a very questionable plan B."

"Tell you what, when we get back, I'll have the limo bring Sandy out to your place. I'll be with her. I'll get out, kick my toe in the dirt—sort of an 'aw shucks' kind of thing—ask Sandy to give you and me a few minutes so we can talk, then I'll slip you the ring and everything will be five-by-five. What do you say?"

"I'm not entirely sure I want Sandy on an airplane with you that's having issues with one of its fuel control units."

"Wow, that's a little harsh. But see, I was right, wasn't I? It came to you."

It did indeed. Virgil ignored the governor's remark and his callous indifference to events that cost the lives of a number of people back in the late eighties. But callous indifference aside, it was suddenly clear to Virgil why Pearson wanted Ron in and him out.

———

"WAS THAT THE GOVERNOR?"

"Yeah, it was. Don't look at me like that, Ron. It's an unrelated issue."

"Really?"

"Really. It's something personal. Listen, I might have an idea of what this is all about. All of it."

"That makes one of us."

"Sit tight." Virgil went into his office, unlocked the safe and pulled something from the back. When he returned to the kitchen, he handed the envelope to Ron. "Take a look at this."

"What is it?"

"Just look."

Ron opened the envelope, pulled out the paper and studied the contents. "A copy of Sidney Wells, Jr.'s birth certificate. This is the broad that was trying to kill the governor. I don't mean to sound ignorant, but so what? That's a closed case. What does this have to do with anything?"

"In all of your years of solving murders, Ron, what have you ever known any of them, categorically speaking, to be about?"

"Same as you. Money, revenge, sex, or power."

"Exactly."

"Which one is this?"

"Let me tell you a little story. You know most of it, but this should give you some perspective…"

———

AFTER HE'D HEARD THE STORY IN ITS ENTIRETY, RON LOOKED AT VIRGIL OVER THE tops of his glasses. "That wasn't in your report, the part about Wells being the governor's daughter."

"You're right. It wasn't."

"Why not?"

Virgil shrugged. "I'm not sure I can answer that, Ron. Lapse in judgment? Professional misconduct? Empathy? Seduction of power? Who's to say? I'd lost my father. The governor had lost his daughter. I was already on the pills by then. But the important thing to remember is what he said to me when I asked him about Samuel Pate. I wanted to know if he—the governor—had sent me down that path…to look at Pate as the prime suspect in the murder of Franklin Dugan. He told me no, that it had been Pearson who suggested I investigate Pate. And that's what I did."

Miles reached up and flattened his hair with the palm of his hand. "What of it?"

"The governor's daughter and Sid Wells, Sr., were going around the city killing people. The first person they killed was Franklin Dugan. But Dugan wasn't really part of why they killed everyone else. All the others were killed for revenge…as payback for what the governor did. But Dugan was different. Sermon Sam wanted him out of the picture because he found out about the child porn. Dugan was also the first to be killed. When that happened Pearson immediately had me looking at Samuel Pate. But what if the reason was deeper than that? What if he had me looking at Samuel Pate not because of *something* else, but because of *someone* else?"

"Who?"

"You already know who, Ron."

Miles thought it over for a moment, then said, "You're talking about Augustus Pate?"

Virgil pointed his finger at him. "Exactly. This private prison thing has been going back and forth in the Indiana house for over a year. What if Augustus Pate knew about his son's predilection for under-aged sex? If he did know and that knowledge became public, he wouldn't have a chance in hell at winning the bid on the lottery deal or the private prison. In fact, if it ever came out that he knew, he'd probably be sharing a cell with his son in the very prison he was supposed to build."

"But Samuel Pate killed himself."

"So what? In the end, Augustus still got what he wanted. His son was no longer a factor and it was none other than Bradley Pearson who made that happen."

"Man, I'm telling you, I did not sign up for this."

"Yeah, you sort of did, Ron. Why do you think they call it the Major Crimes Unit?"

"HERE'S SOMETHING I CAN'T FIGURE OUT," RON SAID. "What does any of this have to do with Nicholas Pope's death?"

"There's a very real possibility that none of this has anything to do with Nicholas Pope."

"You don't really believe that, do you?"

Virgil grinned at him. "No, I don't. I'm saying it's possible that his death is unrelated and as such, that fact shouldn't be ruled out. Look at the facts, Ron: Twenty years ago, I killed Pope's father. A few months ago Samuel Pate gets erased from the map. At the same time, Samuel's father, Augustus is awarded one of the largest construction projects in the state. Shortly after that, one of his other companies takes over the management of the lottery. The lottery is essentially paying to build the prison. You said Monroe and Pearson were lying to you. Monroe was Pope's boss at the lottery. I will personally accept any wager you'd like to offer that says his death is unconnected."

"No bet. So how do we prove it?"

Virgil heard a buzzing sound in his head and for a moment he thought he was having a bad reaction to being off the pills. "Do you hear that noise?"

Miles reached into his pocket, pulled out his phone and wiggled it. "Yeah, it's me. I took a class. It seems I am technologically up to speed." When he looked at the screen a curtain of irritation crossed his face.

"What is it?"

He shook his head. "Our researcher, Becky? She just quit. Who quits via text message?"

Oh boy. "Listen, Ron…about that…"

———

"You and Wheeler hired Becky out from under me?"

"Well, technically we hired her out from under the state, but yeah, I guess so."

"That's about the shittiest thing that's happened to me all week and I've had some shitty things happen to me this week. This isn't some sort of revenge deal is it? I mean, I know you were pissed at me for taking the job, but the truth of it is, you were already gone by then. If I didn't take it, somebody else would have."

"Ron, I can assure you this has nothing to do with revenge. Becky sort of came to us. I think she wanted more hours. Plus, she and I have worked together for a few years now and she…well, hell, I don't know…she knows me. She knows how I think and what I'm looking for. Half the time she knows what I want before I do."

Miles sat there and shook his head. "I don't know how you managed to get anything done. This job is nuts. I've got politics on one side and administrative bullshit on the other. Somewhere in the middle there's some sort of crime happening and I'm almost too busy to notice. Who has time for that?"

"You better get used to it."

"I had her working on something for me and now I'll have to get someone else."

"What was she working on?"

That earned Virgil a suspicious look. "How about you and I come to some sort of agreement?"

"What do you mean?"

"What I mean is, don't play dumb with me, Jonesy. Like it or not you're up to your neck in this Pearson and Pope shit. Pate too. You've got the three-P trifecta going on and I feel like the only way I'm going to make any headway is with your help."

Virgil held his hands in the air. "Who says I'm playing dumb?"

Miles pointed his finger at him. "I do, that's who."

"I think I have an idea."

"I think I've got a headache."

"Why not have the MCU hire Murton and me to handle the research? You've got a discretionary budget. Did you know that? Anyway, we'll handle the research, it'll be like you never lost Becky and maybe we can figure this thing out together."

"What would that cost me?"

"Ah, you don't have to worry about that. We'll take care of you," Virgil said.

"Why do I feel like I'm getting rolled?"

"Welcome to the MCU, Ron."

"I wish everyone would stop saying that to me."

———

"SO WHAT WAS SHE WORKING ON?"

Miles chewed on his lip for a few seconds. "Okay, this is not public knowledge. Are we clear on that?"

"You bet."

"Pope left a message. It was written in blood...his blood and it was under the sofa. The crime scene techs took about twenty different pictures of it."

"What did it say?"

"It listed his killer's name and address. How the hell

do I know what it said? It was some kind of coded message…a series of numbers. No one can figure it out. Becky was going to go to work on it for me."

"Do you have it with you? The picture?"

"No, but I can email it to you later today."

"Do that."

Miles gave Virgil a defeated look. "Anything else I can get you, or do you now have enough information to solve this case?"

"Hmm, that should do it." Then, Virgil thought of something else. "You said you could email me the photo?"

"Yeah, but I have to do it from the office."

"Send it from your phone."

"I didn't know I could do that. It wasn't covered in the class."

"Let me see your phone…"

CHAPTER NINETEEN

"So he hasn't said anything else to you?" Monroe asked. Pearson had a mouthful of toothbrush and didn't answer right away. He rinsed, spat, rinsed again, tipped his head back, did a little gargle and then spit the contents into the basin. He turned the water off without bothering to clean out the sink. They were at Monroe's condo.

"It's been less than a week, Abby, and we've had no reason to speak with each other."

"So, you think we're good? I'm okay in all of this, right?"

"You'll be fine as long as you keep doing what I tell you."

Monroe knew she had a problem, said problem being she didn't quite know how to keep her mouth shut. She had babbled on and on to the cop and that could have hurt her, but it looked like Pearson had fixed that. Except he fixed it by telling him they were sleeping together and she had been ashamed to admit it. *Jesus.* She had to give Bradley credit though. He said never lie to the cops and then he marched right out there and told the truth.

So given that, after the cop left Abby felt like *she* had to tell Pearson the truth. She began yammering on and on until the words were pouring out of her mouth like a runaway freight train. She had already told him about Nicky—how they had been sleeping together—and now she told him how he'd had a plan to cheat the lottery system. She even told him of their plans to take the money and run. After she'd confessed everything to Pearson, she thought he'd be furious with her. Instead, he smiled, put his arms around her and said everything would be fine. All she had to do was follow his direction. Do what he wanted, when he wanted it.

"You can do that, can't you, Abby?" he'd asked her.

In the moment she'd been so relieved she almost cried. Now, not even a week later she thought she'd do almost anything to get out from under him, though she didn't yet know what that something might be. She'd have to figure that out. He couldn't blackmail her forever, could he? What, she was supposed to be his personal sexual assistant for the rest of her life? Fuck that.

"I want you to come over to my place tonight. Pack a bag too. I'd like you to stay for the weekend. I like having a woman around the house."

"Oh, Bradley…I don't know. I'm awfully tired. How about next weekend?"

Pearson smiled at her. "Sure, that'd be fine with me. Do you think you'll be out of jail by then?"

"Jail? *Jail?* Now you listen to me you disgusting little—"

"Careful there, Abigail. Wouldn't want to say anything you can't take back now, would you? Seems you've got a bit of a problem in that area…letting your mouth get the better of you. I know it's certainly got the better of me on occasion. So, let's keep everything nice and friendly, shall we? How does six o'clock sound? And on second thought, don't bother with the bag. I don't think we'll be going out…at all."

———

PEARSON WALKED OUT OF MONROE'S CONDO AND DIALED Pate's number. "We should have a conversation."

"Regarding?"

"A minor complication." Pearson said.

"How minor?"

"Nothing we can't handle."

"Does it impact our arrangement?"

"There is some potential for that."

"I'm at my office."

"I'm on my way."

———————————

PATE'S OFFICE WAS LUXURIOUS. PEARSON HAD BEEN there before, so he knew the way up. The reception area was deserted…Saturday…but Pate's outer office door was open. When Pearson walked inside he sat down and came clean right out of the gate. Mostly clean, anyway.

"Last time we were together, Bradley, if I'm not mistaken—and I rarely am—you indicated to me that you were not romantically involved with Ms. Monroe."

"And I'm not."

"But you are sleeping with her."

"Well, yeah. I mean, wow, have you seen her?"

"Yes, we've met a number of times, you know that."

"Figure of speech, Gus. Listen, none of that matters. In fact, when you hear what I'm about to tell you, you're going to appreciate my initiative. As it turns out, Abby was having an affair with one of her programmers. Care to guess which one?"

Pate was behind his desk. He swiveled his chair ninety degrees to the left, looked away from Pearson and did a few quick calculations in his head. On Monday the unclaimed lottery money would go into the state's discretionary fund. Once there, literally within seconds, the money would be transferred to various API accounts—that had been set up for months now, all nicely written into the legislation and the contract Pate held with the state—so no problem there. But…the dead programmer,

Pope, he would be a problem. If word got out that Monroe had been sleeping with him, far too many questions would be asked. Questions that Pate wouldn't want to answer.

"Yoo-hoo, Gus? Anybody home?" Pearson said.

Pate looked at him. What an idiot. Here was someone who was only days away from his share of millions of dollars and he couldn't keep his pants zipped up long enough to make a bank deposit. Was this all it took to qualify to be the governor's chief of staff? "I can assure you, Bradley, I am most definitely home, as you put it. I'd like to have a conversation with Ms. Monroe."

"She's at her condo right now. I just came from there."

"Not now. Tonight. Can you make that happen?"

"Sure. She's coming over to my place at six. Why don't you stop by after that? We'll be there all night. You know where I live, don't you?"

"Yes, I do. I'll see you tonight."

———

AFTER PEARSON LEFT THE OFFICE, PATE TOOK OUT HIS cell phone and made a call. "Where are we with our side project?"

"I'm heading out there now," Hector said.

"We can't afford any mistakes at this point."

"There won't be any."

"We also have to pay a visit to Mr. Pearson and Ms.

Monroe. Pick me up tonight at home. Eight o'clock. Come prepared."

"Eight o'clock," Hector said.

Pate ended the call without saying anything else. Hector knew the drill.

CHAPTER TWENTY

VIRGIL SHOWED RON HOW TO ACCESS HIS EMAIL FROM HIS cell phone then had him send the picture. The first time he sent it the picture wasn't attached, so he had to repeat the process before it came through. Once he had it, Virgil sent it directly to his printer.

"How do you do that?" Ron said.

"I took a class. Listen…let me get to work on this."

"What exactly are you going to do?"

Virgil smiled. "I'm going to let my researcher handle it."

Miles shook his head. "That's just wrong."

"Says the guy with my old job."

"Speaking of your old job…tell me more about this discretionary budget. No one said anything to me about it…"

NICHOLE POPE STOOD AT THE BACK OF THE MINI-MART, near the candy and chips and bottled soft drinks. She had a clear view of both the parking lot outside and the front counter. She looked in the cooler like she was trying to decide which type of drink she wanted. A little girl pulled her father along by his hand and they stopped right next to her. They were smiling and laughing and teasing each other and as Nichole watched them she realized she felt nothing at all. She had no memories of those types of interactions with her father before he'd been killed...no frame of reference. There had never been any smiling or laughing or teasing for her. There'd been nothing, really, other than the basics, like food, shelter, clothing. There had been a lot of fighting with her mother. She remembered *that*. It hadn't been all bad, though...like that one good birthday when she'd gotten a bicycle...

The man had been speaking to her and she'd missed it. "I'm sorry, Miss, would you excuse us, please? I'd like to get in the cooler right there for a bottle of water."

Nichole stepped back out of the way.

"Are you okay, Miss? You look a little—"

"I'm fine," Nichole said. "Thank you."

"You bet. Have a nice day."

Nichole smiled at the little girl, then looked at the man. "It's far too easy for a father to break his little girl's heart. Those types of wounds take a long time to heal. Sometimes they never heal at all."

The man gave her an odd look, scooped up his child and walked away.

———

NICHOLE WAS SO LOST WITH THOUGHTS OF HER FATHER and the childhood she never really had that she almost missed Pearson. He'd already parked his car and was walking into the store. Her timing would have to be perfect here. She waited until he'd filled a cup of coffee, grabbed a newspaper from the rack, and walked up to the counter to pay. When he took out his wallet she started moving to the front of the store, her head down. Didn't want to attract any unnecessary attention. Not this close.

———

PEARSON PAID FOR HIS ITEMS AND STUCK THE CHANGE IN his pocket. He had a newspaper in one hand and a hot cup of coffee in the other as he moved toward the door. His hands were full so he turned himself around to push the door open with his ass. As he turned a young woman stepped up to the door and said, "Here, let me get that for you." She pushed the door open, stepped outside and held it for him as he walked through. Pearson told her thanks, then he tucked the newspaper under his other arm and reached into his pocket for his car keys.

———————

NICHOLE HELD THE DOOR FOR PEARSON AS HE STEPPED through. She saw him tuck the paper and reach into his pocket. The entire performance was going to last about five seconds. She turned and walked right with him, stuck her hand in the crook of his elbow, and said, "Why, it's my pleasure, sir." She leaned her head against his shoulder and smiled. "Anything for a handsome devil like you."

———————

PEARSON WAS SO SHOCKED BY THE WOMAN'S BEHAVIOR HE stopped and turned toward her. "Do we know each other?"

She smiled even brighter and laughed out loud. Then she placed her other hand across his chest "Nope. I'm just a happy girl. Smile with me. You'll feel like a million bucks."

Pearson thought *what the hell is this?* But he smiled right along with her, it was just that unusual of a moment. Two-seconds later he was laughing as well. Right after that the young woman let go of Pearson's arm, told him to enjoy his life and walked away.

AFTER RON LEFT, VIRGIL DROVE OVER TO MURTON'S house, walked up the front steps and knocked on the door. Becky answered a few seconds later wearing nothing except one of Murton's white T-shirts.

"We're in the kitchen. Come on back," she said. She walked ahead of him and Virgil couldn't help but notice that the shirt was barely long enough to cover her butt.

Murton was at the stove. He had two pans going, one filled with bacon, scrambled eggs in the other. Becky walked up behind him, stood on her toes and kissed the back of his neck. When she did, the shirt rode up on her ass.

Murton turned and looked at Virgil. "When was the last time you ever knocked on the front door before walking into this house?"

"That might have been a first," Virgil admitted.

"Make sure it's the last."

"It's your house now Murt, not some place out of the past."

"Why can't it be both?"

"I don't know. Maybe it can."

"Well, my house means my rules. No knocking for the guy who grew up here."

"If you say so."

"I say so."

The three of them looked at each other for a few seconds, before Virgil said, "So you guys, are…what?"

Becky winked at him. "Hungry. Have a seat."

Murton brought two plates of bacon and eggs with buttered wheat toast over to the table. He set one plate in front of Becky and the other in front of his chair. Once they were seated, the two of them began to eat. After a few seconds, Virgil cleared his throat.

"Yeah, like I need that kind of grief," Murton said with a mouthful of eggs. "Small would hang me by my colon from a meat hook. You're supposed to be juicing. The Gerson thing, remember?"

Becky looked at Virgil. "He's right. And let me tell you this: You can stare at my ass all you want. I kind of like it. Most women do. But if you keep staring at my eggs like that I *will* punch you again. You've single-hand-edly redefined the term eyeballing. It gives me the willies."

───────────

WHEN THEY WERE FINISHED EATING, BECKY GOT UP FROM the table, dug through her purse and pulled out a slip of paper. "Here's what it's going to take, if you want to do it right." She looked at the list for a moment, nodded once to herself then read the items to them. "A high-speed Internet connection. And I'm not talking about one of those low-budget high-speed deals like Comcast is always trying to sell you. What is that, three megs? A three-meg line might be good enough to occupy a neglected second grader while mommy humps the pool boy, but it won't cut it for what I do. Also, let's talk about cell phones. I suggest you go with Sprint. They're about the only ones who really do give you unlimited data anymore. Wait, I take that back. They *are* the only ones. You want to know about computers? Okay. I'm going to need two of the 12-core Mac Pro's. They've got twelve gigs of memory and a one terabyte hard drive each. They're a little pricey, but worth every penny."

"Why do you need two?"

"One for here, and one for the office at the bar."

"How much will all that cost?" Virgil asked.

"Hmm, somewhere between six and eight should do it."

"*Thousand?*"

Becky let her eyelids droop. "No, cents, Sherlock. But like I said, that's if you want to do it right."

"How much to do it sort of right?"

She thought about that for a minute. "Short term, about half that amount. Long term, about three times as much."

Murton rolled onto his left hip, pulled his wallet from his back pocket and handed Becky his Amex card. "Do it right."

She hopped up from the table, kissed Murton and took the card. "I always do. I better go get dressed." Then she wiggled the card in front of us. "Hey, what about my hair? I was thinking about getting it cut anyway…"

They watched her walk out of the kitchen and Murton said, "Boy, she's a pistol, huh?"

———————

FIFTEEN MINUTES LATER BECKY WAS DRESSED AND READY. "I emailed you a photo that the crime scene techs took at Pope's apartment," Virgil said. "Ron gave it to me. Can you take a look at it? You know, research it?"

"The one with the code? I've seen it," she said. "Ron already gave it to me."

"Were you able to figure anything out?"

"Hadn't even started on it yet."

"Let's make that our priority, okay?"

"I'll get to work on it as soon as I get my gear set up."

"Do that."

"Say, shouldn't we hammer out my salary and bennies?"

Virgil gave her a slow blink. "We'll match whatever you were making at the state. I'll let you and Murton work out the, uh, bennies."

Becky frowned. "So, a lateral move then, huh?"

Murton: "Hey, now."

———————

In Virgil's truck. "You sure you know what you're doing?"

Murton set a small duffle by his feet. "I guess I'm not sure what you're asking me, Jonesy. Are you asking about Becky the researcher, or Becky the girlfriend?"

"Yes."

"To be perfectly honest, I'm basing her research abilities on what you've told me. I'm basing her other abilities on firsthand knowledge of the situation as it has been presented to me."

"If you don't mind my asking, when did that presentation begin?"

"About a month and a half ago. Boy, you have been out of it, haven't you?"

Murton was right. Virgil was beginning to notice some of the things he'd missed over the last few months, the medication dulling his awareness and his desire to care. "I guess I have. It looks like she's all but moved in."

"We've been living together at her place for a couple of weeks now. After I found out your dad had left me his place, well, we decided since we were already living together we might as well take the house. A lot more room, that's for sure."

"Seems kind of fast, if you ask me."

"I don't and I'm not...Mr. Small. Besides, my house, my rules, right?"

"Yeah, yeah." Fucking partners.

———————

Virgil dropped the truck in gear, but held his foot on the brake. "So, where to?"

Murton took a slip of paper from his pocket and then entered an address into the truck's navigation system. "Thirty-two minutes…if you drive the speed limit."

Virgil looked at the route displayed on the screen. "That's in Hendricks County."

"Yep."

"What is it?"

"Abandoned warehouse."

"And we're going there why?" Virgil asked.

"Because it's going to catch on fire this morning, or more precisely, someone is going to set it on fire. Probably about an hour from now. Come on, man, take your foot off the brake. We don't want to be late."

"And how, exactly, do we know this?"

"Becky told me, how else?"

They turned out into the street and began driving north. "What? She figured it all out?"

"Uh-huh."

Virgil shook his head.

"Don't do that," Murton said. "She mapped it. If you look at the dates, times and locations of the fires, you'll see there's a little bit of a pattern there."

"A pattern, or a little bit of a pattern?"

"Quit splitting hairs, will you? According to the

computer program she wrote—some C++ bullshit that I don't understand—the next fire is going to be at the address where we're headed. And if you don't stop driving like a little old lady, we might actually get there in time to catch whoever is getting his jollies by burning empty buildings to the ground."

"I see. What's in the bag?"

"Supplies."

A half-hour later they turned into one of Hendricks County's many abandoned industrial parks. The recession had hit the area hard and every single warehouse in the complex was empty. Murton pointed to the left. "There you go, up ahead and just past the intersection. That's the one. Drive on past and let's come around from the back side."

They rolled past and then turned left at the end of the service road and wound their way around to the front of another building one street over from the address on the nav system. "You sure about this?"

"What's not to be sure about? It's billable hours. If she's wrong, we'll keep investigating. If she's right, we earned ten grand the easy way."

"What ten grand?"

"Jerry sent a check over yesterday."

"So we're up twenty grand in two days and we haven't actually done anything yet? We should have done this a long time ago." Virgil opened the door. "Come on, let's go have a look."

"Hold on," Murton said. "Are you carrying?"

"No. I had to turn in my service weapon. I haven't replaced it yet."

He reached into the bag at his feet and pulled out two Smith and Wesson 1911 model .45's. "Remember these?"

Virgil did. They were the same thumb-busters Murton had used to kill Collins and Hicks, the men who'd kidnapped and tortured him.

"Would you prefer Mr. Smith, or Mr. Wesson?" Murton asked. "Wait, never mind. I almost forgot…you're left-handed. You'll want Mr. Smith." He handed one of the guns over, along with a clip-on holster. Virgil pulled the gun from the holster and noticed that its safety, slide release, ejection port and mag release were designed for left-handed shooters.

"Be careful with that," he said. "It's loaded."

"What else have you got in there?"

"When was the last time you were on a stakeout, Jonesy?" He rooted around in the bag and listed the contents. "I've got about a half-dozen energy bars, four bottles of water, binoculars, a camera, and four extra mags loaded with Federal hollow-points."

"Isn't that a little excessive?"

"Only if you don't need it. Boy, I thought the feds were dull. You state guys are like a safe substitute for sleeping pills. Come on. Let's book." He grabbed the bag and hopped out of the truck.

Virgil pulled back the slide, checked to make sure a

round was in the chamber and set the safety. They crept along the side of the warehouse toward the building their part-time researcher and Murton's full-time girlfriend said was going to be the next one to burn. Virgil had a loaded gun tucked into his waistband, his best friend as a partner and suddenly realized for the first time in a long time…he was having fun.

CHAPTER TWENTY-ONE

THE INDUSTRIAL PARK WAS LAID OUT IN THE SHAPE OF A horseshoe with buildings spaced evenly around the inner and outer parts of the shoe. They took up a position between two buildings on the outer edge near a drainage culvert facing the suspect building. Most of the structures were similar in design and appearance. They all had tan or white corrugated steel sides, no windows, a single door in the front, and loading docks for semi-trailers in the rear. If Becky was correct—Virgil had his doubts—they had about fifteen minutes to spare. They crawled down next to the culvert, dug into the weeds and waited.

"This is dumb," Virgil said. "There's no way she could predict this."

"She didn't predict this exact building. It's the one that's in the center of the complex. It could be any of them, really."

"Still, even to pick the right industrial park is a bit of a stretch, don't you think?"

"Who am I to say? It's intel. What's the harm in checking it out?"

Virgil slapped a mosquito at the back of his neck. He thought he felt something crawl up his pant leg. "The harm is I'm getting eaten alive and we've only been here a few minutes."

"Speaking of eating, hand me that bag, will you?"

Virgil tossed the duffle to Murton, then slapped another bug off his neck. "Did you bring any bug spray?"

"Nope. I put some on before we left."

Great. "Give me one of those candy bars," Virgil said. "And don't give me any grief about juicing. I'm starving."

"They're energy bars."

Virgil was starting to get annoyed. "Whatever, Murt, just give me one, will you?"

"Okay, okay. Don't get yourself in a bunch." He pulled two bars out of the bag. "You want the Snickers or the Three Musketeers?"

———

THEY PASSED THE TIME DISCUSSING THEIR OTHER CASE. "I've seen the crime scene photos," Murton said. "That was a lot of blood."

"It was a lot, that's for sure."

"I'll tell you something you probably already know…

when it comes to murder, I'm a little out of my element. That's one of the reasons I wanted you with me. Most of my job with the Feds was pretty basic, either straight-up investigative work—fraud or fugitive tracking, and for me a ton of UC—but since murder isn't a federal crime…at least not yet, I'm not quite sure what to do about Nicholas Pope."

"You know what? I hadn't thought of that," Virgil said. Then he barked out a little laugh.

"What's so funny?"

"Nothing…Boot. I guess I didn't realize that I'd be working with a rookie. Maybe we should reevaluate our partnership agreement."

"We don't have a partnership agreement."

"Not yet."

Murton refused to take the bait. "So teach me about murder. What are the details of Pope's murder that we should focus on?"

"Well, we've got Becky looking into that coded clue and the hope is that she might be able to figure it out. No one else has been able to. Pope obviously had some sort of information that someone wanted. Whether they got it or not is unknown. Clearly he was tortured in an attempt to extract that information."

"So Pope—who worked for the lottery—gets tortured and killed over information he possessed. You think he was trying to scam the lottery?"

"It feels right, but I'll tell you what doesn't feel

right…if you're the person or persons involved in the torture and Pope dies, why take the body? That apartment was covered with blood. It's not like they were concealing up a murder."

"Maybe they took the body to create misdirection," Murton said.

"That's a hell of a risk and what exactly does it misdirect? Doesn't seem like it would be worth it. You go in, you get the info you were after—or maybe you don't— and during the course of that event, Pope winds up dead. Disposing of the body after the fact only adds unnecessary risk."

Murton thought about that for a moment. "Without the body being present though, wouldn't it help delay discovery? No dead body smell, right? Maybe whoever killed Pope needed time…time to do something, or wait for something to happen before his murder was discovered."

Virgil hadn't considered that. "That's a possibility. Nothing else really fits, at least not yet."

"Here we go," Murton said. He pulled his camera out of the bag, pointed it at the entrance of the complex and snapped off a few pictures. The vehicle was an unmarked brown and tan Hendricks County squad car. It crept along the access drive that gave way to the front of the buildings. As the car approached they lowered themselves further out of sight and when it passed, Murton rose up enough to take a picture of the plate and car numbers. He lowered himself back in the ditch. "Hot tip?"

"Must be."

"Unless…"

The implication was clear. Could a county cop be responsible for setting the fires? "I doubt it, Murt."

"Stranger things, Jones-man."

"Let's sit tight and see what happens. There's only one way back out of here. I'll bet you even money he gets to the other side, turns around and leaves."

"And when he sees your truck?"

"What of it? We're not breaking any laws."

Murton shook his head at me. "That's not what I mean. What if this is our guy and he sees your truck and bails? No fire, no crime."

Murton had a point. If for some reason a county deputy was setting the fires, this was their chance to catch him in the act. But if he saw the truck, he would more than likely leave without committing any crime. "So what do you suggest?"

"My professional opinion is that we sit tight and see what happens."

HECTOR, WAS A HALF-MILE AWAY. HE GOT OUT OF HIS car, leaned across the roof, and looked through a pair of high-powered binoculars. The deputy was turning into the industrial park, right on schedule.

If anyone had bothered to ask him—and no one ever

did—he'd have told them it was pure luck. He was following the cruiser with the binoculars and caught the reflection of the camera lens. He froze on that spot and watched for a few seconds before he saw them. Wheeler and Jones. He almost had to smile. They *were* good. Hector took out his phone and made the call. "Don't speak, don't say a word. This is a wrong number. You've got company, drainage ditch at your six o'clock, west side. Hit your lights and siren like you've got a call and get the hell out of there." Then he closed the phone and slipped it back in his pocket.

A second later he saw the red and blue grill lights of the cruiser, then heard the siren. He got back in his car and drove away.

———————

MURTON RAISED HIS HAND HIGH ENOUGH TO REACH THE top of the culvert, kept the shutter button depressed and tried to follow the track of the squad car with the camera. When it was well past, they raised their heads and watched as the cruiser turned out of the industrial park. "What do you think of that?"

Murton was fiddling with his camera. "I think we got made, is what I think. Look at this."

Murton's camera was digital and had a screen on the backside that displayed the photos. He pressed one of the buttons until the proper picture came up. It showed the deputy's face clearly looking right at the spot where they had been hiding. "Coincidence?"

"You're running lights and siren and happen to glance at the spot where we were? Not very likely."

"You may be right." Virgil took out his phone and pulled up Powell's number. "Are you at home or your office?"

"You sound like my ex-wife. It's Saturday, I've got less than two months before the election and I'm down by six points. Where do you think I am? I haven't seen home in so long I'm not sure I'd know how to get there without a map. What's up?"

"We've got a couple of pictures for you to look at."

"Bring them over. I'll let the front desk know you're coming."

"No, no. Don't do that, Jerry. Tell you what, wait about fifteen minutes, then step outside for a smoke. We'll meet you out in the parking lot."

"What's going on, Jonesy?"

"I'll let you tell me. Fifteen minutes, Jerry."

———

HECTOR PULLED INTO THE DRIVE—A GRAVEL PATH WITH weeds growing up between the tire ruts—and turned his car around, then backed up until his rear bumper was almost touching the cruiser. He left the engine running, pulled on a pair of gloves, got out and headed toward

Hendricks County Deputy Frank Brackett's house. The house had no sidewalk, only a worn-down trail through the crabgrass that led to the front door. He walked inside without knocking and Brackett was right there.

"What happened?" he asked.

Hector had his hands in his pockets—he didn't want Brackett to see the gloves. "I am not sure. We think your Sheriff Powell has enlisted the aid of two private detectives. They were there ahead of time waiting for you."

"How is that possible?"

"Again, I am not sure."

"What does Pate say?"

"He says we have no room for error."

Brackett huffed. "Damn straight. I'm about to win this thing and when I do, the county will belong to me."

Hector tilted his head to the side and let the corners of his mouth turn downward. "Hmm. I think it will belong to the man who financed your campaign. Would you not agree?"

Brackett ignored Hector's remark. "I think it's time to ease off the fires. We've made our point. There's too much risk. We've shown Powell's incompetence. I think we can ride it out from here. The voters are not going to be pleased with a sheriff who let an arsonist get away."

"Perhaps you are correct. I will discuss it with Mr. Pate. Do nothing until you hear back from me."

"Hey, no problem. You want a beer?"

"It is a bit early."

"Not if you work third shift." Hector followed Brackett into the kitchen, next to the refrigerator. Brackett pulled the door open and bent over to pull a bottle of beer from the vegetable crisper. Hector thought the crisper probably hadn't seen any vegetables since sometime in the mid 90s, but it was fully stocked with beer. When Brackett stood up and started to turn around, Hector gave him a little zap right on the back of his head with a hand-held stun gun and it dropped him like a bag of birdseed.

Hector looked around the kitchen. The place was a mess. The trash barrel was stuffed with a combination of pizza boxes, Chinese takeout containers and empty beer bottles. The whole house smelled a little like a high school gym locker. Hector put the stun gun back in his pocket, pulled out his phone and called Pate. "I'm at his place. We've got a problem. The burn didn't go. He was discovered. I called it off."

"How did that happen?"

"I believe Brackett was a little too, mmm, predictable with his patterns. Our two favorite private detectives managed to figure it out."

"That will have to be addressed and soon."

"I agree," Hector said.

"What's your exposure?"

"If I am quick, absolutely none."

"You're certain?"

"Yes."

Pate hesitated. The decision to eliminate an inside

source was not something to be taken lightly. "I hate to lose an associate on the inside."

Hector didn't want to overstep, but he knew Pate valued his opinions on these types of matters. "There are two or three others who can be bought. I have a list. Perhaps it is time we set a precedent…for future associates."

This time Pate didn't have any second thoughts. "Do it."

———————

WHEN VIRGIL AND MURTON TURNED INTO THE BACK LOT of the Hendricks County Law Enforcement Center they found Powell leaning against a marked cruiser, a cigarette tucked in the corner of his mouth and a can of Diet Coke sweating on the roof of the car. Virgil pulled up close and buzzed the window down. Powell removed his sunglasses and stuck them in the breast pocket of his uniform. He peered into the window and said, "I don't like surprises."

Murton leaned over from the passenger seat and smiled at him. "What's the matter, Jerry? Aren't you enjoying the job anymore?"

Powell shook his head. "This from a retired fed turned bartender."

"That's bar owner to you, you fat bastard," Murton said with a laugh. "You do know the concept of a tab, right? That's when we give you a drink and at some apparently undetermined point in the future, you give us some money that reduces said tab."

Powell laughed. "If you thought I was good for it, that's on you. Besides, I wrote you a check for ten grand. That ought to count for something. I know you two didn't drive all the way out here to hassle me about my bar tab. What have you got?"

They got out of the truck and leaned against the cruiser, next to Powell. Virgil didn't waste any time getting to the point. "Jerry, our researcher put a little program together that mapped out the fires, their point of origin and the timing. In doing so, she determined that the next fire would be at or near a certain location at a certain time."

"Good for her."

Murton had his camera in his hand and turned it on. After it powered up, he cycled through the photos, then showed them to Powell. "Any idea who that is?"

Powell looked at the pictures. "That's Frank Brackett's cruiser. Looks like he's driving. So what?"

"Is he working today?" Virgil asked.

Powell looked at his watch. "Not anymore. He's third shift. Would have gotten off a couple hours ago."

"You want to tell us about him, Jerry?"

"Yeah. Brackett's an asshole. Consider yourself up to speed."

"What makes him an asshole?" Murton asked.

"For starters, he's the guy running against me. He's

wanted my job for years and now he thinks he's ready. Personally, I don't think he's qualified for chief kennel cleaner at the pound, let alone my job, but I'm running out of time and he's up by five points."

"Hmm, I heard it was six," Murton said.

Powell ignored him and looked at Virgil. "What about Brackett?"

Virgil told him about their surveillance and the brief encounter with his deputy. "Do your guys turn their squads in at end of shift, or do you have them on the take-home plan?"

"We let them take their cars home. They're not supposed to drive them if they're not on duty, but some of the guys do. You know how that goes...wife is at the mall, they're out of beer or need to run to the hardware or what-not...I don't make a big deal out of it."

"But Brackett wouldn't have any reason to run lights and siren out of an abandoned industrial park two hours after his shift ended, would he?"

Powell scratched the fat under his chin. "No, I guess he wouldn't. So you're saying Brackett is the one setting the fires?"

"We're saying it's a possibility, Jerry," Virgil said.

"A pretty strong possibility," Murton added.

Powell turned away and looked at nothing in particular. "This is a problem for me. You understand that, don't you? If you're wrong, I've accused a veteran of this department—asshole or not—of arson and when that gets out I'll be finished as sheriff. There's no way I'd get reelected after that. If you're right, Brackett's the kind of guy that will scream bloody murder and accuse me of framing him because I'm down in the polls and about to be out of a job. My tit's in the wringer either way."

Virgil took a chance. "You knew it was him all along, didn't you, Jerry?"

Powell rolled his lips together and squinted at Virgil. "How did you know that?"

"I didn't. I only suspected it. You confirmed it for me. That's why you hired us, isn't it? You're only weeks away from the election and you didn't want to have to investigate the guy who is running against you."

Powell dropped his cigarette butt and crushed it out with the toe of his boot. "Nasty habit. Can't quit 'em though." He was quiet for a long time before he spoke again. "Yes, that's exactly why I hired you. Except I didn't think you'd get to it quite so quick."

"So what are you going to do, Jerry?"

Powell pulled his sunglasses from his pocket and put them on. "I'm probably going to flush my career down the toilet by taking a drive out to Brackett's house and having a little chat with him. I'll need impartial witnesses. You two are coming with me."

Murton looked at Virgil. "This ought to be fun."

———————

Hector saw Brackett start to stir so he gave him another zap then grabbed his ankles and pulled him from the kitchen into the family room. He placed him in a recliner that sat opposite a flat-screen television mounted on the opposite wall. He made a quick run through the house and checked that all the windows were closed tight, then went into the furnace room and broke the gas line loose. Then he went back into the kitchen, turned all four of the stovetop burners to their highest setting and blew the flames out one by one. After that, he turned the oven on, left the door open, walked out the front door and drove away.

Problem solved. Precedent set.

———————

Virgil and Murton got back in the truck and followed Powell out to Brackett's house. Brackett lived about six miles away, down an empty gravel road that had houses spaced every quarter mile or so. They were tight on Powell's bumper when they turned into the drive—a gravel path with weeds growing up the center—when the house blew apart.

The explosion was so strong it caused Powell to lose control of his vehicle and he drove the cruiser nose-first into an oak tree next to the drive. Virgil hit the brakes and slammed the truck's transmission into park. He heard Murton shout something but his mind refused to register

what he'd said. Virgil was too busy watching the debris
and wreckage that rained down across the whole of Brackett's property. He saw the brick chimney chase from the
side of the house launch itself like a missile, then fall back
and land on top of Brackett's cruiser, crushing it flat. A
refrigerator flew up through a hole where the roof should
have been and landed upside down in the front yard. A
flat-screen television set buzzed over the cab of the truck,
the noise like the sound of a helicopter's rotor blades. An
old-fashioned washtub basin landed in the tree above
Powell's car. A smoking lampshade tumbled past like a
box kite with its strings cut. Murton yelled to him again
and this time he grabbed Virgil's arm and pulled him flat
across the seat, below the level of the dashboard. At the
same time, a chunk of concrete smashed into the front end
of the truck and crushed the hood. A heavy wooden chair
hit the windshield and all four legs of the chair punched
through the safety glass.

All of it happened in a span of less than five seconds.
When the falling debris subsided Virgil and Murton sat
up, worked their way out of the truck and looked at the
devastation. Virgil thought his truck looked like something you might see parked on the back forty of a salvage
yard. Along with the chair that was stuck through the
windshield, the entire front end was demolished, both side
windows were blown out and the front tires were flat.
Steam and liquid coolant gushed from behind the grill.

Brackett's house was gone, reduced to a pile of rubble.

There was no fire, but the smell of natural gas hung in the air and small pockets of wreckage smoldered everywhere. Powell stumbled out of his cruiser, his sunglasses askew, and shook himself like a dog that had jumped from a swimming pool. He kept opening and closing his mouth. When Virgil spoke to him, he didn't answer.

"Jerry? Hey, Jerry. You better sit down here for a minute." Powell began to stagger toward the spot where Brackett's house used to be. Murton caught up with him, grabbed the back of his uniform collar then gently sat him down in the grass and told him to stay put. Virgil walked over to where Powell was and sat down next to him. "You okay, Sheriff?"

Powell wiped the airbag residue from his face and tried to straighten his sunglasses, but they were bent across the bridge and one of the lenses had spider-webbed from the impact. He finally gave up and flung them in the grass. Virgil stood, retrieved the glasses and handed them back. "We're probably looking at a crime scene here, Jerry. We shouldn't contaminate it any more than we have to." He didn't respond and Virgil wasn't sure if he'd heard him or not. "Sit tight, partner. Help is on the way."

Virgil reached inside Powell's cruiser, grabbed the microphone, identified himself and gave the dispatcher their location and a brief description of the situation, then told her to get the fire department and any available deputies headed their way. When he turned back and looked at Powell, he was standing, his hands on his knees.

Murton jogged over from the other side of Brackett's cruiser. He kept looking up at the branches of the same tree that Powell had hit with his squad car. He grabbed Powell's arm and led him a few yards away, closer to what was left of Virgil's truck.

"Let's sit down over here. You took a pretty good wallop, Jerry."

"What the hell happened?"

Virgil had seen this type of reaction before. So had Murton. During their time in Iraq they'd both been near IEDs when they exploded. "Brackett's house blew up. Probably a gas explosion." Virgil noticed Murton staring at him. "What?"

As usual, Murton's remarks were nothing short of factual. "Brackett's legs are stuck up in that tree above Powell's cruiser. What's left of his torso is laying about a hundred feet past the back porch." The three of them looked up in the tree. Then, as if his point might have been missed, he added, "Congratulations, Jerry. You're about to be reelected."

CHAPTER TWENTY-TWO

POWELL REFUSED MEDICAL TREATMENT AND TOOK CHARGE of the crime scene while Virgil and Murton helped where they could, though there wasn't much for them to do. They helped the crime scene technicians identify bits of debris that might be classified as evidence, but everyone knew that any forensic value associated with Brackett's belongings were going to be slim at best. The majority of the pieces scattered around the property would either have to be picked up with a backhoe or a pair of tweezers.

Brackett's body parts were photographed, bagged, and taken away. His squad car was completely destroyed. Both Powell's cruiser and Virgil's truck had to be towed from the scene as well. The crime scene technicians would have a long day. When it was clear Virgil and Murton had done all they could, Powell told them they could leave. Before they did though, he said, "If Brackett had a computer here at the house no one has found it. Not even pieces of it. I don't think he had one. Nobody has found a cell phone yet either."

"Have one of your people pull his cell records from the phone company. His house too, if he had a landline," Virgil said.

"I've already got someone on that. There's no chance this was a suicide, was it?"

"Probably not, Jerry. There are easier ways to go. Ever try to stay in a room with the smell of natural gas? It's all but impossible."

"Besides," Murton added, "show me a cop suicide and I'll show you someone who either ate their gun or went to town on pills. You know that, Jerry. We all do." Virgil felt like Murton made a point of looking away from him as he spoke about the pills. "Besides, why would he take himself off the board? You said yourself he was beating you. He had a real shot at being the next sheriff. It doesn't add up."

"Accident then?"

"Probably not," Virgil said. "At least according to the firemen. Look, Jerry, you don't really believe that anyone is going to try to hang this on you, do you?"

"Brackett and I were on opposite ends of the spectrum. He had the support of the people. We're plenty short on jobs around here and this private prison system the state is moving toward is something that I have opposed since the get-go. It was also something that Brackett was leveraging in a big way."

"How so?"

"Jobs, how else? Jobs to build the prison, jobs to run the prison, jobs to maintain the prison. Brackett was backed by Pate's construction company and the harder I pushed against the idea of a private prison in my county the harder they pushed back. Have you seen any of their TV ads? They turned Brackett's entire campaign into one big job fair for the county. And not only that, they managed to make it look like I was the one pulling the tent pegs out of the ground while everyone was underneath the big-top handing out their resumes."

Murton clapped Powell on the back. "Relax, Jerry. Everything is copacetic. If nothing else, you're going to win by default."

Powell shook his head. "That's not good enough, Wheeler, and you damn well ought to know it. If I don't have the trust of the people I serve, how in the hell am I supposed to be an effective leader?"

"I think Murton is right, Jerry. You might be overthinking it. Everything will work out." Powell stared at Virgil for a moment then shook his head and walked away. After he was gone Murton looked at Virgil. "What?" Virgil said.

"Nothing. All's well that ends well, that's all."

"Really?"

"Yes, really. Jerry's going to get reelected. A dirty cop

is dead. We've invested about four hours tops into our first case and we're walking away with ten grand. What's the downside?"

"The downside is this: Pate is playing us like a couple of rag dolls. Brackett might have won the election but he was going to be Pate's puppet no matter what. That means Pate controls the county, the prison, and all the revenue it's going to generate. While all that is happening, he and Pearson have put together a plan that essentially allows Pate to walk away with every single dime of any unclaimed lottery winnings. Pate not only set himself up in the county, he had his hand in the state's cookie jar."

"Except none of that is illegal, is it?"

"No, it's not. But Pearson has tied himself to Pate, and Pate's company controls the lottery, which is where Nicholas Pope was employed. If we want to find out who killed Pope, we need to go where the answers are. I want you to get together with Nichole Pope and find out everything you can about her brother's job, his background, the works. Nobody gets butchered like that without cause. We've got to figure out what he was up to."

"Didn't I hire you?"

"Yeah," Virgil said. "I'm teaching you about murder investigation. It was your idea, remember? Let's call it on-the-job training."

"So what are you going to do?" Murton said.

"I'm going to go over to the lottery office and interview the rest of the programmers. One of them has to know something."

"We need a ride," Murton said.

———————————

THE RIDE CAME FROM BECKY AND SHE DROPPED VIRGIL AT his house first so he could get Sandy's car. Once inside he spent the better part of a half-hour looking for her car keys. The longer he looked the more frustrated he became until he finally gave up. He went out to the backyard and without purpose began to walk down toward the pond and his father's willow tree. Virgil looked for him under the branches, but he wasn't there, nor did he really expect him to be. He pulled his phone from his pocket and called Sandy. The governor answered. "Hi, Jonesy. How are you?"

"Why are you answering Sandy's phone, Governor?"

"I'm well, thank you for asking. I don't think Sandy is though. If I were you, I'd get her an appointment with the doctor when we get back."

"Where is she now?"

"Still in the bathroom. She took one bite of the hors d'oeuvres and made a beeline for the can. It seems I'm in charge of her purse and her phone."

Virgil sat down in one of the lawn chairs near the edge of the pond. "How bad is she?"

"Hmm, not too bad. I wouldn't say it's anything to

worry about, but she's been a little green around the gills ever since we got here. Can't seem to keep anything down. Maybe she got some bad shrimp at that bar of yours."

"I doubt it, Mac. Listen, have her call me right away when she gets back to, to…" Virgil suddenly realized he didn't know exactly where Sandy and the governor were.

"To our table?"

"Yes. Your table." He said it through his teeth.

"What's the matter, Jonesy? You sound a little irritated."

He took a deep breath. "I am irritated. I cannot seem to find my girlfriend's car keys, which, at the moment I need quite desperately. I was hoping to ask her where they are."

The governor made a clucking noise with his tongue. "Better be careful there. Fiancée is the word you should be getting used to."

"Mac, maybe it's simply my imagination, but you seem to be enjoying yourself lately at my expense."

"My goodness, you're awfully sensitive for a cop."

"See? That is exactly what I'm talking about. I believe you meant to say former cop, didn't you?"

"Yes, yes. Once a cop, always a cop, though. Isn't that what they say? Anyway, have you looked in the ignition? I'm telling you, with God as my witness I couldn't get my former wife to take the keys out of the ignition if I paid her. Did you know the insurance company won't pay on an auto theft claim if they discover you left the keys in the car? I suppose I could get them to pay if I made a claim, given the fact that I appoint the insurance commissioner for the state, but for the average Joe—"

"Goodbye, Governor," Virgil said, then hung up. When he got to the garage and opened the driver-side door of Sandy's car, he saw the keys hanging in the ignition.

———

PROVING HE WAS THE BETTER MAN, VIRGIL CALLED THE governor back to let him know he was correct; the keys were in fact in the ignition. Proving he knew he was correct, the governor refused to answer. Sandy's phone went straight to voice mail. Virgil could actually picture McConnell sitting there, a little smile across his lips. Virgil left Sandy a message and told her he loved her and asked her to call him back when she could.

———

WHEN HE ARRIVED AT THE LOTTERY OFFICE THE FRONT door was locked and the windows were dark. *Well, what did you expect on a Saturday afternoon, Jonesy?* When he walked around to the back of the building though he found two young men standing next to a steel door that was propped open with a wastebasket. Both were smoking cigarettes. "You guys work for the lottery?"

"Who's asking?" one of the men said. They were both young, skinny, and had hair that grew past their shoulders. Both wore T-shirts emblazoned with the names of rock bands Virgil was unfamiliar with, their jeans had holes in the knees and their sneakers were covered with grime. The only discernible difference between the two was the color of their hair. One had light brown, the other black. They were either programmers or janitorial staff. Virgil hoped they were programmers.

"I am. It's a yes or no question."

Black hair looked at brown hair and spoke from the corner of his mouth. "Cop."

Virgil didn't correct him. "I need to ask you guys a few questions about Nicholas Pope. You knew him?"

Brown looked him right in the eyes. "Knew him? Are you kidding? He was my idol. That dude could fly. He taught me everything I know."

"Fly? He was a pilot?"

He rolled his eyes. "No, no. His fingers, man. He could fly on the keys faster than anyone. He was amazing."

"Is that important? With what you do? The speed?"

He laughed. "Not here…not so much. But as any coder will tell you, sometimes…hell most times, you gotta go fast. You gotta stay ahead of the traps. If you don't have the speed, you'll get backtracked and boxed in so fast the cops will be at your door before you can log out and shut down."

Black cleared his throat. "Uh, don't you have to, like, have a warrant or something before we talk to you?"

"What's your name?" Virgil said.

"Mike. Mike Snowhill."

"Okay, Mike, Mike Snowhill. You're mostly right. You don't have to talk to me. But if you don't I have to ask myself, why not? Why wouldn't you? The only logical reason I could come up with is you've got something to hide."

"Hey man, I've got nothing to hide. We've got legit jobs here."

"Uh-huh. And how about after hours? Got anything going on the side, Mike, Mike Snowhill?"

Brown looked at Snowhill, then at Virgil. "My name is Bobby Epps. Maybe we better go inside."

"Sounds good to me."

And Virgil was in.

CHAPTER TWENTY-THREE

SNOWHILL AND EPPS TOOK HIM TO A BREAK ROOM WHERE three other programmers were eating vending machine dinners. All together the five of them looked a little like a Seattle grunge band from fifteen years ago. Epps made the introductions by pointing at the other three programmers and said, "Wu, Myers, Rand." Then he pointed his chin at Virgil and said, "Cop."

Virgil pulled out a chair, sat down at the table and got right to it. "My name is Virgil Jones. I'm investigating the death of your co-worker, Nicholas Pope. Anything you guys could tell me would be a big help."

Myers spoke first. "Might want to get your facts straight. Don't know that I'd call him our friend."

"Why not?"

"He was my friend," Wu said.

Myers ignored Wu as if he hadn't spoken. "Because

we hardly knew him. Most of us have been here for quite a while, hired directly by the lottery, but Pope came over with PTEK. He hadn't been here that long before they sacked him."

"Sacked him? You mean he was fired?"

Rand gave him a dry look. "No dude, it means they put him in a paper bag."

Virgil ignored the jab. "Why did they fire him?"

They all looked at each other but no one answered. "Look guys, let's decide something right here and now. You agree to talk to me and I'll give you my word that whatever is said here stays here. Sound fair?"

"Sounds like cop bullshit to me, that what it sounds like," Wu said. "Wu want no part of it." He stood from the table. "If the rest of you had any sense you no want it either." He walked out of the room.

Virgil looked at Rand, Myers, Snowhill, and Epps, raising his eyebrows at them. Snowhill waved the expression away. "Fuck Wu, he gets all worked up over everything."

Myers shouted into the hallway. "Yeah, fuck Wu, fuck Wu," and they all laughed and high-fived each other. Virgil shook his head.

———————

Wu *WAS* WORKED UP. HE WAS SITTING AT HIS DESK, HIS computer monitor displaying the live feed from the break room. He called Pate. "It Wu. Police are here."

Pate was instantly worried. "Wu? What the hell is going on?"

"Wu told you. Cop. That what going on. Here at lottery office. What you want Wu to do?"

"Hold on." Pate set the phone down, took out his cell and called Hector. When Hector answered, Pate said, "Come to the office, now," then ended the call and turned his attention back to Wu. "How many? Lots of cops? Like a raid?"

Wu rolled his eyes. "Not lots. One."

"Who's he talking to?"

"Some of the programmers. You want live feed? There are security cameras in the room."

"Yes, yes. You can do that?"

"Wu can do. It is not exactly live, live."

"What does that mean, Wu?"

"There is approximately ten-second delay."

"I don't care about that. What do I have to do to get it?"

"Turn on computer."

"It is on. What do I do?"

"What is your IP address?"

"I don't know what that is."

Wu sighed. "Here is what you do…"

"What do you mean, he gets worked up over everything?"

"Well, there's some loyalty there, I think," Snowhill said. "What Wu said is true. He and Pope were friends."

Epps nodded. "They hung out together. Not a lot, but some. He came over with Pope…from PTEK. What I told you earlier? When I said I idolized him? It wasn't only me. Everyone did. Pope was something of a legend and I don't mean only around here. I mean out there…on the net. He's been places the rest of us don't even like to dream about going. I'm talking heavy-duty places that are fire-walled so thick that the Chinese and the Russians don't even bother."

"You mean government systems?" Virgil said.

Rand turned the corners of his lips down. "No, man. I'm talking about cracking the places that really run the country. The corporations. There really isn't any notoriety with cracking the government anymore. That shit's too decentralized after 9/11 no matter what the media says. They go on TV every night and talk about interagency cooperation and communication, but I don't care who you are, it's all bullshit."

Myers agreed. "It's true. They're lying through their teeth every time—"

Virgil cut them off. "Look guys, this is all very fascinating stuff, but we might be getting a little sidetracked here. I'd like to focus on who killed Pope and why."

Rand swished his index finger back and forth like a windshield wiper. "No, no, no, it matters. Don't you see? Pope came up late in the game. Hell, we all did. There isn't much money to be made anymore in hacking, at least in the traditional sense."

"What do you mean by in the traditional sense?"

"What I mean is—and any other hacker would agree —the whole damn thing was never about the money. It's about the game, the challenge. Sure, a lot of guys made a shit pot of money stealing corporate secrets and credit card information from databases—and a lot still do—but the guys that are really good used to do it for the thrill, the rush. The bragging rights. Now they do it to expose wrongdoing and corruption. Look at Snowden or Anonymous. You think they're doing it for the money?"

"He's absolutely right," Epps said. "It's what you might call catch and release for coders. Besides, it's too damned dangerous anymore to steal. Who wants to go to jail?"

"It doesn't matter if you're doing it for sport or profit," Virgil said. "The activity itself is the part that goes against the law. To use your catch and release analogy, the game warden doesn't care if you haven't caught any fish when he pulls his boat up next to yours. If you've got a line in the water, you better have a fishing license. If you don't, it's illegal."

"Only if you get caught," Snowhill said.

───────────

"As much as I enjoy the philosophical debate, none of this helps me find who killed Nicholas Pope."

"That's because we don't know anything," Rand said. "I get that you guys probably hear that a lot, but in this case it's true." The others nodded their heads in agreement.

"Why was he fired?"

"Who knows?" Snowhill said. "I'll tell you this though, it wasn't for the reason they're saying."

"What reason is that?"

"Ah, he smoked a little dope."

"But that's not why they fired him?" Virgil let the skepticism creep into his voice.

"I really don't think so," Rand said. "It's…mmm…tolerated, I guess would be the right word."

"Why?"

"Any number of reasons really, but the main one is simple. Show me a coder who doesn't mellow out at the end of his shift and I'll show you someone who isn't a coder. We all smoke. It's as simple as that. Odd hours, bad food, too much caffeine, no social life…hell, the pot is the only thing that keeps us sane."

"And they overlook it?"

"They have so far. They have to, really. If they didn't

there wouldn't be anyone to do the job. Besides, that shit is going to be legal before too long anyway."

"So all of you believe Pope was fired for something other than drug use?"

More nodding. "Had to be," Myers said. "None of us have ever been drug tested. I can tell you this though, I'd like to know why he got fired. We all would. Whatever he did—and he must have done something wrong—I'd like to know what it was so I don't make the same mistake. I'm not talking about the job, either. I'm talking about getting whacked." He said the word 'whacked' like he'd been watching too much television. "The two things must be connected, right? Him getting fired and then killed?"

"It is possible," Virgil said. "You guys might want to watch your backs for a while. Don't get alone with anyone you don't know." He let them sit with that for a minute before he asked anything else. "Tell me about your boss, Abigail Monroe."

"Like what?" Snowhill said.

"Like what kind of person is she?"

"She's okay, I guess," Epps said.

Snowhill was taking a drink of his Coke when Epps spoke and snorted a mouthful onto the table. *"Okay, I guess?* Christ, Eppy, tell the truth why don't you?"

Virgil looked at Snowhill. "What?"

Snowhill wiped his mouth on his sleeve and shook his head at Virgil.

"She's hot, dude," Rand said. "Epps wants to bang her

only slightly more than the rest of us, and the rest of us want to bang her pretty bad."

Even Virgil had to smile at that. "What about Wu?"

"Well, there's some debate there," Rand said.

"A debate? What do you mean?"

"Ah, there's no debate," Myers said. "Wu's a little gay."

———————————

Wu was giving instructions to Pate on how to receive the feed when he heard Myers say, 'Wu's a little gay.'

What? Gay? Where that come from? Wu not gay. He turned the volume up slightly so he could hear more clearly.

"Wu? Hello, Wu? Are you there?" Pate. He'd forgotten about him. Had Pate heard what they were saying about him? He didn't want that. He killed the outgoing feed. "Wu, what happened? I had it for a split second then it was gone."

Wu thought for a moment. "Mmm, Wu not sure. Check the subnet mask on your router. It is probably not correctly configured."

"For Christ's sake, Wu, I don't know how to do that…"

THAT MIGHT BE SOMETHING, VIRGIL THOUGHT. "TELL ME more about Wu."

"Why, do you lean that way?" Epps said. "You don't look like the type."

Virgil laughed at the question. "That's good to know and no, I don't...lean that way. I'll tell you this though, the crime scene at Pope's was messy. It looks exactly like some of the ones I've seen before. The...brutality of it all. When you get to that level of violence it's often the result of a scorned lover. And when that type of violence is done to a man, it's usually indicative of...well, you can see where I'm going with this, can't you?"

"Well, I can tell you this," Snowhill said. "Wu didn't kill Pope."

"How do you know?"

"He was killed the same day he was fired, right?"

"Yes."

"We were all here, working on the code. Wu was right here with us."

"He didn't leave, go out to lunch, or anything like that?"

"No. None of us ever do," Epps said. "When you're working the code you get into the zone, man. You might be able to step outside for a quick smoke or something, but no one takes the time to get in their car and drive to a McDonald's. You'd lose your rhythm."

"Eppy's right," Myers said. "Besides, that was the day we had the air conditioning problem. It was about ninety-five degrees in here and we were all running around setting up external fans to keep the servers from overheating. Wu was fried by the time we were done. We all were, but he was here. Hey, you know what's funny? That's the day we figured out he was a little gay."

"I'm almost afraid to ask," Virgil said.

"Monroe," Epps said. "It was so hot in the building she was walking around barefoot. It's her feet. Have you ever seen them?"

Virgil assured them he hadn't.

"They're amazing," Rand said. "I don't quite know how to describe them."

"I do," Epps said. "They're the sexiest feet I've ever seen…"

———

"How does that prove Wu is gay?"

"He thought her feet were disgusting," Rand said. He verbally italicized the word 'disgusting.'

Virgil was skeptical. "That's hardly indicative of sexual preference."

They all stared at him for a few moments, then Rand said, "Whatever, dude. Wu's still gay."

"Fine, fine," Virgil told them. "I'm not interested in Wu's sexual leanings. I'm interested in Pope…"

When Wu heard the cop say he wasn't interested in him, he hit the button and released the outbound feed. "What about now?" he said to Pate.

"Yes, yes, I have it," Pate said. "But the picture looks wrong."

"What mean, wrong?"

"Sort of rounded. Like looking through a glass bowl or something. I can't tell who is who."

"Yes. Fisheye lens. Get whole room that way."

"Can you zoom in or something?"

"Yes. You want the cop?"

"No, Wu, I want the microwave. Of course I want the cop. And I can barely hear them."

Wu tapped a few keys on his keyboard to zoom the camera, then upped the audio output. "How that?"

Pate leaned closer to his own monitor. "Yes, that's much better. I can—"

Wu waited for his boss to finish, but the line remained silent. Finally he said, "What wrong?"

"That's not a cop, Wu. That's the man who murdered my son."

Wu had watched Augustus Pate's son, Samuel, commit suicide on national TV like everyone else, but he wasn't about to debate the facts with his boss. "What you want Wu to do?"

Pate was silent for a few moments and then said,

"Nothing. Let's hear what he has to say."

————————

"THE THING ABOUT POPE," Epps said, "IS HE WAS A little shifty."

"Shifty?"

"Yeah, you know, sort of slippery. I never really trusted him. None of us did."

Snowhill, Myers, and Rand all nodded their heads. "Wait a second…earlier you all said you idolized him."

"We do," Rand said. "Or did, I guess I should say. But it was because of his talent. The guy was the best I'd ever seen at what we do, but he was still sort of shifty."

"Shifty how? In what way?"

"I'm not sure I could define it," Epps said. "I don't think any of us could."

Virgil put some gravel in his voice. "Try."

"Hey man…chill," Rand said. "We're trying to help."

"Then help," Virgil said, but he dialed it back some.

Snowhill looked at Virgil. "It's like you said when we were outside. You asked if we had anything going on the side. That was Nick. He always had something going. He was always talking about making a big score, but he never spoke about anything in particular."

"That's true," Epps said. "He was the kind of guy who dreamed big. I don't think there's anything wrong with that, but he was also the kind of guy that might go a little outside the lines to make it happen."

"Maybe more than a little," Snowhill said.

"So. A risk-taker," Virgil said.

"More like a risk maker. And now he's dead."

"Tell me about his sister, Nichole. Any of you guys ever meet her?"

———

HECTOR WALKED INTO PATE'S OFFICE AND STARTED TO SAY something, but Pate waved him around behind his desk, a finger touched to his lips to shush him. He pointed at the monitor. "Live feed from the lottery building."

Hector squinted at the computer monitor. "Where's Wu?"

"That's how we're getting the feed."

Hector pulled a chair around behind the desk and sat down. He caught the end of what one of the programmers was saying…"Nichole, she was here quite a bit before Nick was killed. It was against the rules, but with the jacked-up hours we keep around here no one ever said anything. I liked her. We all did. Easy to talk to, didn't treat us like nerds, listened to what we had to say like she was really interested. Plus, she's good looking…in a hard sort of way. Not surprising, though, given the way they were raised." They all sat with that in silence for a few minutes.

Pate thought he might have lost the sound. It went on long enough that he picked up the phone and called Wu. "Wu, I'm not getting any sound."

"That because no one talking."

"Right," Pate said into the phone before hanging up. He looked at Hector. "That Wu is sort of a smart ass. He gets on my very last nerve sometimes."

"I think some of it is his broken English," Hector said. Then he pointed to the screen. "Here we go..."

———————

"I'M FAMILIAR WITH WHAT HAPPENED TO THEM AS children," Virgil said.

"How's that?" Epps said.

"Nichole has asked me to help find out what happened to her brother."

"So she told you that the cops gunned down her old man while she and Nick sat there and watched?"

"Not exactly."

"What does that mean?"

"She didn't have to," Virgil said. "I'm the one who shot him."

———————

HECTOR LOOKED AT PATE. "DID YOU KNOW ANY OF this?"

Pate shook his head. "Not all of it. Something is going on here. Get me everything you can on Nichole Pope. I want it by tonight before we go to Pearson's."

"You got it, boss."

———

VIRGIL STILL COULDN'T CONNECT WHAT HE'D LEARNED about Pri-Max—Pate's other company that held the state contract to build the private prison in Hendricks County— with the death of Nick Pope. "Tell me about the unclaimed funds," Virgil said. That got them going.

———

WU KILLED THE FEED. HE PICKED UP THE PHONE AND dialed. When it was answered he said, "He knows. It's time to move. Take your emergency exit bag and leave everything else behind. Go now." He hung up without waiting for a reply. Ten-seconds later his phone rang. Pate.

"Wu, I've lost the feed."

"Hold on. Wu try to reroute through a proxy server."

"I don't know what that means, Wu, and I don't care. Get me that feed back."

Wu clicked at his keyboard…a series of meaningless jabs that he hoped sounded like a frantic effort to get the feed back up. "Hold on. Wu trying."

———————

Rand let out a low whistle. "That's why we're all here. Nobody knows yet. Monroe doesn't even know."

Virgil gave Rand a look. "Knows? Knows what?" They were all smiling now.

"We were all called in this morning to authenticate. It's one hell of a process, I can tell you that."

Authenticate? Virgil was so focused on gathering as much information about Nicholas Pope that it took his brain a few seconds to change gears. When he figured it out, he had to smile. "You mean someone came forward? Someone has the winning ticket?"

"We're not supposed to talk about it," Myers said.

"Fuck that," Epps said to Myers. Then to Virgil, "Someone, somewhere, right now, is holding a lottery ticket worth three hundred million dollars."

Virgil thought about that for a moment and had to admit it was with a twinge of jealousy. He'd always had more than enough money...unless he wanted three hundred million dollars. "Boy, that's a lot of money."

"Someone," Snowhill said, "is about to be famous."

"How come your boss...Ms. Monroe doesn't know yet?"

"We haven't called her."

"Why not?"

"The authentication process is lengthy," Rand said. "Grueling, really. You'd be surprised how often the authentication fails. There are numerous steps—all of which have to be completed in the proper sequence, then crosschecked by all of us. If we called the boss every time a winning ticket was in process, she'd wring our necks. So we don't call until everything is verified."

"But you've done that."

"No, we're doing it now," Epps said. "Well, the computer is. We're running the last of eight different electronic verification processes. Each one is more complex than the previous one, but I can tell you this, there's no question. Someone has that ticket."

"Who is it?" Virgil said.

"Don't know yet," Myers said. "It was scanned at a mini-mart self-check station earlier today. That got the ball rolling for us. If everything checks out and believe me, it's going to, the only thing left to do is wait for the ticket holder to show up with the actual ticket. As long as it's printed on official lottery paper, hasn't been tampered with or mutilated, it's a done deal."

"I thought I heard or read somewhere that the deadline was today, though. When I got here, the place was locked up tight. If you guys hadn't been out taking a smoke break, I wouldn't have even known anyone was here. What do you do if someone shows up on a Saturday or Sunday?"

"There's a loophole," Snowhill said. "If the deadline lands on a Saturday, like this one did, then the ticket only has to be verified electronically, which it has. The winner then has until close of business on the following Monday to show up at any lottery office in the state to present their ticket and claim the prize."

"Huh." The whole thing was kind of exciting.

———————

Wu wasn't a little gay, but he was a little panicked. Pate wasn't supposed to find out about the verification until it was too late. Now that the cop knew…

CHAPTER TWENTY-FOUR

Virgil took Murton's call as he was leaving the lottery office. "Our girl Nichole is incommunicado. That's Fed-speak for she wasn't at her apartment, I can't find her anywhere else and she isn't answering her phone."

"Did you ask Delroy if she'd been into the bar?"

"Yeah. He said she stopped by earlier but didn't stay, so I don't know where she is."

"Huh. Well, she just lost her brother. She's in mourning. What would you be doing?"

"You're the closest thing I've ever had to a brother, Jones-man. I can tell you exactly what I'd be doing."

"What's that?"

"I'd grieve for the appropriate amount of time, then, you know, put the moves on Small." There might have been a half-second gap before Virgil heard him say, "Hey, that hurts."

"You're at home, huh?"

"Yeah…I'm working on Becky's sense of humor. Would you stop that, please?"

"Tell her we need that code figured out."

"She's working on it now. I'm helping."

Virgil heard Becky yell to him in the background. "No he isn't."

"Listen, I'm going to go try to track down Pate. Ask Becky for his home and office addresses, will you?"

A few seconds later Murton said, "Hold on, I'm going to text them to you now." Then, "They're on their way."

"I'm convinced he's connected to Pope, but I can't figure out how."

"Didn't Miles say he couldn't get past his lawyers?"

"Yeah, he did. But Miles is a cop. I'm not. I'll tell you something else…I'm starting to enjoy the freedom of that."

"Atta boy. You want some backup?"

"Nah. I'm sure I'll be fine. How would you feel about sitting on Nichole's place for a while?"

"I can do that. Do you think she's in danger?"

"I'm not sure."

"Let me know how it goes with Pate. And Jonesy?"

"Yeah?"

"Watch your back, brother."

"Always."

Wu called Pate. "He is gone. Nothing else of consequence was said."

"You're sure?"

"What Wu say?"

"Don't get snippy with me, Wu. I've got too much at stake here."

"What can I say? He is gone. You heard most of what was said. It sound like he on a fishing excursion."

"Expedition, Wu. It's called a fishing expedition." After a moment of silence: "Can you leave?"

"Yes, We are all but finished here."

"Finished with what?" Pate said.

Careful, Wu thought. "With work. Always things to do."

"Yes, I'm sure. I want you to meet me at my house. Bring your gear. Things are starting to happen."

"Okay, Wu come now."

Sandy walked out of the hotel lobby, then realized she didn't know which direction would be best, so she went back inside and up to the front desk. The hotel staffers were busy assisting other guests, so she had to wait a few minutes before she could ask for directions.

"The closest one is about five blocks north. It's a CVS if that's okay."

"That's fine," Sandy said. "Thanks."

"You know," the young man said, "we have a gift shop on the mezzanine if you don't want to walk that far, or I could call you an Uber."

"I think I'll walk. Maybe the exercise will do me some good. And I know about the gift shop, but I'd like to speak with a pharmacist. I've got to figure a way to settle my stomach. I might need something a little stronger than what you guys have."

The young man gave her a once-over. "Is there anything else I might be able to do for you? Anything…at all?"

Sandy bit down on her lower lip. *He's hitting on me.* She thanked him and walked out the door. He must have been what, at least ten years younger than she was?

Felt better already.

———

Murton parked a half-block away from Nichole Pope's apartment house, got out of the car and walked up to her door. He knocked, tried the knob—locked up tight —then knocked again. He put his ear to the door but didn't hear anything. The place felt empty.

He walked back to his car and settled in for the duration. Took his cell phone out and reported his position to the city police. Nothing ruined a good surveillance quicker than the locals rolling up on you because the neighborhood watch was on the ball…

———————

AFTER A FEW MINUTES OF WAITING IN LINE AT THE pharmacy, Sandy explained her symptoms to the pharmacist, an aging gentleman with thinning grey hair and the start of Andy Rooney brows perched over soft, blue eyes. His name tag read, 'Your CVS Pharmacist: Phil.'

"For how long now?" he asked after Sandy explained how she felt.

"Quite a few days. Almost a week, now that I think about it. It comes and goes, but I'm having trouble keeping anything down. I've got a flight tomorrow morning back to Indy on a private plane and I don't want an…mmm…incident." She practically winced at herself when she said the words 'private plane.' Made her feel like a pretentious snob. "I was on vacation a few years ago and ate some questionable seafood that gave me a mild case of food poisoning. This feels exactly the same."

"Do you remember what you ate before the onset of your symptoms?"

"I don't. I've been thinking about that and nothing really comes to mind. In fact, I'd have to say that it didn't really hit me all at once. More like it sort of snuck up on me. I think I'd already been feeling pretty lousy for a day or two before I really even noticed."

"Fever, chills, that sort of thing?"

"No, nothing like that."

"Are you getting plenty of fluids?"

"Absolutely. I drink water all day long."

"How about a flu shot? Have you had one?"

"No. I don't trust them."

"Good for you. I don't either. If people knew what they put in those things no one would get one. The hell of it is, most of it isn't even necessary. Aluminum. Did you know they put aluminum in there?" He shuddered.

"No, I didn't, but I've heard some horror stories. I stay away."

"I wish more people would." The pharmacist chewed on the inside of his lip for a moment. "You'll excuse the question, but in terms of your bowels…anything out of the ordinary going on there?" He actually reddened a bit when he asked the question.

"Nope. It's all good. I don't know how else to describe it, other than it feels like I've got a ball of acid floating around in there like my digestive tract is on overdrive or something."

"Stress?"

"No more than usual."

He tipped his head to the side and lowered his chin a bit. Sandy caught the expression right away. "Okay, maybe a little more than usual, but I'm a cop. I work for the police academy, so I'm no stranger to stress."

The pharmacist looked at Sandy for a moment. *Studied her.* "Just a moment, please." He left the counter and a few seconds later popped out through a side door and said, "Follow me."

He led Sandy through the store, speaking over his shoulder as he did. "There is a little something going around, but what you're describing doesn't sound quite right for that."

"What does it sound like?"

They'd stopped at the midpoint of one of the aisles and the pharmacist scanned the shelves for what he wanted. He plucked one of the packages and held it out to her. "Have you ever tried this?"

Sandy looked at the package and a nervous little laugh escaped. "No. I never have."

"Works great. Try it first thing in the morning if you can wait that long. And make an appointment with your doctor when you get home."

"I will," Sandy said.

———

SINCE VIRGIL WAS ALREADY DOWNTOWN, HE DECIDED he'd try Pate at his office first, but when he arrived at the API offices he found it locked up tight, with no cars in either the front or side parking lots. He entered Pate's home address into the map function on his phone and saw that it was a thirty-minute trip north. He dropped the car in gear and pulled out into traffic.

Saturday…early evening. Feeling the fatigue. Looking forward to seeing Sandy tomorrow.

He drove on and let his mind float out a few proposal scenarios. Realized how happy he was.

CHAPTER TWENTY-FIVE

MURTON DIDN'T HAVE TO WAIT LONG. HE WAS WATCHING a group of teenaged boys shooting hoops directly across the street from Nichole's apartment when Hector pulled up. Murton knew Hector from his undercover work on Samuel Pate. He was a large man, lean, soft-spoken, and a former special forces operative that followed orders and didn't ask questions. Perfect for a guy like Pate. Unless Hector lived in the same apartment complex as Nichole—which would be quite a coincidence—his arrival was trouble. Murton got out of his car, ducked behind a row of hedges and headed toward the basketball players.

A HALF-HOUR LATER VIRGIL PULLED INTO PATE'S DRIVE. He was surprised when Augustus Pate himself answered the door. He wore tan slacks with a white button-down shirt open at the neck. His hair looked freshly barbered and Virgil could smell his Clubman after-shave. He looked surprisingly fit for a man of his age, his face clear and his eyes bright. Pate stared at him for a moment and Virgil saw the color creep into his neck and his jaw flex with tension. His words bordered on civil. His tone did not. "What are doing at my home? You of all people."

"I'd like to speak with you about the murder of one of your former employees, Nicholas Pope."

Virgil was certain he would slam the door in his face and that would be that, but men of power and wealth are often full of surprises and Augustus Pate proved no different. He pulled the door open wide, then turned and walked into the house. It was a gesture that said at once, 'come in or leave, I don't care either way.'

Virgil followed him inside and closed the door.

———————

PATE'S SHOES ECHOED OFF THE MARBLE FLOOR AS VIRGIL followed him down the long hallway. The sound was oddly familiar in a distant sort of way, but Virgil didn't know why. Something about the cadence of Pate's step, the way the sound reverberated off the walls. They ended up in his study, a richly appointed room that may have been at least half as large as Virgil's entire house. A large desk was positioned in front of a wide set of windows.

Four high-back leather chairs were arranged in a semi-circle with small square end tables between the chairs. On the other side of the room, an ornately carved coffee table was positioned in front of a sofa that faced a stone fireplace. A set of French doors gave onto a patio with an in-ground pool surrounded with white wrought iron tables and chairs.

They sat opposite each other in the high-backed chairs. Pate sipped from a quarter full glass of amber liquid that looked like bourbon or scotch and then set the goblet gently on the table next to his chair. When he spoke his words were direct and left little doubt that Virgil's agenda was not the only issue at hand.

"You've brought nothing but misery and grief into my life, Detective. I hold you personally responsible for the death of my son and daughter-in-law."

"I'm not surprised you feel that way. I can't begin to tell you how many times over the years I've watched people of means delude themselves with a false sense of self-righteous indignation and entitlement at the expense of others. They either wear it like a crown or hide behind it, victims of their own making. You should be congratulated though. I don't think I've ever seen anyone who managed to pull off both at the same time."

"How dare you, sir. You come to my home uninvited and have the audacity to lecture me—"

"Save it, Pate. Your son was a degenerate and a pedophile who burned his own church to the ground to collect on the insurance. When he killed himself he did so because he wasn't man enough to face the consequences of his own actions. And your daughter-in-law? She gunned down my father in his own bar. He was a man of respect who spent his entire life in the service of others. So, yeah, I do have the audacity. Do not try to take my measure in that regard."

Augustus Pate pointed a hooked finger at him. When he spoke, Virgil thought his voice would be filled with rage, but it wasn't. Pate lowered his hand back to his lap and visibly swallowed. "He was still my son." His voice was so soft Virgil had to lean forward in the chair to hear him. "My only child. My only family other than his wife, Amanda. Samuel's mother died during childbirth. Did you know that? The expression on your face tells me you might not. We were very happy, Samuel's mother and I. The plans we had…a life full of hope, a house full of children." He turned his head away and let his gaze roam around the room. "I never wanted any of this. It simply… came to me. I was a steelworker in the union when Samuel was born, when my wife died.

"I'm certain my son turned out the way he did because of me. I was starting a business…the long hours, the lack of attention…I suppose they call that neglect these days, don't they? He grew up alone, without a mother and an all too inattentive father. Is it any wonder he turned out the way he did? Genetics had nothing to do with it. He sought comfort in his religion. He also found fame and fortune.

The children though, the pictures…it was either a way to find his own childhood, to get it back, or a way to deflect his pain away from himself and on to others."

Then something odd happened. A mixture of embarrassment and anger played across Pate's face. He looked like a man who might have just been awakened from a bad dream in front of a room full of people. "Why are you looking at me like that?"

Virgil wasn't sure how to answer.

"Do you think I want your pity? You're mistaken. I want nothing of the sort. In fact, you're wrong on many levels Detective. I wear no crown and I'm no one's victim."

"I'm not going to play your game, Pate."

"I can assure you, I'm not playing games, Detective."

"Then stop lying to me."

"I haven't lied to you. Not once."

"You have. Every time you refer to me as 'detective' it is a lie of omission regarding facts. I'm no longer with the state police and you know that."

He smiled without warmth or humor. "Ah yes, that's right. You're Wheeler's bitch now, aren't you?"

Don't take the bait, Virgil told himself…

MURTON SAT ON A BENCH THAT PLACED THE TEENAGERS between him and the front of Nichole Pope's apartment door. He had the perfect view and if Hector happened to look his way he would only notice a man watching a group of kids play ball.

Hector did almost exactly the same thing Murton had done a few minutes ago. He knocked, tried the knob and put his ear close to the door. But then, instead of knocking or trying the knob again, he straightened his arm and let a small pry bar slide down from the inside of his jacket sleeve. He pressed the bar between the knob and the jamb, put some weight into it and popped the door.

Murton got up from the bench and started running that way.

———

BUT HE GOT TANGLED UP IN THE BALLPLAYERS AND HE ended up on the ground. "Jeez, Mister, you okay?" one of the kids asked. Murton ignored the boys, rolled onto his side and stood up in time to see Hector leaving Nichole Pope's apartment. He turned so Hector couldn't see him, but now, facing the boys, he could see they were getting impatient with him. He made a show of dusting off his pants and straightening his shirt as he backed off the court toward the apartment complex. Once Hector was back in his car and around the corner, Murton began to run to Nichole's door.

Over his shoulder he heard one of the boys say, "Fuck him. Come on, bang out."

When he got to the door Murton wasn't sure what he'd find. His first thought was a body—Nichole's, but Hector hadn't left in a rush. He'd simply walked away like no one was home. The wood was splintered around the jamb, little pieces of it on the ground right below the knob. Murton took out his gun, nudged the door open with his foot and took a quick peek. Nothing there. He went in hard, following his gun sight. Main room empty. He put his back to the wall, spun into the kitchen—a narrow dead-end space with the sink, cabinets and fridge all on one side. Empty. When he spun around he caught his reflection in the bathroom mirror at the opposite end of the hall and almost fired. Two steps toward the bath took him to the single bedroom on his left. Another quick peek. Empty. The bifold closet doors stood open, a variety of women's clothing hanging from the bar. The bed was neatly made. The apartment was empty and Nichole wasn't there.

Murton ran back outside and took off after Hector. He tried to call Virgil but didn't get an answer. He called Becky, told her what was happening and asked her to do a background check on Hector Sigara. "I know he works for Pate, but see if you can turn anything up on him. Check his driver's license, credit history, the works."

"What about Jonesy? He went to see Pate. He's not in any danger, is he?"

Murton didn't have an answer for that. *What the hell was going on?*

Virgil felt his cell phone vibrating in his pocket, but ignored it. "Is that the best you can do? A homophobic remark intended to...what? Make me lose my cool? It won't work. Why was Brackett burning vacant buildings in Hendricks County?"

"I don't know anything about that, although I must say, it's too bad that he won't be our next sheriff. He was a huge supporter of what I wanted for that county."

"You speak of him in the past tense, Mr. Pate. Why is that?"

"Let me ask you something, detective. Do you take me for a fool? Do you think that I don't have contacts in every branch of our various government agencies that keep me informed?"

"I'm sure you do."

"Then you know that I know that Brackett is dead. Natural gas explosion at his house it seems."

"You were quite the supporter of his from what I've heard."

"Nothing illegal about that. Brackett wanted what I wanted."

"I doubt it. Brackett wanted to be sheriff. He may have even wanted to help the people of his county get back to work. It helps with the crime rate. What are you going to do now that your prison isn't going to be built?"

"Oh it will get built, Detective, I assure you."

"I doubt it."

Pate cocked his head to one side. "What are you talking about?"

"Who killed Nicholas Pope?"

"I have no idea. I barely knew the man."

"He was your head programmer on a contract worth millions of dollars and you say you barely knew him?"

"I employ hundreds of people. The fact of the matter is I haven't met most of them. What were you saying a moment ago? What makes you think the prison won't get built?"

"Was it Brackett? Did he kill Pope for you? Was he that deep into you? I don't think Sheriff Powell is going to have any trouble linking you to Brackett, and the fires, and when that happens it won't take too much of a breeze to blow your house of cards apart. You'll be indicted for Nicholas Pope's murder, then sent away for life. If that prison of yours ever does get built, you'll probably be its first customer."

Virgil expected an outburst from him. In fact, he was doing everything he could to make it happen. He was about to tell him what he'd learned at the lottery office earlier in the day; that the ticket had been verified and someone was about to come forward and claim the prize, but Pate interrupted him and that's when everything changed.

"How are you feeling, Detective?"

FACTORING IN THE TIME SPENT IN THE APARTMENT AND then getting back to his car, Murton figured Hector had about a two-minute head start. But to which location, Pate's office, or his house? The apartment complex was only a few blocks from 465, the loop that circled the city, and Murton was now less than half a block away from making a choice. North or south? One would take him to the office, the other to Pate's residence.

He rolled past the first entrance on his right, an easy glide up the ramp and onto the highway. Then he ran the red light, almost got clipped by a woman in a minivan who pounded her horn and shot him the bone before he took the hard right up and around the cloverleaf, maybe ninety-seconds back now.

And maybe going in the wrong direction.

THE QUESTION CAUGHT VIRGIL COMPLETELY OFF GUARD. "What?"

"It's a simple question, Detective. How are you feeling?"

"How am I feeling? In what context?"

Pate took a sip of his drink and made an elaborate show of placing it back on the table just so before he turned his attention back to Virgil. He grinned. "Why, your leg of course. Has it completely healed? Nasty, nasty break, I understand. Any lingering issues? Pain, tingling, difficulty with your medications? Hallucinations, perhaps? Anything like that?" He leaned forward in his chair. "Anything…at all?"

Virgil laughed out loud. "Really? You think you can get inside my head? I'm embarrassed for you."

"Oh, I don't have to get inside your head, Detective. I'm already there. I have been for quite some time. Too bad you've not noticed."

"I stand by my original statement, Pate. You're delusional. Probably psychotic as well."

"Am I?" Augustus Pate picked a piece of imaginary lint from his sleeve then leaned forward and rested his forearms on his thighs. He was close enough to touch. "The entire ordeal…it must have been so very…" he shook his head and let his voice trail away as if he couldn't find the proper words. Then an odd transformation took place. He opened his eyes wide and ran his tongue across his lips. "Tell me, Detective. What's it like to be stripped naked and hung from the rafters like you're being crucified? Were you afraid? I understand you defecated on the floor. I can only imagine the pain, the sense of hopelessness and despair, the humiliation and how that must have…well…you were there, weren't you? Did you find it surprising at how little time it took to have so much damage inflicted upon your person? I have the pictures. Would you like to see them? A little celebratory trip down memory lane? It might offer you a certain perspective that you seem to lack. No, no, let me finish if you please. You were off the mark then and you're off the mark now. Last time it almost cost you your life. They beat you senseless and robbed you of your dignity with no more effort than it took to cut the clothes from your body and hose your pile of *shit* from the floor. Do you think someone like you can simply walk into my home and question me about issues you know nothing about? I'm not the one who is delusional, Detective, you are. I understand you've been having conversations with your dead father. What an experience that must be. Tell me, does he stink yet? Has he rotted through to his core? Can you smell the stench of his soul? It's all in your head, *Virgil*. There are no wrong answers."

———————

HECTOR CAME IN THROUGH THE BACK DOOR AND HEARD Pate talking to someone in the study. He listened for a few moments at the edge of the doorway, then stepped inside. When he saw who his boss was talking to, he pulled out his stun gun and crept into the room, his eyes locked on Pate, waiting for his signal to move.

———————

Pᴀᴛᴇ's ᴜsᴇ ᴏꜰ ʜɪs ꜰɪʀsᴛ ɴᴀᴍᴇ ɪɴꜰᴜʀɪᴀᴛᴇᴅ Vɪʀɢɪʟ, ʙᴜᴛ he was right about something. Virgil *had* missed the mark. It was the sounds of his footsteps as they walked through his house. They were identical to the ones he'd heard the day he was kidnapped and tortured. The rhythm, the length of the stride, the slight shuffle of step were all precisely the same. "It was you, wasn't it? I was still blindfolded. I heard someone walk through the warehouse. I counted your steps."

Instead of pulling away he tilted his head and leaned in closer. "Of course it was me. I wouldn't have missed it for the world. I think about it every day, just as you do, I'm sure. The difference is…oh, what's that saying? One man's pleasure?"

Virgil saw Pate's eyes shift ever so slightly and when they did he jumped up from his chair, pulled his gun, grabbed Pate by the collar of his shirt and pressed the barrel to his forehead. Then he spun sideways so he could see who was behind him. "Who are you?"

The man didn't answer. Instead, he took a step closer and pressed the trigger on the stun gun. Virgil watched a blue arc skip across the metal contacts, the crackle of the electric current a sound he hoped never to hear again.

"His name is Hector," Pate said. "He works for me. He's very good at what he does. Very thorough."

Hector tried to move closer and when he did Virgil pulled Pate from the chair, got behind him and wrapped his arm around his neck, his gun now at the side of Pate's head. The three of them were moving, circling the group of chairs, keeping their distance from each other. Virgil tried to move toward the entrance of the room, but Hector blocked him. Virgil realized that Pate was giving signals to Hector so he spun him around until they faced each other and stuck the barrel of the gun under his jaw.

"Here's what we're going to do, Hector," Virgil said. "First, you're going to set your little toy down on the table behind you. Yes, that's right, that table right there. Good. Now open your jacket and remove your weapon."

"Don't do it Hector," Pate said.

Virgil pushed the gun up, further into Pate's neck. "Shut up."

"Hector, shoot him."

"I said shut up."

"How do you think this is going to end, Detective? You're in my home with a gun to my throat. What fantasy of yours doesn't end with you either dead or in jail? Hector, shoot him, now!"

Hector had his pistol pointed in Virgil's direction, but Virgil kept weaving Pate back and forth blocking his angle. "I don't have a shot, boss."

Murton took three quick steps into the room, grabbed Hector's stun gun from the table, then cocked the hammer on his .45. The sound froze everyone. "I do," he said. He sidestepped to his left to remove Virgil from his line of fire. "I've never missed from this distance, Hector, though

I guess there's a first time for everything. Want to take your chances? How's it going, Jones-man?"

———————

"IT'S GOING FINE," VIRGIL SAID. "I'VE GOT EVERYTHING under control."

"I can see that," Murton said. "Hector, drop the gun."

Hector lowered his weapon then let it drop on the floor. When he did, Murton walked up behind him, touched the stun gun to the back of his neck and gave him a jolt. Hector dropped to the ground, unconscious. "Hey these things pack quite a wallop, don't they? I might have to get one."

Virgil turned Pate around and pushed him through the French doors and out to the patio by the pool. Murton stayed right with them.

"You're fools," Pate said. "Both of you. Do you think you're going to change anything? The bill was passed in both the House and the Senate and then signed into law by McConnell. The prison is going to get built. Thanks to Bradley Pearson and Abigail Monroe, I've got the contract to run it and the entire project is going to be financed on the greed and delusions of the people of the state. Nothing you do here or in the future will change that."

Virgil let go of Pate's shirt, holstered his weapon then

laughed at him. The message was clear; he was no longer a threat in any sense of the word.

"You seem to find something amusing, Detective. Care to enlighten me?"

Virgil shook his head at him. "I'll share some of it with you, Gus. The rest you can figure out for yourself. Pearson has been playing you. He's been three steps ahead of your game from the start. You want to blame me for your son's death? Go ahead. I played a minor part in that tragedy for sure, except it was Pearson who pointed me at Samuel. The only connection your son ever had to McConnell was Amanda's affair with Sidney Wells, Jr., the governor's daughter. Pearson knew if that information ever became public, the deal he was trying to put together with you would fall apart. The first two victims of the Wells' shooting spree weren't even cold when Pearson had me looking at your son. Why do you think that is? He had nothing to do with it. The way I see it, if it weren't for Bradley Pearson, your son Samuel would still be alive. The governor told me as much not that long ago.

"What's wrong, Gus? You look a little bewildered. Let me dumb this down for you a bit. You thought you and your goons could take me out of the picture by torturing and then killing me and it almost worked. But the truth of the matter is you played right into Pearson's plans. When the Feds got involved, instead of facing the music, Samuel took his own life. It's too bad really. A good lawyer and a fat checkbook probably could have saved him, except you wouldn't have gotten your deal with the state had all that played out in the media. My guess is you and Pearson must have a pretty lucrative arrangement on your private prison contract. I really don't care about the legalities of all that. I'm not a cop anymore. I didn't kill your son, you idiot. Pearson did. Everything you had done to me was for nothing."

Virgil shoved him into the pool then held his hand out to Murton. "Let me see that stun gun." Murton handed him the device and Virgil got down near the water's edge. "Want to know how it feels to be tortured, Gus? Want to know what it's like to lose control of your bodily functions at the hands of others? Here's a little taste."

Virgil pressed the trigger on the stun gun and moved it close to the water. When Pate saw what was about to happen he began swimming frantically toward the opposite side of the pool to escape electrocution.

Virgil let him get almost to the other side...

———————

WHEN HE FELT MURTON'S HAND ON HIS SHOULDER RIGHT before the metal contacts touched the water, Virgil released the trigger and stood up. He dropped the stun gun on the concrete and smashed it with the heel of his boot, then kicked the pieces into the water. Pate was still swimming toward the far end of the pool. Murton Wheeler had in all probability saved Augustus Pate's life.

CHAPTER TWENTY-SIX

Virgil followed Murton over to Nichole's apartment. When they arrived a city squad car was parked in front of the building and two uniformed officers were standing on the sidewalk that led to Nichole's door. One of the cops moved to intercept them, but his partner pulled him back, nodded at Virgil, and said, "Hey Jonesy."

"Frank. What's going on?"

"Not sure. Miles and Donatti are inside."

"Crime scene?"

"I don't think so. At least not the kind you're used to. Looks like someone popped the door. You can go on up."

"Thanks, Frankie. Stop by the bar. Haven't seen you in a while."

"I will. You feeling okay these days?" *Translation:* Off the meds?

"Never better."

"Atta boy."

Over his shoulder Virgil heard the other cop say, "Who was that?" Then Frank said, "Go find me a cup of coffee, Boot."

———————

Ron Miles and Ed Donatti met them at the door. "Let's talk out here. I don't think we should be inside."

They all moved back out to the sidewalk and went about halfway to the street before Miles stopped. "What's going on, Ron?" Virgil said.

"When was the last time you saw or spoke with Nichole Pope?"

"A few days ago," Virgil said. "Thursday. The day she hired us. Why?"

"Donatti's got the rotation this weekend," Miles said. The rotation was this: every member of the MCU had to take their turn—at least once a month on the weekend—and be responsible for accepting incoming calls and other important messages regarding open cases. "He called me after Mimi called him."

"What's going on, Ron?"

"That's what I'd like to know. In fact, I've suddenly got quite a few questions I'd like to ask that young lady."

"What are you talking about, Ron? What kind of questions?"

"Where is Nichole, Jonesy?"

"I don't know."

Ron looked at him for a long, hard minute. A cop look. "You wouldn't try to pull a fast one on me, would you?"

"Ron, you hired us. We work for you, remember?"

"I do remember. But I hired you to figure out the meaning behind the coded message. Any progress on that?"

"Not yet."

"I see. Nichole Pope is your client, is she not?"

"Yes, Ron. She is. You already know that. But so are you."

"You're right, I do know that. So I'll ask you again. Where is she?"

"Ron, we don't—" Virgil interrupted himself and looked at Murton. "We don't know, do we?"

Murton shook his head.

Miles scratched at the back of his neck. He looked like he didn't quite believe them. "If you see her, hear from her, or have any contact with her of any kind, I want to know and I want to know right away. Am I making myself clear?"

"Crystal. Now, are you going to tell me what the hell is going on?"

"I'd like to ask her a few questions."

"What questions?"

"Oh, you know, nothing too over the top. The usual

straightforward sort of questions like, 'Where is your brother and why did you try to fake his death?'"

———————

Virgil and Murton looked at each other. *Faked her brother's death?* "Ron?"

"The budgetary cuts have hurt us, Jonesy. You know that. The state lab has been backed up for months. When the crime scene techs processed Pope's apartment some shortcuts were taken."

"What kind of shortcuts?"

"I know you've seen the pictures. That apartment was covered in blood. We got the DNA back yesterday."

"And you're telling us that it's not Nicholas Pope's blood?"

"No, it's his blood. There's no question about that."

"How about you start from the beginning?"

"Mimi was the lead technician that day. Her crew took numerous samples from the apartment and they all matched. Only one person's blood. Then Pope's sister, Nichole comes literally crashing onto the scene. When Mimi heard she was the sister—*twin* sister—she asked Nichole if she'd be willing to give a sample for comparison. The fact that they were twins would mean an exact match. Nichole said yes, Mimi took the blood and that's where we think things started to go wrong."

"Wrong how?" Murton said.

"We'd already collected all the samples by then. Mimi walked Nichole over to the mobile lab, drew the blood, then sent it out for DNA analysis and comparison."

"Yeah, so what? How do the budget cutbacks factor into all of this?" Virgil said.

"Hell Jonesy, you know how it works…if you've got a perfect match on something like we did with Pope's blood, they don't run additional tests unless the prosecution needs them for trial."

Virgil knew Ron was right. Blood work, DNA, forensic pathology, ballistics testing, it all cost money. A lot of money. When the cutbacks were put in place, if you had enough evidence to move forward without additional testing, that's exactly what you did. If your case made it to trial—and many times they did not because of plea bargains or outright guilty pleas—only then did you move forward with additional testing. If the case never made it that far, why spend the state's money if you didn't have to? "So why were additional tests run on Pope's blood, especially if the DNA matched?"

"It was at Mimi's discretion. And we got lucky. She had a class from the academy visiting the lab. One of the things she always shows them is how they do their tests. Earlier today, when the class came in she demonstrated ballistics matchups, fingerprint recovery and basic blood typing. That's when she noticed."

"Noticed what?"

"Pope's blood. The only test that had been done was

DNA. Except DNA doesn't show you anything…visually, that is. It tells you things, but it doesn't show you. If you want to see anything, you have to take the time to look through a microscope and no one had bothered to do that until the academy class showed up in Mimi's lab and she put some blood under the microscope. She used Pope's blood because it was the most current case and she had so much of the stuff. That's when she spotted the problem. All the cells had burst. Every single cell from every single sample was exactly the same."

"What causes blood cells to burst?"

"That's exactly what I asked Mimi. The cells had all burst because they'd been frozen, Jonesy. It looks like Pope's blood had been in the freezer before it ever hit the walls and floor of that apartment. Our working theory right now is that Pope's blood had been harvested over a period of weeks, maybe even months, then stored in the freezer until it was time to use it. And that means someone was trying to fake his death. The question is, was it Nicholas or his sister, Nichole, or both?"

———————

"What the hell are they up to?" Virgil said.

"That's exactly what I'd like to know," Ron said.

The four of them were so caught up in their conversation they failed to notice the young woman jogging up the street. She made it almost all the way to Nichole Pope's

apartment door before any of them took note of her destination. When she got to the door, she stopped dead in her
tracks, looked at the door, then back at them and finally at
the door again.

"Hey, hey," she shouted. "Are you guys cops? You
look like cops. What the hell is going on here? Did
someone break into my apartment?" Then she disappeared
inside.

THEY WALKED TOWARD NICHOLE'S APARTMENT, BUT
Murton grabbed Virgil's arm and pulled him back behind
Donatti and Miles. He spoke from the corner of his
mouth. "Don't say anything. Hector popped the door
earlier. That's how I ended up at Pate's. I'll explain later."

BY THE TIME THEY GOT TO THE DOOR SHE HAD ALREADY
disappeared inside. They followed her in and when she
popped back out from the bedroom the sight of them froze
her. "Who are you guys? Are you cops? Someone has
broken into my apartment."

Ron held out his badge. "Ma'am, my name is Ron
Miles. I'm a detective with the State Police Major Crimes
Unit."

"Are you here because of the break-in?" she asked.

"Excuse me, Miss," Donatti said. "Could we see your identification, please?"

"My identification? Who are you? What the hell is going on here?"

"Ma'am, I already told you. My name is Ron Miles and I'm a detective with the State Police. These gentlemen are with me. Is this your apartment?"

"Of course this is my apartment. Who did this? Have you caught them? My god, look at my door. What does a new door cost anyway? That's going to come out of my security deposit, you know."

"Yes ma'am," Miles said. "I'm sorry about that, I really am, but I've introduced myself twice now. If you don't mind my asking, what is your name?"

The young woman dug through her fanny-pack, pulled out her driver's license and handed it to Ron. "My name is Darla Walker. Would one of you please tell me what the hell is going on here?"

———

WU RANG THE BELL, WAITED, RANG THE BELL AGAIN AND then knocked until his knuckles hurt. When nobody answered he walked around the side of the house and found Pate standing next to the pool, fully clothed and dripping wet. "What happened?"

"Nothing."

"Something. You all wet."

"I was pushed into the pool. It's not important. Go inside and check on Hector."

"What wrong with Hector?"

Before Pate could answer Hector came through the French doors, his hand on the back of his neck. "They gone?"

"Yes, but not before I was almost electrocuted in my own pool. Next time I tell you to shoot, you shoot."

"I didn't have a shot, Boss."

"Bullshit. I've seen you shoot, Hector."

"Didn't have the shot. Couldn't risk it."

Wu wasn't sure what he'd missed and he really didn't care. He moved closer to both men, looked Pate in the eye and said, "Wu got bad news. Somebody claim ticket."

Pate closed his eyes, his fists clenched at his sides. Then he rushed up to Wu, grabbed the hair on both sides of his head and pulled his face so close that for a split second Wu thought he was going to get kissed. "Three hundred million dollars, Wu. That ticket is worth three hundred million dollars. That's my money." Pate let go of Wu's hair and turned away. When he turned back he looked at Wu and said, "We're out of time. We need to find out who has that ticket."

"No."

"What did you say to me?"

"Wu say no. Say no because not need. Not need because already know who has ticket. Come. Wu show you video." He walked into the house. Pate and Hector stared at each other for a moment and then followed him inside.

————————

RON LOOKED AT THE WOMAN'S DRIVER'S LICENSE, THEN her face, then back at the license before he handed it to Virgil, who did the same thing. The picture, description and address all matched with the woman who stood in front of them. Virgil handed the license to Donatti and tilted his head toward the hallway. Ed nodded, took out his phone and stepped outside.

"Hey, where's he going with that?" the woman said.

"He's not going anywhere," Virgil said. "He's running a check on your identification. It's standard procedure." She looked, Virgil thought, like she didn't quite believe him. "Do you live alone?"

"Yes. It's a one-bedroom unit in case you haven't noticed. I'm not married, no roommate, no kids, so yes, I live alone."

"How long have you lived here?"

She furrowed her eyebrows, the math going in her head. "A little over three years or so. Almost four."

Donatti walked back in, handed the license back to the woman, and said, "Ms. Walker. Sorry for the intrusion."

They asked a few more questions to verify her identity and she cooperated, but it felt like the type of cooperation you'd expect if the police were questioning you in your own home over something you knew nothing about. "Ms. Walker, I'd like to ask you a couple of personal questions. You're under no obligation to answer, but if you will, it would be a huge help to our investigation."

"You never told me what you *are* investigating."

Virgil grinned at her. "With all due respect, it's not the break-in of your apartment."

"No kidding. Even I was able to put that together, about ten minutes ago if you haven't been keeping up. So what are you investigating?"

"We're not at liberty to say," Murton said.

"Well, that sounds about right." She crossed her arms, sucked in her cheeks and nodded. "So ask. Maybe I'll answer."

"That's fair enough," Virgil said. "How's your credit?"

"Good enough that I don't have to worry about it constantly. Bad enough that I worry about paying for a busted door."

"Ever have any identity theft problems?"

"Yeah, as a matter of fact. I had my purse stolen from a cell phone kiosk at the mall. I turned my back for maybe ten-seconds and when I turned back around it was gone. That's where the credit problems came from."

"When was this?"

"Right after I moved in here."

"I see."

"What is this about?" When no one answered her question she brushed past them and stood next to her open door. "This place where all of you are standing? It's a crappy little apartment with secondhand furniture and wilted plants and thin carpet and thinner walls and a hot water heater that has the work ethic of a spoiled rich kid. That means it works when it wants to, which isn't all that often. Whatever is going on here has nothing to do with me. This is my home. It's not your crime scene, or your office and clearly I'm not your victim. Goodbye, gentlemen."

Virgil smiled. Couldn't argue that logic.

———

Wu turned the laptop on and brought up the video. Not a video, though. Not really. It was a series of stills taken from a security camera mounted on a light pole outside the entrance of a mini-mart on the city's east side. Wu knew the camera well because he was the one who installed it six days ago. It was the same mini-mart where Bradley Pearson stopped every morning for his coffee and newspapers.

"Wu create program. Program detect winning ticket and trigger security camera." It was all bullshit, but Wu knew they'd buy it.

Pate and Hector leaned in and looked at the screen. "Let's see them, Wu."

A little wheel spun on the screen. "Still loading. Few more seconds. Maybe Wu should upgrade your Wi-Fi."

Before anyone could say anything about that, Wu's phone began to vibrate on the table next to his computer.

"Aren't you going to answer your phone, Wu?" Hector said. "Wow, look at that picture. She's hot. Who is that?"

Wu looked at his phone. "Wife. Wu call back."

They all stared at the little wheel for a few more seconds, waiting for the pictures to show up. Wu's phone began to vibrate again. "For God's sake," Pate said. "Answer the damn phone already."

Wu picked up the phone, swiped his thumb across the screen, held it to his ear and said, "Wu."

———

THE WOMAN WITH THE SECONDHAND FURNITURE AND wilting plants and thin carpet and thinner walls and a hot water heater that had the work ethic of a spoiled rich kid had a name, but it wasn't Darla Walker. Her real name was Linda and she was Wu's wife. Linda Wu watched from the window until the police all got in their vehicles and drove away, then she waited ten agonizing minutes to make sure that they weren't coming back. When they did not, she took out her phone and called her husband.

"It worked, Wu. Exactly like you said it would."

"Good, good. Perhaps you should go now. Pizza will be fine."

"Can't talk, huh?"

"No, perhaps one hour. With traffic I would say go now. Yes, Domino's."

"Gotcha. See you on the beach, big boy."

———————

"Domino's?" Hector said. "Christ, Wu, that's not pizza."

"Wu still like."

"They deliver, you know."

"Wu not trust delivery people. They steal toppings. Here come pictures." The little wheel on the screen had disappeared and the first picture popped up. This was the critical part, Wu thought. If they didn't believe the pictures, he wouldn't make it out of the house alive.

"I thought you said it was video," Pate said.

"Hmm, like video, but not video. Pictures taken at rapid intervals. Five per second. Like choppy video."

"Yes, yes, Wu. Let's see them."

Wu pressed the play button and the pictures began stuttering along in sequence. He didn't need to look at the pictures; he'd spent all day manipulating them on Photoshop, bringing out the clarity, tweaking the contrast, adjusting the brightness and so on. He instead watched the look on Pate's face when he saw the pictures of Bradley Pearson and Nichole Pope walking out of the mini-mart, her hand tucked into the crook of his arm. They stopped right outside the door, exactly as Nichole had intended, their faces framed perfectly for the camera. Then they looked at each other and Pearson said something. The visual was perfect. Nichole tipped her head back, the laughter obvious. Then she placed her other hand on Pearson's chest, both of them smiling like idiots before they walked out of the frame.

They looked, Wu thought, like two people who might have just won three hundred million dollars.

―――――――――――

PATE TURNED AWAY FROM THE LAPTOP, WALKED OVER TO the bar and poured himself a drink. He downed it in two large gulps and poured another before walking back over to Wu. "Play it again." Wu played the slideshow again and when it was finished Pate threw his glass against the stone fireplace, the cut crystal tinkling around the room. "Hector?"

"Yes, Boss?"

"Get the car."

"Yes, Boss."

Pate looked at Wu. "Print me one of the pictures with Pearson and the woman."

Wu pressed a few keys and Pate's printer began to hum. When the printer was finished, Pate picked up the photograph and studied the image.

"What you going to do?"

"I'm going to have a little chat with our Mr. Pearson and find out who this woman is."

"Not need."

"What?"

"Not need. Wu know who. Name Nichole Pope. Nicky Pope's sister."

When Pate heard that it sent him right over the edge and right out the door.

Wu closed his computer, wiped down everything he'd touched—there hadn't been much, so that little detail took all of twenty-seconds—put the laptop in his bag and walked away.

His part was over.

CHAPTER TWENTY-SEVEN

VIRGIL AND MURTON ENDED UP BACK AT THE BAR FOR A late Saturday dinner. The house band had already started playing, and the noise was so loud they could barely talk to each other. They went upstairs to the office and found Becky working at the desk. The office itself looked like a train had derailed. Empty computer boxes were scattered everywhere and little pieces of crumbled Styrofoam were stuck to the carpet, chairs and virtually everything in the room. Murton walked behind the desk, kissed the top of her head and told her that they needed everything she could get on Nichole Pope.

"You want me to stop working on this code thing?"

"No," Virgil said.

"Good, because I think I'm close. What happened with Nichole?"

They spent about fifteen minutes filling her in and when

they finished she shooed them out of the office so she could work in peace. They ended up sitting down to eat at the only spot available…the employee picnic bench outside the kitchen entrance at the back of the bar. Robert brought two plates of food out and a few minutes later Delroy stepped through the back door with two glasses of juice. He set them on the table, lit a cigarette and then sat down. "Busy, mon?"

"Not as busy as you from the looks of it," Virgil said. "Everything going okay?"

"Yeah mon, everyting irie." Then he looked at Murton and said, "'Irie' Jamaican slang. It mean 'everything all right.'"

"I know that."

"Uh-huh." Delroy winked at Virgil.

"You and Robert are coming tomorrow afternoon, right?"

"Yeah mon, yeah."

"Coming where?" Murton said.

"Uh, I almost forgot," Virgil said. "Sandy and I wanted to invite you and Becky over tomorrow afternoon. Little get-together. No big deal."

"I guess not since you're only now mentioning it."

"How does one o'clock sound?"

"It sounds like you forgot is what it sounds like."

Becky burst through the back door. She waved a piece of paper at them. "I think I've got it…the code. You guys better come and take a look."

Pate had the cut-down 20 gauge with a pistol grip and Hector had a throw-away .32 fitted with a suppressor. They'd leave the .32 behind, minus the suppressor, of course. They'd worked out the plan—impromptu as it was —on the way over. In a way, Pate was disappointed. He had it in the back of his head that Pearson could be saved, that they could continue working together, except no one had ever screwed him out of three cents, much less three hundred million bucks and Pearson wasn't going to be the exception.

They walked up to Pearson's door and Hector gave a polite little knock, the kind a neighbor, or pizza delivery person might make. *Tap, tap, tap.*

When Pearson opened the door a few seconds later, Hector was on him like a malnourished pit-bull. He grabbed him by the throat, stuck the gun against his forehead and backed him right down the hall. Pate closed the door and followed them in.

"It's octal," Becky said. "The code. It was right there the whole time. I finally figured it out."

"What the hell is octal?" Virgil said.

"It's a numerical numbering system built on a base

eight platform using the digits zero through seven," Murton said.

Virgil and Becky stared at him.

"What? I'm educated."

Virgil looked at Becky for verification. "He's right," she said. "Boy, that makes me a little wet."

"Becky…"

"Yeah, yeah. So I was completely stumped at first. I mean, it's nothing more than a random set of numbers right? So I started thinking, what if the numbers corresponded to map or grid coordinates. Let me tell you, it didn't take long to figure out that that wasn't right, unless the meaning of the code had something to do with the Sea of Japan at thirty-thousand feet. Then I thought, maybe it's as simple as the numbers matching up with letters of the alphabet, you know, like the numeral one is equal to the letter 'A' and the numeral two is equal to 'B' and so on. Except that didn't work either because there were too many zero's in there unless you factor in that zero was equal to 'a' and one was equal to 'B' but that didn't work out either, so I went back to the basics. Pope was a programmer. A coder, right? So I looked at all the basic coding systems like ASCII, HEX, and octal. ASCII and HEX didn't pan out, but when I got to octal—"

"Becky?"

She tilted her head to the side and batted her eyelashes. "Yes, Virgie?"

"What does it mean?"

She pointed at the paper and said, "I broke the number sequence down into groups of three. The first three numbers...one, zero, and two? It's actually the number one hundred and two. In the octal system, that number corresponds to the letter 'B.' the sequence breaks down to five letters: B, P, C, o, S."

Virgil took the paper from her and looked at the letters. "Is that a zero, right there between the 'C' and the 'S,' or is it the letter 'O.'"

"It's the lower case letter."

"That's what I thought." Virgil pulled out his phone.

"What is it, Jones-man?"

"It's Pearson. Those letters stand for Bradley Pearson, Chief of Staff."

"How do you know?" Murton said.

"He notices things like that," Becky said.

———

VIRGIL LISTENED TO PEARSON'S PHONE RING FIVE TIMES before it clicked over to voice mail. He hung up without leaving a message.

Murton was skeptical. "You know those letters could mean almost anything. Maybe they stand for British Petroleum Community outreach Services. Or, Borrow Plunger, Commode over Stuffed."

Virgil ignored him and dialed Pearson's number again.

As the phone was ringing he heard him say, "Baked Pretzel Cheese on Side…"

———————

ABBY HAD A FULL BOTTLE OF BORDEAUX—THE GOOD stuff from the rack, not the cheap kind Pearson kept in the kitchen cabinet—and when she came around the corner and saw Hector holding the gun to Bradley's head she let out a yelp, dropped the bottle and ran for the back door. Pate said, "Go," leveled the pistol grip on Pearson and backed him right onto the living room sofa. "If you say one word, make one fucking noise, you will die right here and right now. Look into my eyes and tell me I'm lying. Nod if you understand."

Pearson swallowed, then nodded.

———————

VIRGIL LOOKED AT MURTON. "LET'S TAKE A RIDE."

"Let me guess," he said. "Over to Pearson's?"

"It's about five minutes from here."

"Only three if I drive. That leaves me two minutes to eat my dinner."

"Murt…"

"Yeah, yeah." He looked at Becky. "I love him, I really do, but everything's always an emergency. Get used to it."

"Be nice," Becky said. "Besides, it's kind of exciting. Can I come?"

"No," Murton said as he stood up.

"Why not? I can handle myself."

"I'm sure you can. But it's going to take us three minutes to get there, thirty-seconds to see that there is nothing to see, and three minutes to get back."

"So?"

"So I need you to guard my dinner. I'm starving."

"Can we go now?" Virgil said.

"Yeah," Murton said. "I'm waiting on you."

———

HECTOR FOLLOWED MONROE OUT THE BACK, SAW HER scramble over the neighbor's fence two houses away, and took off after her. He got to the fence right as she was turning the corner next to a detached garage that backed up to an alleyway. When she tripped over a downspout extension and went down, Hector leveled the .32 across the top of the fence rail, aimed in the fading light at the spot where she would be when she stood and waited no more than a half-second before he pulled the trigger three times.

Abby stood and when she did she felt the slugs hit her in the back. She didn't know that she'd been shot, only that something had hit her from behind—hard—pushing her into the side of the garage. Her knees gave out and she slid face-first against the siding. When her head slipped past chest level on the way down she saw her own blood, but it didn't register with her.

A dog began to bark not far away. Porch lights from the house on the far side of the garage lit up. Somebody opened a back door and shouted "Hey!" but Hector was already gone.

———————————

"I'M GOING TO ALLOW YOU TO SPEAK NOW, BRADLEY. Do not disappoint me with your answers. There may be a way out of this for you. Admittedly, I'm having a little trouble with that particular scenario, but I don't deny the possibility of its existence. Are you with me so far?"

Pearson nodded, his brain working almost as hard as his heart. "Gus, I don't know what's happening here. Why are you—"

"Don't think, Bradley. Thinking right now would be a mistake. I'm going to ask you some very simple questions and you're going to give me some very simple and truthful answers."

Hector came through the back door and into the living room. "We're out of time, Boss."

"This should only take a moment."

"We don't have a moment."

Pate ignored Hector and kept his focus on Pearson.

"Boss…"

"I said just a moment, Hector. We're almost finished here."

"Interesting choice of words."

"Bradley, where is the lottery ticket?"

"What? What ticket? Gus, I don't know what you're talking about."

Pate took the picture from his coat pocket and handed it to Pearson. "This is a security camera photo of you and Nichole Pope leaving a convenience store together only seconds after the winning ticket was electronically verified. Don't make me ask you again, Bradley. Where is the ticket?"

Pearson looked at the photo and when he saw the woman on his arm, her smiling face, the way they'd looked at each other for that split second, he knew he'd been played by the Pope twins. Had she been in possession of the ticket the entire time? How was that possible? Wu would have told him. *Ah, Wu.* He was with the twins. Jesus, how long had they been working him? He shook his head. Knew he'd never get the answer to that even as he played his last card. What did they call that in Vegas? Going out?

"Nichole has it. She played us, Gus. You and me both."

Pate gave Hector a quick look. "That may or may not be true, but you know what the difference is between you and me, Bradley?"

"What's that, Gus?"

"I'm going to live to agonize over it."

Pate stepped back and when he did, Hector put the gun to the side of Pearson's head and pulled the trigger.

———————

THEY TOOK SANDY'S CAR AND HEADED FOR PEARSON'S house. "Maybe it stands for Bring Pastries, Croissants or Strudels."

Virgil didn't answer.

"Bad Puppy Chewed on Sofa."

"Would you give it a rest, please?"

"I'm just saying, it could mean anything, like, Bug Problem Caterpillars on Screen."

"I get it. Don't make me pull this car over. I will let you out."

"You drive like an old lady. I would have had us there by now. Maybe it's Bowel Problems, Can't order Sushi…"

———————

PEARSON WAS DEAD ON THE COUCH. HIS BODY WAS slumped sideways, like he'd fallen asleep, or passed out drunk, except for the blood and brain tissue splattered everywhere. "Quickly now," Hector said. "Stand back." Pate moved out of the way and Hector folded Pearson's hand around the grip of the pistol, then fired into the wall opposite the sofa. The suppressor worked well. The loudest sound was the cycling action of the gun. He let Pearson's arm fall to his side. "I am certain the police are already on their way. The woman made some noise when she went down. What have you touched?"

"Nothing. Not one single thing. Wait, that's not right. I closed the front door. The inside handle."

"What else?"

"Nothing, I'm sure."

"The picture. Leave it or take it?"

Pate thought for a moment. "Leave it. It points away from us. Adds confusion."

Hector took a cloth napkin from the table and wiped the photo then let it fall to the floor. "Let's go then. Right now. Do not touch anything on your way out."

"This isn't my first party, Hector."

"Still, touch nothing." Hector wiped the door handle, first inside and then after pulling the door shut, the outside. He tried turning the knob to make sure the door was locked—it was. They walked to the car, got in and drove away. They saw no one and no one saw them.

"We may need alibis, just to be safe," Pate said.

"It is already taken care of."

"We have to find this woman, Hector. This Nichole Pope. And it has to happen before Monday morning."

"Yes, Boss. I'm taking care of that, too."

Virgil pulled the car to a stop in front of Pearson's house and saw a number of lights on inside. It looked like he was home. He heard sirens in the distance. Murton looked at the clock on the dash and did the math. "Seven and a half minutes. I should probably call Becky. She might be getting worried."

"You're a regular riot sometimes, you know that?"

"Sometimes?"

They got out of the car and made their way up the sidewalk. Murton said, "Tell me more about this shindig you're having tomorrow afternoon."

"It's not a shindig. It's a little get-together with friends."

"Huh."

"What?"

"Nothing. Big Party Coming on Sunday."

Virgil thought, *dear God.*

Murton knocked on the door with the side of his fist...a cop knock. They waited a few minutes then knocked again but no one answered. Virgil tried the knob, but it was locked. The sirens they'd heard a few moments ago were now much closer, less than a block away. Then, abruptly, they stopped. Virgil walked around to the side of the house and saw the blue and red flashers bouncing off the houses where the backyards met. Pearson's kitchen window was right next to him, above a flower box filled with weeds. When he peeked into the kitchen window he saw the broken wine bottle on the floor. The rest of the kitchen looked normal, but he was getting a bad feeling. The layout of the house prevented him from seeing into any of the other rooms. He went back around to the front and saw Murton trying to look through the front window, his gun in his hand. "What is it?"

"Pearson's either the worst housekeeper on the planet or those are the filthiest sheer curtains I've ever seen. I can't see inside so I'm not sure, but that looks like blood spatter on the drapery."

"We've got to find a way inside," Virgil said.

Murton took a giant step backward, raised his right foot and kicked the door. Hard. The door splintered and swung inward and when it did he looked at Virgil and said, "Found one."

Virgil pulled his gun and they entered the house. When they turned into the living room Virgil saw Pearson's body on the couch, the gun still in his hand. "Ah, shit."

Murton looked at Pearson, then Virgil. "Bradley Pearson, Chief of Staff."

CHAPTER TWENTY-EIGHT

TWO CITY SQUAD CARS WERE THE FIRST TO ARRIVE, followed by Metro Homicide, then three more city cars, along with paramedics, the coroner and the crime scene investigators. Miles, Donatti, and Rosencrantz showed up somewhere in the middle of it all. They separated Virgil and Murton for questioning, which was standard proce-dure. Donatti took Murton's statement and Rosencrantz took Virgil's. When they were finished, Miles came out of the house, asked them a few repetitive questions, then went back inside for a few more minutes.

"Where's Cora?" Virgil said to Rosencrantz.

"Hell if I know, dude. Miles said he hasn't been able to reach her."

"Saturday night."

"Yeah."

Virgil tilted his head toward Miles. "How's he doing?"

Rosencrantz thought about the question. "I'll tell you something, Jonesy, he's a fine investigator. He really is. But the political aspects of the position might be a little more significant than what he anticipated. Culture shock I'd say."

"I know the feeling. Would you excuse me for a minute, Rosie? I've got a couple of calls to make."

"You bet. Tell her I said hello."

"Say, listen, if you're not doing anything tomorrow afternoon, you and Donatti should stop by my place around one. Tell Ed to bring his wife and kid."

———

VIRGIL CALLED CORA BUT SHE DIDN'T ANSWER. HE LEFT her a message and asked her to call him back, or preferably Ron Miles as soon as possible. He didn't say why and did his best to keep the tension out of his voice. Then he called Sandy. "I love you, Small."

"Hi, Baby. I love you too. How are you?"

"Missing you, that's how I am."

"Do you pine for me?"

"You have to ask?"

"Nope. But I do like to hear it."

"I do. I am. Pining. Listen, how long would it take you to get packed up and ready to go?"

"Wow, you really *do* miss me, don't you?"

"I do, but—"

"I'm already packed, Virgil. We leave at six tomorrow morning. The governor's got some sort of prayer breakfast or something he needs to be back for."

"Yeah, okay. Where's the governor right now, do you know?"

"He's in his room. I just talked to him. What's up?"

"Okay, listen, out of respect for the governor I'm going to ask you to do something for me…for him. I want you dressed and ready to go. Unless I'm mistaken, you'll be coming back tonight."

"Oh Virgil, what's happened?"

"It's Pearson," Virgil said, and he then told her the rest of it. "What I'd like you to do is wait two minutes, then go knock on his door. He may need your…support, your guidance."

"Are you and Murt okay?"

"That, Small, is why I love you. Yes, I'm fine. Murton's fine. We're all good. Two minutes, Sandy. And I'll see you later tonight."

———

THE GOVERNOR ANSWERED ALMOST IMMEDIATELY. "IF YOU were to ask me what I'm doing right now, Jonesy, I'd have to lie to you, so don't ask."

"I won't, but now I am going to wonder."

"Oh, what the hell, I'll tell you. But you've got to promise that you won't tell anyone. It'll destroy my tough-guy image. I'm ironing my boxer shorts. Well, not only my boxers. I'm ironing everything. Shirts, pants, the works. Even my socks. I've been doing it for years, actually. It's something of a meditational process, I think. I know I enjoy it. I always have. I'll tell you something else; I do not think that makes me weird, no matter what my housekeeper might tell you."

"Governor, in about thirty seconds or so, Sandy is going to knock on your door. I asked her to. I thought you might need some…support."

"Support? Support for what?"

"I'm afraid I have some bad news, sir…" In the background, Virgil heard the knock on the governor's door.

———

THE GOVERNOR OPENED THE DOOR AND ONCE SANDY WAS inside he put the phone on speaker and set it on the table in the corner of his suite. The two of them sat down, the governor took a breath then said, "Tell me."

———

HE SAID THE WORDS 'TELL ME' AND SUDDENLY VIRGIL didn't quite know how to say it. In the brief pause that developed the governor said, "It's Pearson, isn't it?"

"Yes, sir, I'm afraid so. If you'll pardon the question, how did you know?"

"If it were anyone in my family the call would come from the state police chaplain. If it were Cora, or perhaps any member of the House, Senate, or my cabinet, the call would come from Bradley. An act of terrorism in the city or anywhere in the state would prompt a call from the Indiana Director of Homeland Security. The fact that you are calling me means…well, it means I'm correct, aren't I?"

"Yes, sir. I'm afraid so."

"Just a moment, Jonesy." Then Virgil heard him say, "Sandy, let me see your phone for a minute, will you?" After another brief pause he said, "Rich, yeah, it's me. Are you guys sober? Okay. I need to be wheels up inside of sixty minutes for Indy. Can you make that happen? Good. See you then."

"Okay Virgil, I'm back. Tell me. Tell me everything."

And that's what Virgil did.

―――――――――――

NINETY MINUTES LATER THEY GOT OFF THE PLANE AND came through the security gate next to the parking lot. Sandy gave Virgil a hug and a kiss.

"I brought your car," Virgil said to Sandy. "The keys are in the ignition. We'll be right there."

When she turned her back the governor reached into his pocket and handed Virgil the ring. "I don't think I've ever met two people who belong together more than you and Sandy. Everybody thinks that when they first get together, but with the two of you it's actually true, right down to the core."

Virgil stuck the ring in his pocket. "Thank you, Governor."

He pointed his finger at him. "Don't fuck it up."

"No, Sir. I won't."

"Let's go then. It's late and I've got a long night ahead of me."

Virgil and the governor tossed the bags in the trunk and the three of them piled into the car, the governor in the back seat. Virgil put the car in gear, touched eyes with the governor in the rearview mirror and said, "Office, or home, Sir?"

"Neither. Take me to Bradley's house, Detective."

They rode mostly in silence. The governor stared out the side window and watched the city lights move past. When he spoke it was mostly to himself. "He was… necessary. Guys like Pearson always are. Make no mistake, I knew what he was. He was a player, a manipulator, a backroom dealmaker and a political operator of the highest order. That's not necessarily a compliment. He was all of those things but he was also my friend. We came up together. I wouldn't be here without him, so it's probably safe to say he wouldn't be dead right now if it weren't for me."

Neither Virgil nor Sandy said anything in response and they all rode in silence the rest of the way to Pearson's house. They were stopped a block away by two city squad cars parked nose-to-nose in the street. One of the officers made a motion with his hands, a back up and turn around motion, but Virgil crept forward anyway. The look of anger on the cop's face was evident and when Virgil buzzed the window down he heard it in his voice as well. "What part of turn around and go the other way don't you understand?"

"Back your car out of the way, Officer. We need to get through."

The cop took a half step back and unsnapped his holster strap. "Sir, turn the car off and step out. Keep your hands where I can see them."

The governor leaned forward from the back seat. "Remember when cops used to be the good guys, Jonesy? They used to be friendly and kind and considerate and helpful and caring. Serve and Protect used to mean they served and protected *us*. Now if you don't do exactly what they say when they say it, you get a gun in your face. What's wrong with people anymore?"

"I'm not sure, Governor."

"Neither am I. It's less than a block. I think I'll walk from here."

The cop had drawn his weapon. "Sir. I will not ask you again. Step from the vehicle. Now."

"Pearson wouldn't kill himself. Not in a million years. Suicides are cowards. Everyone knows that. No matter what you or anyone thought of Bradley Pearson, I can tell you this: He was many things but he was not a coward. I expect you to find who did this. Do you hear me, Jonesy? You. I expect *you* to do it. You'll have the full weight and support of my office, badge or no badge. Anything you need."

"Yes, Sir."

McConnell opened the back door, got out and walked up to the city cop. "My name is Hewitt McConnell. I'm the governor of the state of Indiana. Bradley Pearson was my chief of staff and my friend. I'm going to walk up to his house now and I don't need or require your permission. Before I do though, let me ask you this: What is your name, young man?"

Regardless of the circumstances, Virgil had to smile when he saw the look on the cop's face. He turned the car around and drove home.

CHAPTER TWENTY-NINE

Virgil pulled the car into the garage and moved to grab Sandy's bags from the trunk, but she stopped him before he got the lid open. "Later," she said. "Let's sit and unwind a little, if that's okay. I'd like to talk to you about something. It's important."

"Sure. Why don't you head down by the pond? I'll grab us a couple of Red Stripes and be right there."

"Hmm, it's pretty late. Just water for me."

"No problem. I'll be right down."

Virgil grabbed two beers for himself and a couple of bottles of water for Sandy, put them into a small cooler with ice and went down to the pond.

He had the ring in his pocket and his future wife was waiting for him.

———————

He handed Sandy a bottle of water, opened a beer for himself, lit a fire in the pit and then sat down next to her. "It sounds like you've had a busy couple of days," she said.

Before he could even respond his phone rang. "Sorry," Virgil said.

"It's okay. A lot going on. Go ahead and take it."

Virgil looked at the screen before he answered. "Hello, Cora. Thanks for calling back."

"Would you kindly tell me what in the hell you were thinking?"

"Is there any chance that you could be a little more specific?"

"Who takes it upon themselves to pick up the phone and call the most powerful man in the state while he is out of town on official state business and inform him of the death of one of his closest advisors? Who transports him around in their personal vehicle without protection, all while bypassing standard emergency protocols—protocols I might add, that you happen to be intimately familiar with. If that's not enough for you, who in their right mind lets the governor of the state of Indiana out of the car and allows him to walk a full city block through a residential neighborhood, right out in the open past God knows how many media people and onto a crime scene in the middle of the night? Who does all of that? Have you lost your mind?"

"My first call was to you, Cora. I got your voicemail. I left you a message to call me, or preferably Ron Miles as soon as possible. Have you spoken to Ron? Based on your attitude and your characterization of the governor's actions over the last half hour or so, I'd say you have."

"You would be mistaken. I was at the movies. When I walked outside after the show and turned my phone on it was already ringing. I found out about your little cluster-fuck from the governor himself when he called me."

"My clusterfuck? How exactly does this land in my lap?"

"It lands in your lap exactly this way: You and your partner broke into a private residence, destroyed a crime scene and obliterated any chance of gathering meaningful and untainted forensic evidence directly related to what may turn out to be a capital murder case, the victim being one of the highest-ranking officials in the state."

"It was a judgment call, Cora. We didn't know if Pearson was dead or not. Murton and I gained entry into the residence, discovered his body, cleared the house, backed out and made the appropriate calls. One of those calls was to the governor. He asked me to pick him up at the airport. What would you have done?"

"Don't you question me. You are in no position what-soever to—"

"Cora?"

"*WHAT?*"

"What's wrong?"

"*What's wrong?*"

"I mean what's wrong between you and me? I don't know what to do. I don't know how to repair our relationship. I've made some mistakes, I realize that and I'm doing everything I can to make that right. But my mistakes...they were in my personal life and I don't know why you've been so angry with me. Help me understand what it is. Tell me what to do to make it right and I promise you I'll do everything I can to fix it."

She hung up without responding.

Virgil was so caught up in his conversation with Cora that he'd failed to notice Sandy as she stood from her chair. After Cora hung up, he turned and saw her as she was coming out from underneath the branches of the willow tree. "What the heck is this?" she said.

———————————

SHE HELD A PACKAGED TOY FISHING POLE IN HER HANDS. It was the same toy pole that the young boy, Wyatt, had been carrying when Virgil had encountered him in the park. The same pole that he had dropped on the hill before he ran off...the same pole Virgil had carried back to his truck. Earlier in the day the tow-truck driver had given Virgil his card with a cell phone number on the back. He punched in the number and waited for the connection to go through.

"Virgil, what's going on?" Sandy said.

"I'm sorry, baby, this will only take a second."

Virgil got the driver on the phone and asked him to check the truck. A few minutes later he came back on the line with an answer Virgil didn't know how to process.

"You're sure?"

"Positive. I'm sorry Mr. Jones, but it's not there. I looked under the seat and behind it, too. Nothing on the floor or in the bed. If you think the fault is ours, we've got insurance to cover this sort of thing."

"No, no, that's all right. I'm sure I must have misplaced it. Thank you."

Virgil took the pole from Sandy and examined it carefully, deciding it was definitely the same one Wyatt had carried in the park, the same one he'd taken with him in his truck. Try as he might though, he could not remember if he had seen the pole anywhere inside the truck when he and Murton drove to the industrial park, or to Brackett's house. He set the pole in the grass. "Let's sit down."

"You didn't answer me. What's with the toy pole? Getting back to basics?" Sandy said with a smile on her face.

"Maybe."

"I've got something I need to tell you, Virgil. It's important. Can we turn the phones off and put all the drama of Pearson and the governor and Cora and everything else aside for a few minutes?"

The night was one of the most beautiful summer nights Virgil could remember. A blue moon hung full and bright in the sky, the air was still, the tree frogs were croaking, the bass and bluegill were feeding across the surface of the pond, the firelight flickered around them, and as he glanced at the toy fishing pole at their feet, Virgil suddenly knew what Sandy was going to tell him.

"Do you trust me?" Virgil said.

"Of course I do. You know that."

"I have something too. To tell you…ask you. I'd like to go first."

Sandy let her eyelids droop. "Why am I not surprised?"

"I had all these different scenarios laid out. All kinds of different ideas and plans, some of them simple, some of them grand, but they all seemed so…contrived." He got down on both knees in front of her. "This one isn't. This is me, Virgil Francis Jones, talking to Andrew Small's daughter. I've waited my entire life for you, Sandy. I know I've put you through hell these last few weeks and months, but if you ever find yourself doubting or wondering how much I love you, all you'll ever have to do is remember this very moment. I love you, Sandy. With my whole heart, I love you." He pulled the ring out of his pocket and held it out to her in the soft glow of the firelight. "Will you marry me?"

SANDY TOOK THE RING FROM HIS HAND, HELD IT IN THE light for a moment, smiled in a melancholic sort of way, then closed it inside her fist. "Virgil, it's beautiful and I love you. I do. I know you know that. But…"

And Virgil thought, *oh no…*

"I CAN'T ANSWER YOU," SANDY SAID. "AT LEAST NOT yet. You should have let me go first. I have to tell you something and it matters, Virgil. It matters more than anything else you and I have ever been through. It wouldn't change my answer, nothing could. But I have to know if it would change the question."

"Sandy…"

"No, Virgil, you've got to let me say it. I don't think it will affect your proposal, but I can't live my life wondering. I can't answer you until you hear what I have to say."

"Would you be upset if I told you I already knew?"

Sandy made a funny noise with her lips. "No, I wouldn't, because you don't know this."

"Yes, I do."

"You couldn't possibly, Virgil. Nobody knows. I haven't told a soul."

Interesting choice of words, Virgil thought.

"I'm pregnant, Virgil."

He wrapped his arms around her and kissed her hard on the lips. "I know, baby, I know. I don't think I've known for long, but I have known. I simply wasn't paying close enough attention."

"What? What do you mean?"

"It will be a boy. We'll name him Wyatt. He'll have one blue eye from you and one green eye from me. I'll teach him to fish right here in this pond and you'll show him how to love and be loved, just like you've taught me."

"How did you know? I didn't even know until earlier today."

Sandy's back was to the willow tree. A moment ago, before he'd gotten down on his knees, Virgil saw his father as he stood behind Wyatt, his hands on his grandson's shoulders. He wasn't sure what would happen, but he took the chance. "Turn around and look at the tree."

CHAPTER THIRTY

THEY SLEPT LATE THE NEXT MORNING AND PROBABLY would have slept later were it not for the buzzing noise Virgil's phone was making on the nightstand. He rolled over, hit the button, and said, "What?"

"Good morning to you too, Jones-man."

"What is it, Murt? I had sort of a late night last night."

"Yeah, me too. As a matter of fact, I haven't been to bed yet. I hung out most of the night with the crime scene weenies while they did the GSR tests on Pearson. He fired the gun all right. Had powder residue all over him. His prints were the only ones on the weapon, too. Here's something else…you know those sirens we heard last night? The flashing lights from a block or two over?"

"Yeah."

"That was from a shooting as well. Want to guess who

the victim was? No? Okay. It was Abigail Monroe. They found some brass at the scene. According to the preliminary report she was shot with the same gun that Pearson used on himself."

Sandy got out of bed, went into the bathroom and closed the door. Virgil thought he heard her vomit. "They're sure?"

"According to Mimi—and let me just say, wow, what a voice on that broad—it's about a ninety-eight percent certainty. Firing pin and ejection port markings are exact."

Virgil hit the speaker button and let the phone rest on his chest. "So Pearson goes after Monroe, shoots her in the back, then goes back to his place and kills himself? The governor isn't going to accept that, Murt."

"He won't have to. I had a little chat with the medics. She never made it to the hospital…she ended up DOA, but she was semiconscious, sort of in and out of it on the ride there. The medic said she kept saying, 'pain' like she was really hurting, which you would expect from someone shot in the back multiple times. He told me he was pumping her full of morphine as fast as he could get it into the syringe. In fact, he was giving her so much that he had to call in to the hospital docs while they were still en route to get permission to give her more."

"So?"

"So thanks to lawyers everywhere, no one wants to get sued over bad advice or miscommunication. The hospitals are required to digitally record those transmissions. I drove over to the hospital, made some noise and got them to let me listen to the tape. You can hear Monroe in the background. She wasn't saying, 'pain.' She was saying, 'Pate.' I think Pate murdered Pearson, Jonesy. Miles agrees with me."

"What'd you do with the recording?"

I had the hospital's IT guy make two copies. I've got one, the hospital has the other and Miles has the original. The search warrants are already being served for Augustus Pate and Hector Sigara. Dying declaration. They'll both go down for multiple murders."

"That's great work, Murt. Top-notch."

"Ah, I got lucky, that's all. I think we've built up some goodwill with Miles and his department though, not to mention the governor himself."

"Since you're on such a roll, how about you go find Nichole Pope. I'd like to ask her a few questions." Sandy came out of the bathroom, naked as the day she was born —though clearly more developed—and hopped back into bed. She took the phone and said, "Hi, Murton. This morning he's mine. See you at one." Then she hung up.

"Want a little morning fun? We won't have to worry about me getting pregnant."

"Are you up for it? I thought I heard you getting sick in there."

"I did, but only a little. Right now I feel fine."

"Hmm, you did brush your teeth, didn't you?"

Women, it seemed, enjoyed punching Virgil.

———

VIRGIL SPENT THE REST OF THE DAY PREPARING FOR THE party. He went to the grocery store, bought burgers and brats for the grill, a large bag of charcoal, buns, and a case of Mountain Dew. Then he stopped at the bar and grabbed three cases of beer, a large bottle of Appleton Estate rum and four large bags of ice.

By the time everyone began to show up, he had the lawn chairs set out in the backyard, the grill lit and the drinks in the cooler. Delroy and Robert were the first to arrive and even though they had decided to make one big announcement to everyone regarding their engagement, when Sandy saw them she ran over, gave them both a big hug and stuck the ring right in their faces. "Look!" she said. "We're getting married."

They'd also decided they weren't going to tell anyone about the pregnancy until Sandy had a chance to go to the doctor and make sure everything was okay. Virgil wondered how long that would last, mentally putting his money on sometime around two in the afternoon.

At his own insistence Robert took over the grill duties. "I've seen you cook, mon. Go. Relax. Da professionals are here. Respect."

Over the next half hour or so Virgil and Sandy spent

their time greeting everyone, listening to the ooh's and ah's regarding her ring and generally having more fun than they'd had in a long, long time. Then someone unexpected showed up.

_____

"When I saw all the cars I almost turned around and left, but then I realized that I recognized most of them…"

"It's okay, Cora. I'm glad you're here. I was going to invite you, but…"

They walked down the slope of the backyard and stopped at the midpoint, away from the noise. Cora looked at nothing before she spoke.

"My father drank himself to death," she said. "That's a polite way of saying he was a raging alcoholic. He wasn't mean or abusive or anything like that and it didn't matter if he was drunk or sober, he was a good and kind and decent man. But he had this huge problem and no matter how hard he tried, Jonesy, he couldn't get past it. It was their twenty-fifth wedding anniversary. He took her to the nicest restaurant he could afford and over the course of the evening he had quite a few too many. I don't know why my mother wasn't driving, only that she wasn't. They never made it home. This was back before airbags and seatbelt laws and Mother's Against Drunk Driving. They swerved off the road and when they hit the tree head-on they died instantly."

"Ah, Jesus, Cora, I'm sorry."

"Let me finish if you would please. I'm trying to apologize. My only sibling, my little sister…she was five years younger than me at the time…and it landed on me to take care of her. She became my responsibility. Something happened to her that night, Jonesy, the night our parents died. Something in her head clicked off. Have you ever seen the light go out of someone while they're still alive? I have. I hoped I'd never see it again. I did everything I could, everything I knew how to do, but nothing worked. Eventually, I took her to the doctor. He put her on some pills…antidepressants and tranquilizers. She began to take more and more, much more than she was supposed to and three months later I buried her too."

She turned away from him for a moment and Virgil watched as she choked down a sob. "I'm a fifty-seven-year-old overweight black woman with absolutely no one in my life. I've no family, very few friends and even fewer people that I've let get close to me. Big surprise, huh? But you're different, Jonesy. You're the only person I've ever known besides my parents and my sister that I consider family. When you started on those pills I was concerned. When you didn't stop I became worried. When you tossed your badge in the pond the look on your face was identical to the one I saw from my sister before she died. The light had gone out of your eyes, Jonesy, and I couldn't bear it.

I'm sorry for the way I've been behaving. I'm sorry for the things I've said, and done. I'm sorry for...well, I'm just sorry. I'm going to go now. I didn't mean to intrude on your party."

Virgil grabbed her arm and pulled her close. He felt her resistance, but only for a moment before she put her arms around him, pressed her face to his chest and sobbed. After a few moments she pulled back, wiped her eyes, straightened her blouse and walked away.

She didn't get far, though. Sandy intercepted her, showed her the ring and led her to a chair. Virgil watched them talk for a minute and then Cora took out her phone and made a call.

———

No more than a half-hour later Virgil heard the sirens and the rumble of the Harley-Davidson State Police motorcycle protection detail. The governor knew how to make an entrance. When he climbed from the back of the limo he waved to Virgil and Sandy, then walked over. Sandy gave him a big hug and showed him her ring.

"My goodness," the governor said. "Isn't that fantastic? Congratulations to both of you. I couldn't be happier." He admired the ring for a moment, winked at Virgil, then said, "I understand Cora is here. Would you two mind if I stayed for a bit. I need to have a word with her."

"You're welcome anytime, Governor," Virgil said.

Sandy led the governor around to the backyard and Virgil walked over and invited the uniformed state cops back as well. They wouldn't drink, of course, but he knew they could eat.

And so it went…

————————

A SHORT WHILE LATER VIRGIL CHECKED HIS PHONE AND noticed that it was after two o'clock in the afternoon. He punched in Murton's number and it went straight to voice-mail. He tried Becky's number next and got the same result. Cora and the governor had taken two chairs and walked them all the way down to the water's edge where they sat in the shade of the willow tree. The chairs faced each other and both of them were deep in conversation, their forearms against their thighs. Politics. Pearson would have to be spun.

Someone had turned the music on and Delroy was dancing in the grass with one of the female motorcycle cops and Virgil wondered if life could be any more strange and beautiful at the same time.

Fifteen minutes later he tried both Murton and Becky again with the same results.

————————

He found Sandy sitting with Ed Donatti's wife, Pam. "Listen," Virgil said, "We've got quite a few more people here than what I planned on. We're running low on food and drinks, not to mention ice. I'm going to make a quick run to the store. I'm also going to swing by Murt's and find out what the hold up is. He should have been here by now."

Sandy turned and looked at the table where the drinks were set up, then over to Robert who was still working the grill. "I think it looks like we've got enough."

"Well, you can't have too much."

They stared at each other for a long minute. Pam straightened her skirt and looked like she was pretending that the conversation taking place between Virgil and Sandy was as normal as any she'd ever heard. "He'll probably be here any minute now," Sandy said.

Virgil leaned over and kissed her goodbye. "I'm going to go check. I'll be back before you know it." He made it about three steps away before he heard Pam call out to him.

"Jonesy?"

"Yeah?"

"Why don't you take Ed with you?"

Virgil turned and looked out across the lawn. Donatti was near the edge of the pond with his young son, Jonas. Earlier, Virgil had set out some fishing gear and a small bucket of earthworms. He watched for a moment as Ed baited a hook for his son, then tossed the line out into the water before handing the pole back to Jonas. "Ah, look at him, Pam. He's having the time of his life. Let him be."

"I'll watch Jonas. Take Ed with you. Every time one of you guys go out alone anywhere it makes me nervous."

Virgil smiled at her. "Well, I guess we can't have that, can we?"

CHAPTER THIRTY-ONE

Virgil let Ed drive because Sandy's car was hopelessly pinned at the front of the house by all the other vehicles. The traffic wasn't bad and they made it to Murton's house in less than thirty minutes. "Looks okay to me," Donatti said.

"Check the back, will you?" Virgil said. "I've got the front."

"Are we up against anything here?"

"I don't know. I don't think so. There are warrants out for Pate and Sigara. It's a snake hunt now and Miles is on it. But I should have heard from Murton by now."

Virgil moved about halfway up the walk and waited until he saw Donatti get around to the back of the house. He stepped up on the porch, heard the familiar creak of the second step, noticed the uniform gap between the deck boards under his feet, the missing bolt at the base of the wrought iron handrail, the cement patch on the foundation under the front door that his father had to patch year after year. This had been Virgil's home and he was as comfortable here as any place he'd ever been in his entire life.

But it wasn't his home anymore no matter how familiar he may have been with the smallest of details. So against the previously stated wishes of his best friend and brother, against everything he should have been paying attention to and wasn't, Virgil did what he thought was the appropriate thing to do.

He knocked on the door.

———————

IT HAD HAPPENED LIKE THIS: MURTON WAS FRESHLY showered and ready to go exactly thirty minutes before they were supposed to be at the party, but Becky was running late. These earrings or those? This dress, or that one? Murton didn't mind. He spent the time cleaning up the boxes and the bits of Styrofoam off the carpet from all the new computer equipment Becky had moved into the house. He stacked the boxes—four of them in all—and carried them to the back door. Tomorrow was trash day.

The boxes were stacked high enough that he could almost see where he was going. But he'd grown up in this house and knew his way without looking. He got all the way through the kitchen to the back door, then, balancing the boxes with one hand he twisted the knob and pulled the handle. When he did, Hector kicked him in the groin and then interlocked his fingers and brought both hands down across the back of his neck.

Murton landed face-first on the back steps of the porch, knocked out cold.

———————

HECTOR GRABBED THE BACK OF MURTON'S COLLAR AND pulled him into the living room like a dog that might have just peed on the carpet. He hefted him into a chair then taped his hands and legs together and stuffed a rag into his mouth.

Then he stood still and listened.

The shower.

He moved up the stairs and followed the sounds to the end of the hall. When he walked into the bathroom he spent a few minutes admiring the shape of the woman behind the shower door. When the water turned off, Hector pointed his gun at the door and waited. When the woman stepped out he put his finger to his lips in a shush fashion. Her jaw dropped and before she could make a sound, Hector punched her square in the face. She dropped to the floor, out just as easily as the fed downstairs. Then he thought, here was a beautiful woman, naked and unconscious. What would be the harm? She was going to die soon anyway. Why not have his way with her? That's when he heard Pate's voice behind him. "Get her downstairs, Hector."

Hector grabbed her by her hair and pulled her naked body down the steps, her feet and ankles banging off the polished hardwood planks. Halfway down she started to moan and he hit her in the face again, this time with the butt of his long gun. That shut her up. He propped her in a chair next to the fed, taped her arms behind her back and her ankles to the legs of the chair, then stepped back to admire his work.

"What now, Boss?"

"Now we wake them. First we're going to cut on the woman some. Not much, but enough to show them both, especially Wheeler, that we are serious. When we have their attention, they'll tell us where Nichole Pope is, we'll get the ticket and then come back and finish them. Go in the kitchen and get a sharp knife. No, no, wait. I've got a better idea. See if you can find a potato peeler. The peeler always makes them talk."

"Yes, Boss."

———————

MURTON FELT THE CONSCIOUSNESS WASH OVER HIM, heard the sounds from the kitchen, someone rattling around in the drawers. He opened his eyes and saw Pate staring at him. When he turned his head he saw Becky, naked and taped to a chair, her face bloody and swollen.

He shook his head to clear the fog, spit the rag from his mouth and said, "Hey, Gus? I hope you've enjoyed your life. You're going to die today."

Pate opened his mouth to say something, but the knock at the door caused him to turn away from Murton's words. He leveled his shotgun at the front door and emptied both barrels from a distance of less than three feet.

———————

VIRGIL WOULD HAVE DIED RIGHT THEN AND THERE EXCEPT Pate had loaded the shotgun with slugs instead of buck-shot. The first shot blew through the door and Virgil jumped sideways, landed on his shoulder, rolled and then spun back around as Pate fired the second shot. Virgil drew his weapon, leaned around the corner past the shat-tered door and saw Pate standing next to Murton, the shotgun pointed directly at Murton's neck.

Murton gave him the slightest of nods, no more than a quarter inch at the most but that was all Virgil needed.

Had he thought about it, he might have hesitated.

You've got people in your life who are going to need you, Son.

He didn't think about it.

Virgil fired three shots and Pate was dead before he hit the ground. When he rushed inside, Murton said, "Hector. Out the back."

That's when Virgil heard three more shots.

———————————

DONATTI WAS ALMOST AT THE BACK STEPS WHEN HE heard the shotgun blasts. He yanked the Glock from his ankle holster, ran up the steps and barreled through the back door. Hector was right there. They ended up on the floor in a pile, snarling and scrapping for survival, but Donatti had already had a few drinks at the party and wasn't quite as fast as he could have been. Hector rolled him, got Donatti pinned on his back and buried the sharp, pointed end of the potato peeler in the center of his neck, right below his Adam's apple. Just as he did, Donatti began pulling the trigger on his Glock. He got off three shots before he didn't have the strength to pull the trigger anymore.

———————————

VIRGIL RACED DOWN THE HALL, HIS .45 LEADING THE way, made the kitchen in about three-seconds and found Hector on top of Donatti. He pulled him off, rolled him over and saw the bullet wounds in his chest. He was breathing, but just barely. When he looked at Ed, Virgil saw something sticking out of his neck. Donatti was trying to pull at the handle, but his strength and coordination were fading. Blood was pouring from the wound and his shirt was already soaked. His lips and the skin around his eyes were starting to turn blue.

Virgil grabbed a knife from the rack, ran back to the front room, screaming Murton's name along the way. He cut him loose as fast as he could. "It's Ed. He's down. In the kitchen. It's bad, man. Really bad. He's been stabbed in the neck. I've got Becky. Go!"

Murton had medical field training in the Army and Virgil knew he was Donatti's best hope for survival. Virgil cut Becky loose, carried her to the sofa and covered her with a blanket. She was a mess, but she'd live. He pulled out his phone and dialed 911 as he ran back into the kitchen.

"Stop yelling," Murton said. "They won't be able to understand you."

Virgil tried not to shout, managed to relay their location to the emergency dispatcher then let the phone drop to the floor. "Tell me what to do."

"It's not good, Jonesy. His airway's blocked and from the amount of blood he's probably got arterial damage. I don't know how bad it is. If I pull the knife he'll either drown in his own blood or bleed out. If I don't he's going to suffocate."

"He's turning blue, Murt. We've got to do something."

Murton looked up at the counter. "There are plastic straws in the silverware drawer. And get me the paring knife from the rack. Hurry, get right down here with me now, right on the other side."

Virgil handed Murton the knife and the straw. Murton took the knife and said, "Hold the straw. Give it to me when I ask for it."

Virgil had his hand on Ed's chest and could feel his heart. It felt like it was beating way too fast. "What are you doing?"

"I've got to open him up. It's the only way to stop the bleeding and get him some air."

"Ah, Murt."

Murton ignored him, touched the blade to Donatti's neck right below the handle of the other knife and began to cut.

Virgil listened for the sirens, but didn't hear any.

———————

MURTON MADE AN L-SHAPED CUT IN DONATTI'S NECK that intersected with his wound. He set the knife aside, said, "Ready with the straw," then pulled what turned out to be a potato peeler from Ed's neck. A burst of blood sprayed out and Murton said, "Straw." Virgil handed him the straw and Murton pushed it into the hole where the peeler had been. Ed's chest instantly began to rise and fall. He was breathing, but the blood was pouring from his wound. "Get me some paper towels. We're not out of the woods yet."

Virgil grabbed the roll of towels and peeled off a wad and held them out. Murton grabbed the wad and said,

"Not like that. Take one sheet at a time and fold it over until it's as small as you can get it."

He did what Murton told him and when he had the paper towel folded the proper way, Murton took it and said, "Just like that. Keep 'em coming."

Virgil began to tear and fold as fast as he could. He'd hand the towels to Murt and he pressed them to Donatti's neck and they turned red and were completely soaked through before he was finished with the next.

"Faster," he said. Somewhere in the back of Virgil's mind it registered how calm Murton was. "It's not working. He's breathing, but he's losing too much blood." Then Virgil witnessed something he was sure he'd never forget no matter how long he lived. Murton picked up the knife and sliced more skin and tissue and muscle from around the wound, stuck two fingers inside Donatti's neck, and just like that, the bleeding slowed to no more than a trickle. "I've got it pinched off. Put your hand right over the top of mine and hold it in place."

No more than five-seconds later two city cops ran down the hall, stopped at the entrance to the kitchen and leveled their guns directly at Virgil and Murton. "Nobody move. Show us your hands, show us your hands!"

"We can't show you our hands unless you want this cop to die," Murton said. "Stop pointing your guns at us and get the medics in here right now."

CHAPTER THIRTY-TWO

THE MEDICS DIDN'T WANT TO RISK MURTON LETTING GO of the artery so he held the wound all the way to the hospital and right into emergency surgery. The doctor walked up, placed his hand on top of Murton's, and said, "On three now, nice and slow. You're going to open your fingers and let me guide your hand back. Okay? Good. Here we go. One, two, three…"

VIRGIL CALLED SANDY, TOLD HER WHAT HAPPENED, AND asked her to get Donatti's wife, Pam, and their son, Jonas to the hospital as quickly and safely as they could. He also told her he was okay and that he loved her and after they hung up he went and checked on Becky.

————————

SANDY RAN DOWN TO THE WILLOW TREE WHERE THE governor and Cora were still speaking with each other. She gave them both the short version of what had happened and the governor took it from there.

Three minutes later, Pam Donatti and her son, the governor, Cora, Rosencrantz, and Sandy piled into the limo and made it to the hospital in less than twenty minutes, which will happen when you don't have to stop for a single red light. The twelve state police motorcycle cops made sure of that.

————————

BECKY WOULD BE OKAY. SHE HAD TWO VERY LARGE AND swollen black eyes, a split lip and she'd lost two of her bottom teeth, right in front. They had her sedated and when Virgil and Sandy found him, Murton was right there by her side, listening to the doctor. "She'll recover completely," the doc said. "The x-rays came back clean and the teeth shouldn't be a problem either. They can do things with implants now that are absolutely amazing. Going to be sore for a few weeks though." He made a few notes on a clipboard, nodded to everyone and stepped out of the room. Two-seconds later he stepped back in and said something else to Murton. "From what I hear that was pretty amazing…what you did to try to save that police officer's life. Not too many people would have done that. You should be proud."

And Virgil thought, *try to*?

Then, down the hall he heard a woman scream. Sandy said, "Oh, no," and ran from the room. Virgil looked across Becky's hospital bed and watched as Murton closed his eyes and put his head face-down on the mattress.

━━━━━━━━━

INDIANA STATE POLICE MAJOR CRIMES UNIT DETECTIVE First Class Edward James Donatti was buried the following Wednesday. It rained all day. When the service was complete and everyone had gone except Pam and Jonas, Sandy walked to the car to wait for Virgil, who had moved around to the front of the tent. He sat down next to Pam.

"I did this," she said. "I sent my husband to his death."

"You've done no such thing. He was a brave and decent man who never backed down from anything or anyone." Virgil didn't want to be harsh with her, but he did want her to hear the truth. "Don't disrespect his memory or the good he did by thinking otherwise."

"I killed him."

"That's simply not true."

"Jonesy…I can't talk to you right now. Maybe not ever. Please go away. I'm sorry."

Virgil didn't know what to say. He started to stand but Jonas came over and crawled into his lap. "It's okay Mr. Virgil," he said. "My daddy loved you, so I do too." Then he threw his arms around Virgil's neck and began to cry. When Virgil looked past Ed's casket he saw Sandy standing next to her car, her face buried in her hands.

The rain came harder still.

———

IT FELL SO FAST AND THE WIND BLEW SO HARD THAT EVEN though they were only a mile or so from home, Virgil had to pull the car over to the side of the road. The clouds had turned coal-black and the early afternoon sky was as dark as night. Lightning flashed all around them and the thunder clapped so hard Virgil thought the windshield might shatter. The wind gusts were so strong Sandy's car rocked on its springs. Visibility had been reduced to the point that they could barely make out the front end of the vehicle. "Are we okay here?" Sandy said.

"I think so. Storms like this...they blow over pretty fast." Then, only a minute later, the rain stopped and the visibility improved. Not much, but enough that they could continue driving. "See? No worries," Virgil said as he reached for the gear lever.

"Tornado." Sandy said.

"Nah. Only a strong summer—"

She pointed. "No, Virgil. Tornado!"

Virgil looked in the direction she was pointing and saw the funnel. It spun out of the cloud base less than half a mile away. "Ah shit. Come on, out of the car."

They scrambled out the driver's side door, crossed the road and got down in a culvert that was barely big enough to hold them both.

Thirty-seconds later it was over. They inched their way out of the culvert, stood up and brushed themselves off, though the effort itself was futile. They were both covered in mud and bits of debris. Sandy had a small cut on her forehead. "Here, hold still, you're bleeding a little bit," Virgil said. "Are you okay?"

"Yeah, I'm fine."

"What about the...the..."

She actually laughed at him. "The baby? Boy, I'm going to have to get you a book. The baby is a little clump of cells that you might be able to see with a microscope. The baby is fine. So am I. Let's go home."

Virgil looked behind her. "Hope you don't mind walking. Take a look at your car. That right there is exactly why you never want to try to ride out a tornado in your vehicle."

Sandy turned around and discovered her car had been rolled about a hundred yards into the field on the opposite side of the road. It was upside down, the windows were smashed out and the hood was missing.

Sandy shook her head and said, "Motherfucker."

Virgil raised his eyebrows at her.

"What?" she said. "I'm a little hormonal."

———————————

NO MATTER THE CIRCUMSTANCES OF THE PAST WEEK, OR even the past few hours, Virgil and Sandy had what could only be described as a pleasant walk home. They held hands, talked about their future, and in many ways, Virgil thought, made peace with the damage and drama that had found its way into their lives. He was mildly concerned that their house may have been damaged by the tornado, but when they walked up the drive and saw the house, they discovered it wasn't too bad. Quite a few shingles had been torn off...maybe as many as half. The porch swing had cracked one of the front windows before being torn from its support. The gutters hung askew and the downspouts were completely gone. But structurally the house seemed fine. "Looks like I've got some projects for the weekend."

"Maybe a few weekends," Sandy said.

"Let's check the back." They walked around the side of the house and when they got to the back corner Sandy saw it before Virgil did. He heard her sharp intake of breath and when he followed her gaze, he felt his knees weaken. Virgil sat down on the wet grass, his back against the side of the house and let his head hang down. Sandy sat down next to him and neither one of them spoke. What was there to be said?

Mason's willow tree had been snapped in half about three feet above ground level.

AFTER A FEW MINUTES VIRGIL GATHERED HIMSELF together and they walked down and looked at the tree. He pulled a few of the feathery leaves from the branches and held them in his hand before dropping them on the ground. Then he turned and began walking toward the shed. He came back with a pair of work gloves, goggles, ear protectors, and his chainsaw.

"You don't have to do this now, Virgil."

"Yeah, I think I do."

"Don't you want to change your clothes first? You'll ruin your suit."

"A lot of things have been ruined lately, Sandy. What's one more?"

She stood on her toes and kissed him hard on the lips. "You want to be alone?"

"I think I do."

She nodded, turned away and moved toward the house.

"Sandy?"

She stopped and turned back. "This was the best thing anyone ever did for me, when you guys planted this tree. The absolute best."

"I know, Baby. I know. Do what you've got to do."

Virgil had his back to the fallen tree as he checked the condition of the saw. He made sure the gas and bar oil tanks were full and that the throttle and choke were adjusted properly. He set the saw in the grass and put on his goggles and work gloves. Right before he pulled the starter cord, Virgil said, "Sorry, Dad."

"Don't be," Mason said.

Virgil spun around and saw his father sitting on the trunk of the tree, right next to where it had snapped. He patted the trunk with his hand. "This was a good thing. Nothing will ever change that. But things happen, Son. Life goes on."

"Does it?"

"What a ridiculous question. Of course it does."

"You saved my life."

"At the risk of sounding like a broken record, I believe I told you that there are people in your life who are going to need you, did I not?"

"Yeah, Dad, you did."

"You should check the tension on that chain."

"I will."

"I came here to tell you four things, Virg. The first is this: I'm proud of you, Son. We all are. You got off those pills and now we don't have to worry about that anymore, do we?"

"No, you don't."

"Good. Here's the second thing. Don't plant me any more trees. Plant one for the child you're about to have."

"I will." The tears were beginning to roll down Virgil's cheeks and he couldn't have stopped them if he wanted to.

"You said you needed to know something else."

"I don't know what you mean," Virgil said.

"That first day we spoke. Right at the end of our conversation, you said there was something else you needed to know. What was it? I'll answer you if I can."

"I wanted to ask what it was that you were trying to say to me when you passed. You were choking on your own blood and I don't know what you were trying to tell me."

"I wasn't choking on the blood, Son. I was choking on the words. That's why I never said them. I didn't want to seem selfish."

"What do you mean?"

"I mean I had a hold of your hand and I knew my body was dying. I wanted to ask you not to leave me even though I knew I was about to leave you. What kind of man does that make me? Who does that?"

Virgil smiled through his tears. "Humans, I guess."

Mason smiled back.

"What's the fourth thing?" Virgil said.

"You have to ask?"

"No…but I do want to hear it one more time, even if I never hear it again."

"Never say never," Mason said as he stood from the trunk and waded out into the pond.

"What are you doing?" Virgil said.

"I'm going for a swim. See you around, Son." And then he said it. "Dad loves you."

Virgil closed his eyes. "Dad loves you too."

When he opened his eyes and looked at the water, his father was gone.

Virgil wiped the tears from his eyes and fired up the saw.

———————

HE CUT THE MAIN PART OF THE TREE AWAY FROM THE three-foot-high stump, then began to trim the branches back. Three of the branches were particularly long and straight and he set those aside without cutting them down to size. He spent the next hour cutting the rest of the tree and stacking the wood. When he was finished he moved to put the saw away, but then, as an afterthought, he pulled the starter cord and fired it back up. He cut four vertical strips from the stump to turn it into a thick square post. Then he made two vertical cuts from the top down, equal distance from the center. Then four horizontal cuts, then finally two more vertical cuts from the bottom section down to the ground. When he was finished, he was left with a flawed, yet somehow completely perfect cross. He carried the saw back to the shed, grabbed his hammer and a chisel and went back down to the tree. He carved the name 'Mason' on the front of the cross and Jones on the side that faced the water.

After a few minutes he walked up to the house, got undressed and threw his suit in the trash.

CHAPTER THIRTY-THREE

OVER A WEEK HAD PASSED SINCE DONATTI DIED. BECKY was on the mend and Virgil and Murton worked the bar with Delroy and Robert, thankful to get back to the business and regularity of their lives. It was Saturday afternoon, well before the evening rush and Virgil was sitting alone at the bar when Nichole Pope walked in and sat down next to him. They stared at each other in the bar mirror for a few moments. "You want to know something?" Virgil said.

"Sure."

"I'm wondering whether I should laugh or scream."

"Maybe the answer is somewhere in the middle."

Virgil took a sip of juice. "You've got brass, I'll give you that."

"I'm sure I don't know what you mean."

"You're here, aren't you?"

"Why wouldn't I be?"

"What are you going to do with all the money?"

"Who says I have any money?"

"I do."

"And you're the final say, are you?"

When Virgil didn't answer, she reached into her purse and pulled out a thumb drive and set it on the bar. "This is every scrap of evidence we ever gathered on Bradley Pearson. There's some interesting stuff on Pate in there as well. Do whatever you want with it."

"There's nothing to do. They're all dead."

"Then burn it, crush it, or erase it. I don't really care."

They sat quietly for a few moments. "Let's say I believe you, that you don't have the money, even though I don't. What do you get out of all of this?"

She thought about the question. "I get my life back. So does Nicky."

"At what cost?"

"I'll be able to sleep at night, Jonesy, I assure you."

"Keep telling yourself that."

"Spare me the philosophical psycho-babble. Everyone got what they deserved."

"I think you lost more than your father that day, Nichole. I think you lost your soul."

"Mmm, you may be right. Perhaps that gives us something in common."

"I don't think so. The problem with people like you is that you think no one else suffers, no one else has problems or fears or loss or heartache in their life. But here's the thing, Nichole: everyone does. I know I sure as hell do. Even after everything I've been through, everything I've done that's ever hurt anyone, I know I've turned out okay."

She leaned in close and whispered in his ear. "Have you, Jonesy? Have you really?"

Virgil pulled away from her as if he'd been slapped. "Get out, Nichole. I better not ever see you again."

"Or what? You'll take another Pope off the board?"

"I shot him to save someone's life."

"And that turned out just swell, didn't it?"

"I've got a dead cop who had a wife and a young son. Now that boy will never get to know his father, a man who was as good and kind and as decent of a man the likes of which I don't believe you'll ever know or recognize if you did."

Nichole laughed, but Virgil wasn't having it. "What's so funny?"

"You'd rather have me as a friend, Jonesy. I guarantee it. It's all on the thumb drive. Things you can't imagine."

They both let a moment pass before Nichole said, "And what about James Pope?"

"What about him?"

"He was my father, you miserable prick."

When Virgil refused to acknowledge her insult, she stood and turned to walk out of the bar. He grabbed her arm and yanked her back onto the stool. "Wait here."

Virgil went upstairs to the office and came back with a copy of the picture of her and Pearson outside the mini-mart.

"So what? It's a picture of two people sharing a moment. It proves absolutely nothing."

"You're right. But it's not about proof, and that's the part you don't understand. Bradley Pearson was a snake. He manipulated, maneuvered and used people to get whatever he wanted, whenever he wanted it. But as far as I know, he never killed anyone, Nichole."

"Neither have I. Too bad you can't say the same thing." She stood from the stool again and walked away. After a few steps she stopped and looked over her shoulder. "And it's not Nichole anymore, Jonesy. Thanks to you, all the Pope's are gone."

Virgil thought she was going to say something else, but she never did. Instead, she simply walked out the door and in every way imaginable, Virgil considered that a blessing.

━━━━━━━━━━

NICKY POPE—WHO WOULD FOR THE REST OF HIS NATURAL born life be known as Brian Addison—sat in a chaise lounge on the beach, his sister, Nichole Pope, a.k.a. Chloe Addison, sat next to him. "It was a hell of a risk," he told her, sort of pissed. "The longest two days of my life."

Nichole nodded. "You're right, there's no question.

But a lot of people are dead and even though we've covered our bases, I still felt like it was something that had to be done. If not, I had the feeling we'd be looking over our shoulders for the rest of our lives...or worse, we wouldn't be looking at all and that's when they get you, Bro, when you're sitting in your chair watching the waves break and sipping a margarita. You'll have four or five federal agents walk up and say something like, 'Excuse me, sir, is your name Nicholas Pope?'"

"Ah, that's TV drama," Nicky said.

"Maybe, maybe not. But I can tell you this: We're golden now."

He turned in his chair and looked past his sister. "Speaking of gold, here comes the money."

———

RON MILES PARKED HIS CAR, REACHED INTO THE BOX AND pulled out the plastic statue of the Virgin Mary. *What a joke*, he thought. It was one thing to return evidentiary property to their rightful owners, but quite another when the property was a cheap plastic statue that wasn't worth the cost of the gas it took to drive it over.

He grabbed the statue from the front passenger seat, got out of his car, walked up to Mrs. Ibarra's apartment and gave the door a good old-fashioned cop knock. When no one answered a few minutes later, he knocked again. After the third time, the door to the right of Ibarra's opened and an elderly Mexican man with a cane in one hand and a bottle of Dos Equis in the other opened his door. "Señor?"

Miles showed him his badge and said, "My name is Ron Miles. I'm a detective with the Indiana Major Crimes Unit."

"Si?" the man said.

Ron heard himself say, "Si," and winced a little.

"You are looking for Señora Ibarra?"

"Yes. Do you know where I can find her? I have some of her property that I'd like to return to her."

The man smiled and did a little wiggle. "You have not heard?"

"Heard what?"

"Señora Ibarra. She has won the lottery. The big drawing. She had the ticket, Señor. The one worth mucho dinero. She is rich and I tell you this: she is gone."

And Ron thought, *son of a bitch.*

———————

IBARRA CARRIED THE MONEY IN A LAPTOP BAG THAT HELD no actual money, just a laptop that had access to the money.

"Everything go okay?" Nicky asked.

"Oh yes. Everything go exactly like you say it would. The funds were transferred...all three hundred million dollars worth." She handed him the laptop and Nicky punched the keys.

"I told you I'd do it, didn't I?"

"Si, but I never quite believed you. Where is our gay little Wu?"

Nicky pointed out to the water. "He's out there, snorkeling with Linda. Why does everyone think Wu is gay?"

"Hmm, I am not sure. I do not like the way he looks at my feet..."

EPILOGUE

Later that evening when Virgil got home he walked down to the pond and stood next to Mason's cross. He stared out at the water and thought about his dad, his grandfather, Ed Donatti, and especially his unborn son, Wyatt. As much as he was loathed to admit it, Nichole Pope was probably right...at least about one thing: The answers were not in the extreme, but somewhere in the middle.

He still had the thumb drive she'd given him. He pulled it from his pocket and studied it under the light of the moon before setting it on top of the cross. He bent over and picked up a few rocks and skipped them out across the water, wondering what was on the drive and more importantly if it really mattered anymore. It would be easy enough to find out. He could take the drive up to the house, pop it into the computer and read everything it contained. But to what end? Pearson and Pate were dead, their misdeeds and malfeasance no longer an issue or a problem in Virgil's life. Why dive into the past when it was the future that really mattered? Wasn't that the message his father had been trying to convey all along?

Ultimately Virgil decided to take Nichole's advice. If she didn't care, why should he? He'd destroy the thumb drive, leave Pearson and Pate to rot in hell and let the Pope twins deal with their own demons down the road.

He tossed one final rock into the pond then turned to grab the thumb drive from the top of the cross, ready to crush it under his boot. But when he looked at the cross, the thumb drive was gone and his badge—the badge he'd thrown into the pond—sat there in its place.

And Virgil thought, *Dad?*

Thank you for reading State of Betrayal. If you're
enjoying the series, then there's good news:
Virgil and the gang are back in State of Control!
As Mason would say, "Stay tuned…"

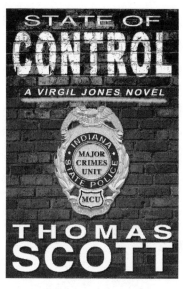

*State of Control - Book 3 of the Virgil Jones Mystery
Thriller Series*

Virgil Jones thinks his life is back on track and he's in
control of his future. But he's not. In fact, he's about to
discover he doesn't even know the meaning of the word
control.

On a quiet Sunday afternoon Virgil's former boss calls
and tells him the governor wants a private meeting. Why?
Virgil has no idea. And frankly, he doesn't care. He was

fired from the state's Major Crimes Unit by the governor himself eight months ago. Besides, his life is going just fine.

But Virgil is about to discover that time isn't as linear as it appears and events from his past are about to repeat themselves. And when they do, he'll come face to face with pure evil, and be forced to make the kind of choice no man should ever have to make.

You've felt the Anger...

You've experienced the Betrayal...

Now...it's time to take Control!

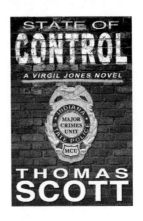

— Also by Thomas Scott —

The Virgil Jones Series In Order

State of Anger - Book 1
State of Betrayal - Book 2
State of Control - Book 3
State of Deception - Book 4
State of Exile - Book 5
State of Freedom - Book 6
State of Genesis - Book 7
State of Humanity - Book 8
State of Impact - Book 9
State of Justice - Book 10
State of Killers - Book 11
State of Life - Book 12
State of Mind - Book 13
State of Need - Book 14
State of One - Book 15
State of Play - Book 16
State of Qualms - Book 17
State of Remains - Book 18
State of Suspense - Book 19

The Jack Bellows Series In Order

Wayward Strangers - Book 1
Brave Strangers - Book 2

Visit ThomasScottBooks.com for further
information regarding future release dates, and more.

ABOUT THE AUTHOR

Thomas Scott is the author of the **Virgil Jones** series, and the **Jack Bellows** series of novels. He lives in northern Indiana with his lovely wife, Debra, his children, and his trusty sidekicks and writing buddies, Lucy, the cat, and Buster, the dog.

You may contact Thomas anytime via his website ThomasScottBooks.com where he personally answers every single email he receives. Be sure to sign up to be notified of the latest release information.

Also, if you enjoy the Virgil Jones series of books, leaving an honest review on Amazon.com helps others decide if a book is right for them. Just a sentence or two makes all the difference in the world. Plus, rumor has it that it's good for the soul!

For information on future books in the Virgil Jones series, or to connect with the author, please visit:

ThomasScottBooks.com

And remember:
Virgil and the gang are back and waiting for you in State of Control!

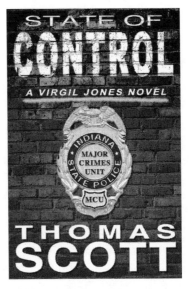

State of Control - Book 3 of the Virgil Jones Mystery Thriller Series

Grab your copy today!

Made in the USA
Middletown, DE
01 March 2024

50663822R00255